MW01257066

PATRIOT DAWN

The Resistance Rises

Max Velocity

Web: www.maxvelocitytactical.com

Email: maxvelocitytactical@gmail.com

Blog: maxvelocitytactical.blogspot.com

Copyright © 2012 by Max Velocity

ISBN-13: 978-1480139688
ISBN-10: 1480139688

CONTENTS

Contents

Prologue

The election on November 6 2012 had been the mortal blow to the ideal of America. The stakes could not have been higher or more straightforward: a choice between freedom or coercion, individualism or collectivism, modern civilization or uncivilized brutalism.

America, those of her voting and abstaining majority, chose the latter option in each case. The forces of this late modern brutalism had been at work in America for a long time and had, of course, scored many victories. The progressive beast had slowly eaten away at America's educational establishment, the character of her people, and moral virtue, leaving little of the true American values behind. The sad thing was that the indoctrinated generations did not even realize what they had lost, while they tinkered over minor social issues.

With the election behind them, certain elements within the Administration continued their agenda to attain total control. Plans were put into motion.

The terrorist attack was carried out by jihadist fighters. They came in by chartered airliner, landing to disgorge several hundred terrorists into an assault on Washington D.C. This was not a hijacking, but a legally scheduled charter.

The flight plans of the terrorist controlled aircraft had called for a scheduled landing at Washington's Dulles International Airport. However, that was considered too far away from DC, the Capitol and key targets such as the Pentagon. Reagan National was chosen instead.

The pilot of the aircraft was a US/Saudi joint citizen with impeccable English who had worked as a commercial pilot extensively in the US; he had plenty of experience landing at US airports, including Dulles and Reagan National.

As the pilot flew south towards DC, he put out a bogus Mayday call, citing engine power failure, and announced that he was going to have to put the plane down at Reagan National, thus diverting from the scheduled landing cleared for Dulles.

The control tower at Reagan declined, ordering him to continue to Dulles, but he simply told them that he was experiencing power failure and that they needed to clear the runway because he was coming in hard and fast. They obliged and scrambled the emergency services.

The Boeing 777 came in on the difficult river approach from the north, passing close to the Washington Mall; the pilot brought the plane in for a hard landing and began to taxi towards the terminal. He tried to ignore the instructions of the ground guide vehicles but soon had his way blocked by airport police vehicles who had been alerted by the tower. International flights were not cleared to land at Reagan National, and this was highly suspicious.

Still out on the taxi-way, the terrorists pulled the emergency release on the doors and activated the emergency exit slides. Somewhere around two hundred fighters began to pour out onto the tarmac, fueled by drugs and fanaticism and heavily armed with Kalashnikov assault rifles, rocket propelled grenades and improvised explosive devices, including a number of suicide vests. They opened fire on the emergency crews and police and started to run towards the terminals.

Some split off from the main group and commandeered airport pickup trucks on the tarmac and headed out onto the pan to where the delayed passenger aircraft were waiting at the end of the runway to take off.

They drove along the taxi way, stopping only to fire volleys of RPGs into the aircraft, which were loaded with passengers and fuel. The planes began to burn and as the jet fuel ignited they began to explode. The resulting fire and explosions were apocalyptic and soon the taxi way was engulfed in a conflagration of flames and burning fuel.

Meanwhile, the main body smashed their way into the terminal buildings and began to kill as they fought their way through to the passenger drop off and taxi ranks at the front. The armed security did not stand a chance. The fighters began to commandeer vehicles, any one would do. Civilians were shot down and murdered out the front of the terminal buildings and teams of four fighters stole the vehicles and started to head out into traffic and towards the city.

There was mass panic in the terminals, but as the crowds tried to escape they were engaged by assault weapon fire and hundreds were murdered. Pipe bombs had been dropped in the terminal on timers and as the fighters began to move away in their stolen vehicles the bombs began to detonate.

Each group had a specific target and objective. They had studied transit maps, photos and satellite photos on Google Earth. They had objectives but they realized that not all of them would make those objectives – if so, the plan was simply to keep going for as long as possible, causing as much damage as they could before they were stopped.

A group of fifty did not even bother to look for cars; they ran towards the Pentagon, which was only about a mile away just across the I-395. The group simply formed a file on each side of the road, trotted up the airport access road, turning north along the Jefferson Davis Highway until they passed under the Interstate.

As they jogged along, they engaged any resistance with automatic fire, AKs carried at the hip. Passing under the I-395 underpass they fanned out into their assault teams and attacked the Pentagon. They used RPG rockets and breaching charges to blast their way in and began to fight their way through the corridors inside.

Meanwhile, the alert had gone out to the Washington DC Metro police, who responded rapidly and called for back-up. Within fifteen minutes they had a cordon up around the city. Although true that there were a large number of armed federal agents, working for numerous 'alphabet' agencies within DC, they were not really prepared for the sort of savage urban conflict that these jihadists brought, straight from the battlegrounds of the Middle East.

Local SWAT teams from the DC Metro area were first into the battle, reinforcing the uniformed police units caught in the ground, rapidly joined by the FBI Hostage Rescue Team from Quantico, Virginia, who came in by helicopter to join the fight.

By this time the jihadists had smashed the police roadblocks and fought their way across the bridges into the city. Those that found themselves in the open parklands around the capital did not fare so well, but others fought their way into the city and infested the urban environment.

Mass panic ensued and it took the callout of a US Marine battle group from Quantico and the addition of two available Navy SEAL teams from Norfolk to turn the tide of the fight and clear the jihadist fighters out from where they had gone to ground.

It took a week and the deaths of thousands of Americans before the terrorist threat was eliminated.

The terrorist attackers were reported to have been recruited, abetted, directed and sponsored by Iran, although the details were unclear and it appeared that an investigation was not the top priority of the Administration.

How had the terrorists managed to charter this plane, which had apparently originated in Dubai on a one stop flight to the US, loading it with two hundred heavily armed fighters, without alerting any suspicion?

However, the focus following the attack was not international but domestic, and the priority was the 'safety and security' of the public by the accelerated implementation of the massive domestic surveillance and policing drive.

Fear was paramount and the masses were even more convinced that giving up their freedom and rights was in their best interests for their 'safety and security'. Many internet bloggers and alternative media sites were describing the attack as a 'False Flag', abetted by the 'Powers That Be', but those crackpots were soon shut down by the Department of Homeland Security, in order to prevent further 'panic mongering'.

The attack also provided the justification for war against Iran. However, that war was prosecuted by the Administration in the form of a primarily naval and air campaign that limited the involvement of ground troops.

This limitation allowed for the deployment of troops as convenient to the agenda of the Administration and the military-industrial complex, but ensured that sufficient active duty units remained available for domestic operations.

The attack on Iran was however the final straw that preceded the total meltdown of the Middle East.

As part of the 2012 National Defense Authorization Act, measures were in place to allow Posse Comitatus laws to be ignored domestically. This was activated by executive order and active duty and reserve U.S. Army units were used to reinforce the National Guard in operations against domestic terrorists and sleeper cells.

The terrorist attack had precipitated the final mortal blow to liberty and the destruction of the United States of America as a Constitutional Republic. It was true that the erosion of liberty and the Bill of Rights had been going on for some time; the Constitution was viewed by many as a dead document, and the measures had already been put in place for the implementation of a state of emergency.

The attack had been a terrible thing, but at the same time it was so convenient to the agenda of the Administration. Everything since the attack had been the death rattle of liberty as the police surveillance state was fully imposed.

Due process and Habeas Corpus were suspended, and the NDAA allowed arrest and internment without probable cause or trial on the simple suspicion by the authorities that someone posed a terrorist threat; a system that was easily abused.

Everything in society was now centered on compliance and obedience to authority. Questioning of the orders of those in authority positions was not tolerated. America was no longer the land of the free, but anyone with a mind had seen that coming for a long time.

Anyone with ideas counter to the official line, or who argued or challenged authority, was labeled a 'domestic terrorist', arrested and interned in 'corrective and reeducation facilities'.

Following the activation of the NDAA by Executive Order, a state of emergency was implemented. It was necessary, because another terrorist attack could happen at any time, and anyone could be a terrorist. There was a lot of talk about sleeper cells and many citizens were arrested and interned without trial. 'Extremist terrorist' organizations, including Patriot and conservative organizations such as the Tea Party, were outlawed.

It wasn't really clear to the general public exactly what happened next, given that they only got their information from the Administration via the heavily state directed mainstream media, and the internet was now under heavy lockdown. However, the economic dangers that had been looming and fueled by the continuous policy of 'Quantitive Easing', or money printing by the Federal Reserve, finally came home to roost.

The economy went over the cliff. There was much discussion that the actual precipitator of the plunge was the cabal of bankers who were the real power behind the

Regime; they had pulled the financial plug, causing a massive run on the banks and hyperinflation, just like they had done in 1929 to cause the Great Depression. But who really knew, given the lockdown?

The effect was ultimately to cripple the economy, destroying the middle classes. What better way to turn the screws of citizen compliance when so many were now reliant on entitlement handouts?

The 'progressive' agenda of collective socialism was nearing its ultimate fulfillment; coerced redistribution of wealth, except now no-one was generating any wealth to feed the monster of the dependent welfare classes.

Statist authoritarian big central government was the order of the day, even though those policies spelled the death of the country. Many 'progressives' yearned for that, so that the 'United Socialist States of America' could rise from the ashes.

The government of the United States of America was no longer an 'Administration'; it was a totalitarian Regime.

However, what the Regime had not predicted was that the Chinese, themselves suffering from the global financial collapse that ensued from this, then decided to take action.

For years China had infiltrated American cyber networks. They had perfected the cyber-attack and had penetrated into all aspects of American networks. They were able to 'weaponize' the cyber-attack, taking control of infrastructure such as power plants and programming them to fail while causing widespread outages and damage to power grid infrastructures.

There was no longer any reason to need America anymore, now that there was no money to be made from the previously symbiotic relationship. China and Russia were best served by destroying America and the petrodollar, carving out their own spheres of influence in the new world order.

Three months after the terrorist attack and the beginning of the run on the banks, China simply took down the North American power grid.

It was not a permanent or total attack, but it did enough damage and would be time consuming to repair, given that most of the replacement equipment would have to be shipped in from abroad where it was manufactured, mostly in China. This resulted in massive infrastructure failure with essential commodities such as food and fuel unable to be distributed.

When the shortages hit the stores, combined with the inability of the Regime to distribute and honor electronic benefit checks to the entitlement classes, the effect was massive civil disorder and rioting, on a scale that the Regime could not fully control. The collapse was self-promulgating; it was not easy to fix once the dominos started falling.

The main rioting took place in the urban centers where the mass of entitlement dependents resided. The Regime was brutal in its crackdown on its 'children'. Millions perished from a combination of lawless violence, the brutality of the Regime's response, disease and starvation.

The Regime wrested control back in the main urban centers across the country. By executive order exception was written to Posse Comitatus, invoking the Insurrection Act, thus declaring Martial law. The Regime commenced to consolidate its power. Given the general food shortage, it aided the Regime that they controlled the food reserves, and according to the 'dictate' of the executive orders and the NDAA, Federal agencies such as FEMA and the DHS were able to commandeer private and commercial food reserves.

Many citizens 'bugged out' of the urban centers into the countryside to escape the violence, and thus out of the immediate control of the Regime, which precipitated another crisis of refugees and transit gridlock by those unprepared and bugging out to 'nowhere'.

Out of the ashes of this disaster, the Regime was able to rise. Federal safe zones were created under martial law, along with FEMA camps where food rations were distributed. While the grid was being rebuilt, the FEMA offices and camps ran on emergency generators to support the registration and tracking process.

Outside of those zones were the contested areas where military operations were conducted to subdue the population. The Regime concentrated on controlling these main zones as well as mobility corridors connecting them.

Outside of the zones, the country was divided into sectors of martial law, each sector the responsibility of a military governor backed by a political commissioner from the Regime. The Department of Homeland Security was responsible for domestic military operations. National Guard and active duty units were allocated to the DHS as necessary.

FEMA also made use of the FEMA Homeland Corps. This was primarily a youth organization of armed paramilitaries, formed before the collapse, which was trained and indoctrinated by the Regime and given paramilitary police powers. They were not old enough to understand the real history of the United States beyond the propaganda taught in the school system and they had no familiarity with the Constitution or the Bill of Rights.

They became inoculated against brutality and were used for the more flagrant breaches of liberty, such as house raids to confiscate weapons and food stores, where often whole families were killed. In their blue SWAT style overalls, these young thugs became known as the 'blue shirts'.

The majority of the country's armed forces remained under Regime control, with the exception of the 'enlightened' that were already awake to the reality. Why was this? The country was under attack, now under martial law. The soldiers were indoctrinated to obey orders; they were in the system, part of the machine. In the same way that the mass of the people were fed their news from the mainstream media, so was the military.

True, there were mass desertions when the collapse happened, with many army National Guardsmen staying home to look after their families. But by and large, the active duty units remained on their bases, loyal to the system. The chain of command never flinched: orders came down as usual, situation briefings were given, and before they knew it, the active duty army was deployed domestically under martial law, protecting the country from terrorism. Why would they think any differently?

In fact, the Regime did experience problems with many of the actual combat veterans among the ranks of the National Guard, active duty army, and even law enforcement. Some of them took their oaths seriously and refused to act illegally against citizens. These types were severely cracked down upon, those that had not deserted or escaped out of the zones.

Those deserting veterans that were captured or those who dissented, refusing to obey illegal orders, were often taken into mental institutions against their will, on the pretext of mental illness or PTSD, for 'treatment' that often involved severe drug therapy that left them mentally incapacitated, shadows of their former selves.

Others saw the writing on the wall and deserted, getting out and away from the zones, often taking weapons and equipment with them.

However, there was a flip side to the refusal to obey orders to fire on citizens: as good Americans, many of these veterans actually found it easy to fire on the entitlement 'eaters' that they came across in the worst of the inner city riots. In their eyes, these eaters were the antithesis of how America was intended. Once they had pulled the trigger though, there was no going back, and they were lost on the slippery slope.

A new constitution was written, termed the 'Homeland Charter'. This new document rejected the original Constitution and declared all those supporting it to be domestic terrorists.

There was much deliberate obfuscation between sleeper cells allegedly related to the 'Iranian' terror attack on DC, and domestic 'constitutionalist' terrorists, who were often simply Patriots and preppers.

The old Constitution had led to the destruction of the country, according to the revisionist agenda of the 'progressive' Regime and the 'doublethink' mental illness that plagued America. Individual liberty was the enemy; the only salvation was in the collective. The agenda of the progressives was complete.

'New Citizens' had to swear an oath of allegiance to the Regime, to obey all laws and orders given to them by those in authority. They were fitted with subcutaneous RFID chips containing all personal information. Cash and firearms were outlawed and the chips allowed the GPS tracking of people. It was therefore easy to determine someone's status simply by scanning their forearm, and if no chip was present they were an outlaw, to be arrested or shot on sight.

As part of this new direction, the flag was redesigned. Rather than the stripes, there was a red and white sunray effect radiating out from a central, slightly offset to the left, sun-like circle in blue and white. The lower part of the 'O' like circle had an effect similar to the radiating red and white stripes, but more horizontally across the bottom of the 'O': A shining symbol of the bright future of collective socialism. The new flag was supposed to signify 'hope' or some similar progressive garbage.

The star spangled banner was relegated to the newly demonized 'Patriots' and subversives. Patriots, constitutionalists, libertarians and anyone who had prepared for the collapse were targets of the Regime, to be tracked down. Those who were not sworn to the new regime were either interned or executed if they were under direct Regime control.

The citizens of the new Regime lived hand to mouth on government handouts, working in State sponsored jobs and living in camps or state controlled housing, cowed but grateful that they were being kept safe from the outlaws and terrorists outside of the zones.

Many who had not been aware of the true danger of the creeping progressive agenda were rudely awakened after the collapse. 'Normalcy bias' was swept away and their eyes were opened to the true horror of where their great country had descended to.

The FEMA camps were no holiday camp: those who had elected or been forced into them found that due to a combination of corruption, incompetence and simple brutality, rations were meager and conditions basic. They were more like concentration camps, with oppressive rules enforced by sullen guards, quick to violence. Many in the camps were simply taken out and killed for being trouble makers, tossed into mass graves and left to rot in piles.

Many could not understand how the military could be used against citizens. With rioters, it was easy. For the innocent preppers and Patriots who were considered domestic terrorists, it was also easy: it was all a matter of information management. Regime strike teams under the DHS were simply briefed that a 'target' housed 'domestic terrorists' who were harboring food, weapons and even explosives.

The targets were hit hard in 'no knock' raids with unrestrictive rules of engagement, often resulting in everyone at the target being killed, including whole families in some cases. If the target was found to contain innocent preppers, it was no problem. It was not the first time, even before the collapse, that the wrong address was hit or 'intelligence' was found to be incorrect. Heavy handed SWAT 'kill squad' tactics were fine as long as 'department procedures' were followed.

Chapter One

Before the DC terrorist attack, Jack and Caitlin Berenger were thirty-something professionals living in the Northern Virginia suburbs. They had three children; a teenage boy and two toddlers. The eldest, Andrew, was sixteen, Connor was four and the youngest, Sarah, was two.

Jack was a former Captain with the Army Rangers, a veteran of multiple deployments to Iraq and Afghanistan, where he had gained considerable combat experience. He was very tactically adept and he continued to keep himself fit since resigning from military service, despite his sedentary job as a crisis management consultant. Caitlin was a veteran with a military intelligence background, now working as a civilian for the Department of Defense.

They had always been an active and outdoors type family, hiking and camping often. Jack also liked to keep his hand in with shooting and they owned several firearms, which he had also been training Andrew to use.

More recently, they had woken up to the fragility of modern society, the threats faced by the potential for economic collapse and the advance of the socialist agenda of the progressives in the supposedly free United States. They were both Patriots who had served their country and sworn the oath to protect the Constitution from 'enemies foreign and domestic'.

They had started to make more extensive preparations for a potential collapse, like many other preppers, and had been stocking up on food and supplies. They were shocked to find that this otherwise sensible endeavor would categorize them as potential 'domestic terrorists' for having more than seven days' worth of food, among other things.

The sane answer to this was that they were simply making preparations for potential hard times ahead. They were loyal citizens and bore no ill intent towards their country; in fact it was just the opposite. But the lunacy appeared to be spreading, and there was no other way but to ignore and resist the madness.

The Berengers lived in a relatively well to do middle class area, some twenty five miles south of the DC beltway. The sub-division consisted of a maze of residential back roads situated in a forested area. It was actually very beautiful, surrounded by lakes and woods and giving no hint of the nearby urban sprawl. However, the malls and shopping centers were only a short drive away, and the I-95 was only five miles to the east.

Their house was a two story four bedroom colonial from the 1980s, with basement, on a half-acre wooded plot, similar to most of the other surrounding properties. They were situated on the north west corner of a residential four way junction, with the house itself set back about thirty to forty meters from the road, oriented towards the junction to the south east, with the wooded yard to the rear and extending along the two roads to the left and right of the property.

The house was on a slight rise and looked down towards the junction, which was a four way stop where the kids congregated in the mornings to wait for the school bus.

The slope down to the two roads was grassed with a couple of wooded islands that gave some cover from view from the road, but otherwise there was just a drainage ditch and grass between the house and the two roads. The driveway was on the right side as you looked towards the road and sloped up over about thirty meters towards a double garage on the right side of the house.

The neighborhood was a mix of professional and retired types, some families with kids and others living in empty nests. One of the big problems the Berengers had encountered, when they got into prepping following the purchase of the house, was the local Homeowners Association.

The HOA, although ostensibly well meaning, was in fact a microcosm of the problems in the country. It appeared to attract to its employ those petty authority types who enjoyed wielding power over others in the small tyrannies.

Go against the HOA at your peril, because they had the money to afford the attorneys, which funnily enough came from the dues that those same homeowners paid for the HOA to serve their best interests. Sounds familiar? It was almost laughable if it were not so tragic.

The presence of the HOA was another reason that they had to keep their prepping low key. Operational security, or OPSEC, was always a factor in prepping anyway. But if they had lived in the country they could have aspired to a vegetable garden, goats or cows for milk, and chickens. Instead, the prepping was confined to the purchasing, and storing in the basement, of food and equipment.

The Berengers had discussed this problem at length but they were not financially positioned to sell up and move to a rural retreat, they were too tied to the golden handcuffs of the beltway rat-race, with the kids in school and all the rest.

They always said that if the slide began, it would get to a point that the HOA would not matter anymore, and they would get chickens and goats then. They had heirloom seeds ready to start a garden. But in the end it had all happened so fast there was no chance to buy any animals.

Luckily, they had about a years' worth of food stored in cans and buckets in the basement.

As part of their prepping, Jack had worked diligently on the tactical side: defense of his family. He had two 5.56mm Colt M4 rifles, two Remington 870 pump action shotguns and three Glock 23 handguns, chambered for .40 caliber rounds. He had amassed a sizeable quantity of ammunition for all the firearms, plus an ACOG x4 magnification combat optic for his M4.

He had acquired a set of body armor plates and he had used them recreate his old rig from his Ranger days, creating a tactical plate carrier vest in ranger green. He had ammunition pouches attached across the front of the vest, allowing him to carry eight magazines, along with some other utility pouches for various items.

As well as the plate carrier rig, he had created a battle belt using a tactical belt, a padded hip pad, and several types of pouches. On the battle belt he had his handgun and spare magazines, three double rifle ammunition pouches allowing carriage of six thirty round magazines, and a dump pouch for used magazines, plus several other utility items in their own pouches. He could wear the battle belt on its own or with the tactical vest, allowing him to rig himself according to the situation.

Basically, Jack stuck to what he knew and felt comfortable with. For him, weapons and equipment had always been tools that he had been 'issued', so he stuck to familiarity and he was by no means an expert on all the various firearms, optics and equipment on the market.

Jack had also collected various amounts of web gear and other tactical supplies that he fitted to Caitlin and Andrew for when the time came. They both had battle belts, Andrew's rigged up just like his, while Caitlin's was specialized for her handgun and also shotgun ammunition carriage. Andrew also had a chest rig for carriage of additional ammunition for his rifle.

Jack worried about having only one set of ballistic plates but whenever they discussed, or more rarely ran through a tactical situation, they practiced for Caitlin to act as protection to the young kids, while Andrew moved to cover and a fire support position with one of the M4s. Jack would always do the maneuver and thus it seemed right that he wore the set of armor.

Whenever they went and did paintball games it always worked out that Andrew liked to stay back and snipe from cover while Jack would always run about doing bounding over-watch like he had been trained to do in his soldiering days, which inevitably got him killed in paintball, usually by a twelve year old hiding in a bush.

Jack was terrified of any harm coming to the kids. He worked on close protection drills with Caitlin as much as he could, and although they both understood the need to prep, it was never easy with inter-marital politics to actually train together. Wives and teenagers did not make ideal training buddies, and it was all too easy for him to put his foot in it and unintentionally cause offense.

He was also very mindful that Andrew was a teenager, his son, with no combat experience and he wanted to keep him safe as much as possible. He always had him in a fire support role working from cover.

Andrew was actually a very good shot. He wasn't an experienced combat shooter like Jack, but he had the basics and had been on the air rifle team with the ROTC before Jack had introduced him to range shooting with the M4.

One of the aspects of preparing his family that Jack gave a lot of thought to was their mental preparation. Although he did not want to discuss specific aspects of his combat experiences with them, he felt a strong need to try and make them understand what it may be like, and what could be at stake, should violence come to them.

He talked to them and had them visualize combat situations, attackers coming at them bent on their destruction. He explained that in the absence of law and order, and facing armed marauders, it was a simple 'them or us' situation. On the range, he had them fire at photographic and realistic targets, and when simulating combat through training such as paintball, he had Andrew actually aim and fire his 'weapon' at the 'enemy'.

Jack explained that if or when it came, the violence would likely be sudden and unexpected, and they would probably not be ready for it. They needed to visualize their reactions in advance, train muscle memory, and be ready to 'turn it on' in an instant should the need arise.

In the three month period between the terrorist attack and the Chinese attack on the power grid the Berengers had found themselves out of work. Jack worked as a consultant for a corporation and as such he was one of the first to be let go, before the full time employees.

Caitlin should have had a secured job with the DoD, but what happened was that government employees were not fired, but put on furlough without pay 'until further notice'.

They had planned to fall back on their savings but the hyperinflation that followed the bank run soon wiped those out and they were solely reliant on their preparations and food stocks.

They had never got as far with their prepping as buying precious metals, but they figured that you couldn't eat them anyway so what was the use? (Better to buy more ammunition.)

When the grid went down, Jack wished they had been able to afford the generator they had planned for, but by then it was too late. It was the beginning of fall and luckily they had a wood fire, a woodpile, plenty of propane and some camping style wood burning stoves and a rocket stove.

Jack had also stockpiled enough gas to refill both their cars once each. They had a Suburban and a Dodge grand caravan, and when the lights went out they moved the two vehicles to the rear of the house to keep them out of sight.

The plan, given that they did not have an alternative place to go, was to hunker down in place. None of their family was near and the only suitable place that Jack could think of was the farm belonging to their friends Bill and

Cindy, who lived out in the country past Manassas towards Shenandoah. But they had made no plans and they did not want to impose uninvited. How would they feel if the roles were reversed, after all?

Bill was an old friend from Jack's army days. He had fully embraced the prepper thing, but had gone beyond that to writing a libertarian blog highly critical of the Administration. Jack agreed with him, but given that he and Caitlin worked in DC and had security clearances, he didn't want to make any waves.

Jack and Caitlin worked on getting their place ready to sit out the coming chaos following the cyber-attack. They did not in fact know it had been a cyber-attack, they just knew that the power had gone out and that it appeared to be widespread. They were getting FEMA updates on their wind-up radio, which were mainly transmitting locations for FEMA refugee camps and food distribution areas.

There was no more fuel in the gas stations so there was a network of pickup points for FEMA buses that would take people in. The unofficial word was that firearms were now outlawed and you had to turn them in, and anyone in receipt of handouts had to be RFID chipped.

Apparently, you did not have to go into the camps permanently, but if you took food handouts and returned home on the buses, you had to be chipped and file your address and details with FEMA.

Initially after the blackout their street had been pretty social, more so than in normal times. The situation had drawn a lot of neighbors out of their homes to talk and pass around information and rumor. There was talk of mass exoduses from the cities and gridlock on the roads, with many ignoring FEMAs request to concentrate under their control.

They had not seen much traffic, either foot or vehicle, through their sub-division and so far no rioting or looting had spread their way. However, there were rumors of mass violence as the mobs tried to get out of the cities into the surrounding country.

The remainder of the utilities had all shut down a couple of days after the power went out. There was no longer any water service. As the days dragged into weeks this took its toll, along with the beginning of starvation, and activity dropped on the street. Some families drove to the FEMA reception center downtown, or took the bus there instead. Others decided to head out and try to make it to relatives or simply into the country. Many stayed in place.

Jack had boarded up his ground floor windows internally with plywood and barricaded his front door, including moving an upright piano from the opposite wall in the foyer to block the doorway. They had shifted to cooking on propane tanks on a camping stove in the kitchen. It was the start of fall and they had firewood, but it wasn't really cold enough to need it yet.

Jack had an old camping shower tent that he set up in the yard over a deep drop latrine that he dug. They would go potty in a bucket, and tip it into the hole, with the adults simply going out to this improvised outhouse for 'number twos'. He was using biocide to tackle the waste in the hole and gradually filling it in with dirt; he would start another hole and move the tent when it was full.

They still had plenty of drinking water in 55 gallon drums in the basement, and there was a small lake that had fish nearby that he planned to replenish from, filtering and boiling the water as necessary. Jack had rain barrels attached to the downpipes on the corner of the house, and they had initially used this water to flush the toilets before they decided to block them as a defense against backflow and gas.

They were even able to shower, using the rainwater heated up over a wood stove to fill a solar shower. Jack had rigged a bar up over the shower in the master bedroom to hang the solar shower from, and it was fairly comfortable to use. The bath in the main bathroom was still occupied by the 'water bob' that they had filled before water service stopped.

It was not really practical to run a watch system, and there really did not seem to be much going on. Jack relied a lot on their German Shepherd family dog, Jasper. He barked without fail whenever anyone approached the house.

Jack took to stashing his tactical vest and rifle in an easily accessible central place. He had started wearing his battle belt with his handgun and some magazine pouches all the time anyway, and Caitlin and Andrew wore their battle belts also. Jack always slung his rifle on his back when he went outside.

The rifles and shotguns were moved room to room inside the house to keep them close, and the 'Alamo' was in the basement. They put the weapons up on six inch nails Jack had hammered into the walls, to keep them available yet safe from the young kids.

They ran the kids through 'bad guy' drills for taking cover in the basement. When they weren't doing chores in the house or the yard, Jack and Andrew often took turns sitting in a chair by an open window in an upstairs bedroom, just listening and observing the junction. Between that and Jasper, they hoped to avoid being taken by surprise.

There had been some gunfire in the distance from time to time, sometimes the sirens of emergency response vehicles, but none of those lately. It was plain from the rumor mill that although FEMA was determined to concentrate everyone at their reception centers and camps, it was not working out like that. Many had gone in to the camps; others just used the distribution centers, handing over their firearms and getting chipped for the privilege.

Jack had expected more of a problem in his area from looters and marauders, but although he could hear the evidence of the gunfire in the distance, they had not really seen anyone transiting through the neighborhood. It was true that their sub-division was off the beaten track, it was not an obvious transit route so may have been bypassed.

Jack also wondered whether it had something to do with the high proportion of ranking government workers and those in the employ of the various DC alphabet agencies who resided in the area. Perhaps the area had been a higher focus for protection by law enforcement agencies?

There were some bad rumors spreading around about treatment at the FEMA camps. Because of this, many had headed out to the countryside or remained at home in their properties outside of the zones.

Of course, incompetence and corruption before the collapse had transferred to the current Regime. Progressive socialism with its doublethink logic went hand in hand with cronyism, incompetence and corruption. Those that actually handed over their guns in return for registration and food made the mistake of thinking the Regime was all-knowing, when in fact it was mostly a confidence trick. The corruption worked both ways, it benefited the cronies but it also created gaps for those wishing to evade the oppression.

Some four weeks after the power went out the family was eating lunch in the kitchen when they heard loudspeakers out in the streets. Jack cautioned them not to show themselves and left the kids with Caitlin while he and Andrew went to look out. They saw four military Humvees, two of them parked in the middle of the four-way junction. They seemed fairly innocuous, they were unarmored and they did not have weapons mounted on top.

One of them had, in place of a weapon, a large loudspeaker array mounted on top. It was blasting out a message: "THIS IS A FEMA MESSAGE. THIS AREA IS NOT SECURE. FOR YOUR SAFETY AND SECURITY WE REQUIRE YOU TO MOVE TO THE NEAREST

FEMA COLLECTION POINT. YOU ARE AT RISK FROM EXTREMIST ELEMENTS AND CRIMINALS." and so the message continued in a similar vein until it looped around again.

"That's a psychological operations unit," Jack said to Andrew.

Just down the street across the junction were parked the other two Humvees. The soldiers were going door to door knocking and when there was an answer they were handing out boxes of MRE rations. They seemed to be taking notes in conversation with those households that chose to show themselves.

"So," Jack said, "That's probably a civil affairs team."

"But Dad, you said they could not operate here in the States?"

"Yep, but they are. Ok, keep it quiet, we are not announcing our presence. Go tell Mom and keep Jasper and the kids quiet, I'll stay on watch."

The civil affairs team moved across the junction and knocked on their door, but they made no response, Andy keeping Jasper quiet. They moved on, going door to door down the street. Finally, the teams packed up and moved off. Jack could hear the distant voice from the speakers coming from further up the road, at the next junction, as the military teams continued their mission.

Chapter Two

A couple of days later, it was mid-morning and Jack was sitting up in the watch position. He was reading a book with one ear on the street, glancing up occasionally. He could hear Caitlin in the kitchen, where Andrew was helping her with a chore, and the two young kids were playing down in the basement.

The junction was to his south east, and the road that ran away from the junction in a south easterly direction dropped off into some dead ground as it ran off downhill.

He heard the sound of a powerful car engine and looked up to see a small convoy of four vehicles crest the hill from the south east and stop some two hundred meters away in front of the Johnson's house. There were two black Suburbans and two pickup trucks.

As the vehicles came to a halt a number of men jumped from them and split, some headed towards the Johnsons house on the right and the others across the

31

street to another house; Jack didn't know who lived there. He did know that the Johnson's had decided to stay.

The men were dressed in a variety of civilian and tactical type clothes but they were all well-armed and wearing tactical vests. On the one hand they appeared scruffy and non-uniform, on the other they moved like experienced operators. They reminded him of security contractors he had come across on deployment; their appearance was like a mix of civilian paramilitary and SWAT.

Jack saw that remaining in the passenger seat of one of the black Suburbans was a man in a dress shirt and tie. From what Jack could see of his head and shoulders through the windshield he was wearing a set of black civilian body armor over his shirt. Jack eyed him through his x4 scope and he looked like a pasty faced bureaucrat.

Interesting.

"Cat, bad guys, stand-to!" Jack shouted down to Caitlin as he shrugged his tactical vest on and closed the Velcro sides.

"What was that Hon?" Caitlin called back, in the process of making lunch.

"Bad guys! Get in the basement!" Jack repeated as he moved to the bedroom door so he could be heard.

"Ok, moving! Kids, bad guys! Basement, let's go, go, go!" replied Caitlin as she hustled towards the basement door.

As Jack turned back towards the window he heard the sound of gunfire from down the street. He moved back to the window, bringing his M4 up to the ready position to scan through the optic, but being careful to stay back in the shadows.

There was something going on at the house on the left; that was where the gunfire was coming from. At the same time, the group approached the Johnsons house and there was the crash of a shotgun as someone inside fired out at the armed men. They returned a fusillade of fire and rushed the door, kicking it down to enter, then dragging a bloodied Mr. Johnson out of the house and throwing him down.

One of the gunmen appeared to be the leader and he was stood back from the house out on the front lawn. Next, his men returned dragging Mrs. Johnson and their sixteen year old daughter, Sarah. Mrs. Johnson appeared to be pleading with them but one of the men punched her to the ground.

They brought Sarah to the leader and he grabbed her hair, blatantly inspecting her, then he reached up and ripped her shirt open, at which point Mr. Johnson got up and charged, to be felled by a burst of fire from one of the thugs. The girl tore herself from the leaders grasp and ran to her mother, where they both crouched in each other's arms while the thugs stood around laughing.

At that point Jack forgot all thoughts of remaining low profile. It was simply not in him to let this continue. He raised the rifle and took aim, firing and hitting the leader center mass, dropping him. He then followed with several more shots into the leader's body as he sprawled on the ground, and then switched fire to the other gunmen.

As his shots rang out, the thugs reacted by bomb-bursting for cover. Jack took some rapid shots and hit another as he ran for the cover of some bushes. He then began scanning for targets. Mrs. Johnson and her daughter had been frozen in place and then after a short delay they reacted and ran to Mr. Johnson, hysterically rolling him onto his back and trying to help him.

There must have been around fourteen bad guys, less the two that had already been hit. They had dispersed to cover and were now hard targets. It was clear that they were trained shooters, but clearly not infantry.

They had not yet located his firing point and he saw one taking cover by the rear wheel of one of the Suburbans, facing the wrong way. Jack took aim and squeezed off a shot, taking him in mid torso through the side of his vest, avoiding the ballistic plates and dropping him instantly.

One of the enemies must have seen his muzzle flash from within the bedroom window and a shout went up as the target indication was passed out. Suddenly, a squad automatic weapon (SAW) opened fire from the cover of a landscaped embankment and the room around Jack came alive with the violent crack of passing high velocity 5.56mm rounds and the smacking and splintering as the rounds passed through the thin bedroom wall.

Jack threw himself to the floor and crawled out through the bedroom door as the rounds passed through the room like some sort of lethal hornets' nest, throwing bits of plaster and dust into the air. He crawled along the landing and headfirst down the stairs.

Jack ran through the foyer to the top of the basement stairs, wrenched open the door, and called down to Caitlin, "Cat, we're under attack. I'm going out back with Andy. Keep the kids down. Have you got the shotgun?"

"Yes. Hon, for God's sake, be careful!" she called back from the bottom of the basement steps, shotgun held at the low ready. "I love you."

"I love you too," said Jack as he headed towards the back door, where Andrew was waiting, M4 in hand and battle belt on, as they had planned. "Ok, as we discussed Andy, stay in cover and protect the rear. This is gonna get sporting - don't hesitate. If they come round, take them out. They're wearing armor, so aim hips and heads. If you get in trouble, call me."

They jogged out the back door and across the deck, Andrew running to a wood pile at the rear of the property and taking a position to cover the left rear of the house. Jack turned left and ran around to the right front side of the house, heading towards the edge of the wooded yard where it ran along the top of the bank before the open grassy easement as it sloped down to the road.

From among the trees he could cover the junction to his front and also the front of the house, to his left, with enfilade fire. Andrew was covering to the rear left of the house. The main weak spot was the left side of the house, that was blind to both of them, but there were two small windows behind shrubbery at ground level that accessed the basement. If the bad guys got to that wall and tried to breach those windows, Caitlin would have to stop them with the shotgun.

Now that Jack had moved from his fire position in the window, the bad guys must have thought they had him suppressed. They continued to demonstrate fire superiority and they had started to maneuver towards the house. There was a huge volume of fire ripping into the house and he was thankful for the basement and the hard cover that his wife and kids were in down there below ground level.

The enemy firepower was simply tearing into the house and they were firing through all the windows and even through the walls as they shot the place to pieces. They had not spotted him out there on the right flank in the tree line.

Jack saw a group of four break cover and run in single file from left to right across the far side of the junction towards the house opposite his. He engaged the rear guys first, making sure to give them an appropriate lead. He shot three of them in rapid succession, working up the line, the guys in front not realizing what had happened.

The front guy reached cover and turned to look for his guys behind him. He was only about a hundred meters away and his look of incredulity as he saw his team sprawled out on the road and on the verge was cut short as Jack shot him through the head.

They were all wearing body armor and Jack was trained to aim 'center mass.' He had reverted to his training. Sometimes his high velocity rounds found their way in past the front and rear ballistic plates, other times they did not. One of the guys was just winded and was rolling onto all fours to try and crawl to cover when Jack hit him with rapid fire, after which he switched fire onto the other two to make sure they stayed down permanently.

Hips and Heads. Get a grip.

The bad guys still had not spotted his position but the killing of the four man team spurred them to further efforts to suppress the house.

One of the pickups drove out into the junction and stopped there with a SAW gunner in the back, resting the machine-gun on the cab while he poured fire into the house, firing long bursts from a box of two hundred rounds. Jack ripped into the vehicle with his rifle, changed magazines, and then he went to rapid fire again, smashing the driver and gunner.

Jacks rage was growing.

My family, my kids, my house and these bastards are trying to wipe out everything that is precious to me.

He had knocked the SAW gunner back into the truck bed and he saw him getting up and trying to roll out the back. Jack riddled him with fire and expended the magazine shooting into the vehicle.

Ok, calm down, steady it down, hold the rage close, but think. If I screw this up, we are all dead.

He dropped the empty mag off the weapon and was pulling a fresh one out of one of the pouches on his vest when he heard the roar of the second pick up as it gunned towards the junction, supported by a massive weight of fire from the dismounted enemy.

The truck came towards the junction as Jack fitted the fresh magazine to his weapon. He could see a couple of guys in the back. Just then, he became aware of Andrew shouting from the back of the house. He got up and ran towards him; he could hear gunfire coming from over where Andrew was, and from the left side of the house.

As he rounded the corner, his view of the rear left corner of the house was blocked by the deck but he could see Andrew firing from a crouched position behind the woodpile to his left. He ran around the deck and Andrew's head swiveled towards him. His eyes were wide and his mouth was open with a kind of slack dazed expression. Seeing his dad he turned back and continued to fire to the left.

Jack came round the deck and saw one of the bad guys lying on the ground. Another was firing from the corner of the house; they must have sent a flanking team to the left also. Jack just kept on going, weapon up, walking forward rapidly, engaging the enemy gunman until he went down. Just as he looked back to see if Andrew was ok there was a massive crash from the front of the house.

"Stay here!" Jack shouted, running towards the back door, "Cover the rear!" As he ran, he dropped the magazine off his weapon, letting it fall to the ground, as he whipped another out of a pouch and slid it home.

Caitlin was in the basement covering the two babies with her body as she heard the men shouting outside of the windows, which were up high at ground level on the left side of the house. The windows were large enough to let someone crawl through.

She could hear the intense violence of the firefight going on above with the rounds cracking and whipping through the house. Jack had not covered the basement windows with plywood, to let light in during the day, and they were simply covered with curtains. Jasper was barking like crazy at the windows.

Suddenly one of the widows exploded inwards. She was instantly up on her knee pointing the shotgun at the opening and she heard one of the men outside shout "Fire in the hole!" before silhouetting himself in the small window.

Caitlin fired the shotgun and the '00' Buckshot smashed into the shape. There was a scream of agony and then the flash-bang went off outside, followed by a stream of curses from the attackers outside. She kept pumping and firing the shotgun through the smashed window, and also into the walls to each side, before she reloaded with spare shells from the side rail.

With one hand she reached for the kids who were both crying and screaming, "It's ok, it's ok, mommies here - it'll be ok." she repeated, as she kept the weapon trained on the window.

Around the front of the house, the two guys in the back of the truck jumped clear just short of the front door and the truck accelerated, bumping through the shrubbery and smashing into the reinforced front door. The door went flying back out of its frame and the reinforced bull bars on the front of the grill smashed the piano back and it skewed across the foyer with a ringing crash of discordant notes.

The truck reversed and the two dismounted guys ran in through the smashed doorway. One of them carried a SAW with a box of two hundred rounds on it and as he stepped to the right of the doorway, the other guy going to the left, he unleashed a long burst of fire, swinging the weapon in an arc. The long burst spewed across a large arc in front of him, smashing through the walls and passing through into the back of the house.

Luckily, he had not aimed the weapon down through the basement floor. His next arc was aimed up, chewing through the roof and into the upstairs rooms. The two guys from the truck cab joined the two already in the house and they prepared to stack up and move through the house.

Just as the last roar of SAW fire died away, Jack burst through the back door. He had line of sight through the archway where the basement door was situated, central to the house, and into the foyer.

He came on with righteous fury.

The piano was between him and the three men preparing to clear through the house, the SAW gunner was out of sight to the left. He came on with the M4 in his shoulder, both eyes open, firing rapidly and instinctively into the three men in front of him. He saw his rounds hit at least two of the men; one was hit in the throat and his blood sprayed out across the foyer closet, the other took a round through the skull, snapping his head back.

Jack pushed through the archway and as he did so he saw the third guy behind the piano break and try to run through the broken doorway. He instinctively laid the weapon onto him and pulled the trigger rapidly, dropping him in a sprawl as the corpse slid over the concrete step and into the shrubbery.

Jack was still walking forward firing and as he rounded the arch he heard the distinctive 'clunk' empty sound as he expended the last round in his magazine and the bolt locked itself to the rear.

Shit.

At the same time, he caught sight of the SAW gunner out of his peripheral vision to the left.

Jack dived behind the piano as a burst of fire ripped through the wall above him. He ended up sprawled on the ground, cheek pressed to the decorative tile, looking into the eyes of one of his daughter's dolls, incongruous in the violence.

He rolled, reached and freed the Glock from its holster, low crawled and moved to the right side of the piano as the SAW rounds continued to smash through it, the gunner trying to annihilate him. Jack popped around the piano and shot the guy rapidly in the legs, working up into his pelvis; as he fell to the floor Jack was up on one knee, firing into the gunner, before moving rapidly forwards and finishing him with a double tap to the head.

Jack realized that he was now exposed in the open doorway and he moved quickly back to the archway, holstering his handgun and putting a fresh magazine in his rifle. Suddenly there was silence, except for the crying of his babies in the basement and the barking of Jasper.

He ripped open the basement door, "Hon, are you ok? The kids?"

"Yea, we're good. You ok - and Andy?"

"Yea, we're good," he replied.

"Thank God. I've got bad guys round the side, trying to get in the windows."

"Ok, stay there, I'm gonna check it out."

Jack headed out back. "Ok, cover me," he shouted to Andrew, 'are you ok?"

"Yea Dad. Wow that was some crazy stuff."

"Ok, keep it focused, you did real good son. I'll clear the side of the house; we'll take it from there."

Jack moved up to the corner of the house. He could see the guy on the ground that Andrew had shot, and then laying out from the corner was the one he had got. As he approached, he put a round into each one, to the head, to make sure they were dead.

No live enemy left behind him.

As he neared the corner he stayed back from it and circled out to the left, keeping his weapon back from the corner but scanning carefully as he 'sliced the pie' and

42

brought more and more of the area beyond the corner into view. Eventually, he could see two men lying by the broken basement window, one moaning in place and the other trying to drag himself away across the lawn, both legs shredded and bleeding. They got the same treatment, double taps to each, then again, until they stopped moving.

Jack did not want to move up to them because he would be exposed to fire from across the road to his left. He was already exposed but having cleared the left side he moved back to the corner. He wasn't prepared to expose Andrew and himself by moving out with bounding over-watch to where the enemy had been. Such a clearance patrol would have been the only way to ensure there was no enemy out there, but it was too risky to expose Andrew. Anyhow, the two Suburbans were no longer there, they must have bugged out during the fight in the foyer.

"Ok, let's secure the house," he said to Andrew as he moved back to him. "We'll confirm the bad guys are dead and get them out of the way so the kids don't see them. Then, we'll get the hell out of here. Andy, you realize we can't afford to let any of these guys live right, it's just too dangerous?"

Andrew nodded.

They moved through into the foyer and dragged the bodies to the door, pitching them out. They took anything of value, their weapons, ammunition and body armor, in particular the SAW.

As they were picking up the last guy from the foyer Andrew noticed a chain round his neck and what looked like an ID badge stuffed inside his shirt. He brought it to Jack's attention. Pulling it out, it was a (Department of Homeland Security) ID badge, current.

They checked the others, they all had them. Civilian clothes, unmarked vehicles, with state of the art tactical vests and weapons, with full auto capability; it all made sense now. These bad guys were not marauders at all. They were FedGov, Regime thugs.

The currency of the Regime was fear. What better way to spread it.

Chapter Three

The only choice was to leave, to bug out. Not only was the house uninhabitable, shot to pieces and covered in blood from the attackers, with the front door hanging off, but the discovery that the marauders were in fact all part of the Regime fear machine made it doubly worrying. Had they called in the address with a 'contact report' during or after the battle?

The Suburbans had gone, so at least a couple had managed to run away. There were no emergency services anymore outside of the zones, no 911 call, flashing lights and police sirens coming to their aid.

The family had bug out bags ready to go and they started to load the two cars. Jack had already mostly loaded the trailer with their stored food for just such an eventuality, leaving it loaded in the garage, and together

45

with Andrew they started collecting the rest of their gear and bug-out bags and rapidly throwing it all either into the trailer or into the cars. They grabbed personal bags and also family camping gear and loaded up the vehicles and the trailer. Caitlin was grabbing the kids' clothing and all the various ancillaries that they needed, throwing it into bags.

They moved as fast as they could. They could have just jumped in the cars and left, but Jack felt they had to take the gamble that the marauders were a 'deniable' asset without immediate backup, because they needed to pack their supplies and equipment if they were to survive out there and not become refugees.

During the packing, they saw no-one. Not a single one of their neighbors had helped, nor did they come out of their houses now, those that were left.

Fear.

Even the Johnsons were no longer around, and Jack did not want to go down there and get involved in their grief. It looked like they had moved Mr. Johnson off the front lawn, probably taking him inside the house.

The Berenger's plan was to put the seats down in the minivan, which made a large cargo space, and load it up. Jack would drive it, alone, as the lead vehicle. The Suburban would be driven by Caitlin, towing the trailer, Andrew riding shotgun with the kids and dog in the back,

They would keep a 'tactical bound' behind Jack, the theory being that a tactical bound was not a specific distance, but depended on the ground. In close country it was shorter, in open country longer, the idea being that the distance of the tactical bound would prevent the family vehicle being caught in any contact that Jack might drive into up front.

They knew that the streets were not deserted, and although traffic was limited by the fuel situation, there was still traffic around. So although it was not completely unusual to be out driving, it was sufficiently unusual to be noticeable. Particularly if they were tied to the battle that had just taken place and ended up on any law enforcement BOLO lists.

They simply could not trust any law enforcement given what had just happened and given that they were armed and weapons were being confiscated; being stopped, questioned and searched would not go well for them.

Jack and Caitlin agreed that their best plan would be to go to Bill and Cindy's farm, if not to stay with them at least as a goal to get out of town and see them on their way. They knew that the great danger of bugging out without anywhere to go was that they could end up as refugees. They did have supplies, so long as they could keep them out of other people's hands, but without a solid base anywhere they went would be tenuous.

In fact, that first afternoon they didn't go anywhere far. They drove to one of the outdoor swimming pools that the HOA ran in their neighborhood, open only during the summer months. This particular pool was a couple of miles away and down a secluded lane, without having to leave the network of suburban back roads.

Jack cut the padlock on the gate and, once they had driven through, replaced it with a spare. He had collected breaking tools for just such a purpose. They drove into cover at the back of the pool buildings and got the cars into the trees. Jack figured that if law enforcement worked out what had happened at the house, and that the family had bugged out, it would be easy to catch them in a net of roadblocks.

They set up the tent in the woods and still had plenty of propane to cook with before they would have to use an open fire or the rocket stove. For the kids, it was another camping trip. They even got to watch a movie on the DVD in the Suburban. Caitlin concentrated on the kids while Jack and Andrew took turns with a roving watch throughout the night, accompanied by Jasper. The only thing the kids missed from their normal camping trips was an open fire.

Later that evening, when the rush was over and Sarah and Connor had gone to sleep, it was the quiet time. Jack noticed Andrew pacing nervously and he walked over to him, placing his hand on his shoulder and squeezing it reassuringly. Andrew looked at him and started to shake, and then he began to sob uncontrollably as the adrenaline come-down from the day's events began to take over. He hadn't stopped to think since the battle and the rush to evacuate, with the possibility of being chased or found. Now, he had time to reflect.

Jack pulled him into his chest and held him, "Its ok son, you did great, you didn't freeze, you did real good, I'm proud of you."

Caitlin came over and hugged them both, tears running down her face. She took Andrew and sat with him cradled in her lap as she comforted him, his soft sobbing more under control now. She gazed down at him under the fall of her blonde hair, just as she had when he was a baby. Jack took the watch.

How had it come to this?

The next morning they were up and packing at dawn. Jack had worked out a route solely along minor back roads. I was a little circuitous and he thought they had about fifty miles to go. They had battle cleaned all the weapons during the night, one firearm at a time, and reloaded all the magazines. They wore their battle belts and Jack wore his tactical vest; they wore civilian clothes, jeans and outdoor boots, and had not yet put on the tactical and camouflage clothing that they had for the backwoods.

Jack had a light jacket and put it on over his vest, so that at first glance in his car he would not appear to be kitted out. They all wore their handguns holstered on their battle belts and the rifles and shotguns were kept down resting by their legs so they were accessible but out of view. The idea was to move slowly so that they would not run into anything by surprise around a bend.

For this reason, and also so that they could get the kids out quickly if they had to, they did not use the child seats for Connor and Sarah.

They had a couple of two way 'walkie-talkie' VHF radios that they kept in the cars, recharging in mounts plugged into the 12 volt cigarette lighter socket. Jack wanted to stay off the radio as much as possible. In case something happened and he did not have time to grab and talk on the radio they arranged that he would use the hazard lights and/or the horn to indicate any trouble ahead.

Caitlin would stay a tactical bound behind and if Jack stopped she would reverse out to a safe spot, turn around, and wait for him to reverse out. If his vehicle was immobilized for any reason he would fight back on foot, with cover fire support from Andrew if possible.

The idea of going slowly was so as to not be taken by surprise and therefore they would hopefully be able to stop short of any trouble, reverse back, turn around and drive away. Jack did not want to be ramming or attempting to drive through any ambush or road blocks: not only did this have the potential to be a catastrophic fail, but it would force Caitlin to follow through after him, unless they were to get split up, and this would put the kids in danger.

The vehicles were not armored in any way and high velocity rounds would pass through them like a knife through butter. The only effective protection to be had from the vehicles was from the engine block and the metal parts of the wheels. The tires on the cars were also standard, not 'run-flats' and thus could be easily punctured, thus immobilizing the cars.

The drill for if they got stopped, maybe as a result of their vehicles being immobilized or trapped under enemy fire, was to get out into cover on the opposite sides of the vehicles from where the fire was coming from. They would return fire and then use fire and the cover provided by the ground to move out of the enemy kill zone and escape. Caitlin would run close protection on the young kids, while Jack and Andrew provided covering fire and 'leap-frogged' out of the kill zone by bounds, working as a buddy pair.

The route they had chosen avoided obvious main thoroughfares and kept to the smaller back roads, sometimes going in the wrong direction in order to get to a junction to take a minor road heading the right way. They got into the countryside south of Manassas.

Whenever they drove over a junction with a main road they saw evidence of the panic and the evacuation from the cities. Gas stations had run dry and were closed and many vehicles were abandoned by the side of, or even on, the road. Down the back roads there was less evidence of this, but there was still a trail of abandoned vehicles.

Occasionally they drove past parking areas that had become impromptu refugee camps, tents or tarps set up back in the woods or people simply living in their cars. They did not get much interest from the hopeless eyes of many of these starving beaten people.

Sometimes they saw evidence of violence, abandoned and occasionally burned out cars, bodies laid by the side of the road surrounded by the detritus of their looted possessions. They passed some groups of exhausted refugees, shambling along carrying their meager possessions, often pushing children in strollers also loaded up with what they could carry from their homes.

It seemed that, a month after the power had gone out, much of the violence had already happened; leaving the survivors starving, hopeless and exhausted, prey to gangs.

They were passing through a mix of open fields and forested areas, typical of Northern Virginia, when they entered a wooded area where the road started winding a little more. Jack came around a right hand bend at about twenty five miles an hour and saw the roadblock ahead, about one hundred meters distance.

It looked like two military armored Humvees, parked on each side of the road, staggered, so as to force vehicles to slow down; the turret mounted machine-guns facing opposite directions up and down the road. There were a couple of uniformed soldiers standing around.

Jack stepped on the brakes and put the car into reverse, as he did so he saw the guard in the road shout, raising his weapon. The turret gunner popped his head up behind the armored glass shield and trained his weapon on Jack's car. The troops at the roadblock opened fire.

The first burst from the turret gunner tore into the road in front of Jack, ripping up the asphalt in a storm of noise and violent impact. Jack ducked his head, using the wing mirror to reverse towards the bend. Rounds came cracking through his windshield, leaving white snowballs and cracks in the glass as they passed through.

Caitlin had been following Jack as they drove along. Andrew was scanning out to the sides. She had closed up a little to Jack given the close nature of the road in the trees and she did not want to lose sight of him. The tactical bound had shortened.

Sarah had started crying and Connor was asking for chocolate milk, which she didn't have. She had turned in the seat to try and console the kids when Andrew yelled out. She turned, took in the sight of Jack stopped and the roadblock ahead, and slammed on the brakes.

The heavy SUV with the trailer came to a slewing stop and she put it into reverse as Jack started to reverse back towards her, the sound of gunfire erupting from the roadblock. In her haste, she forgot the trailer, and as she reversed it jackknifed behind her, slamming into the tailgate, stopping her. She had only managed to get partially back round the bend, and was still in line of sight of the roadblock. She slammed her palm onto the car horn to alert Jack.

Jack saw the Suburban stopped in his rear view and turned the wheel to the right to angle the minivan across the road, stopping right there. He grabbed his rifle with one hand and opened the door with the other, rolling out into the road, slamming the door and popping up behind the hood of the car, by the wheel well. He brought his weapon up and started to engage the roadblock with rapid fire.

Without turning he shouted "Contact front! Andy push out right! Cat, get the kids into the ditch!"

Andrew grabbed his rifle and sprinted out to the right. There was an embankment on the right of the road, on the inside of the bend, overgrown by trees and covered in leaf litter. He scrambled up the slope, using one hand to steady himself, until he found a good tree to use as cover. He got down behind it; his rifle pushed out round the right side of the tree, and got a sight picture on the roadblock, opening rapid fire to support Jack down on the road.

Meanwhile, Caitlin had exited out of the passenger side of the vehicle, opened the rear door, grabbed the kids and scrambled with them into the ditch on the right of the road. Jasper darted out of the vehicle and joined the kids in the ditch. She had forgotten her shotgun, so she ran back to the vehicle with high velocity rounds cracking past her, grabbed it, and ran back to the kids. She told them to crawl and they were able to move back in the ditch out of line of sight of the roadblock.

Jack emptied a magazine, crouched into cover behind the wheel, removed the mag and put it into his dump pouch before grabbing another and reloading his M4. He glanced back, heard Andrew firing and saw that the kids had got out safe.

"Cover me, moving!" he screamed as he sprinted for the embankment, rounds slamming into the hood of the car and cracking overhead around him.

What they really needed to do was get away. But the problem was that both their vehicles were now immobilized in the kill zone and under enemy fire. All their stores and equipment were on board and if they tried to head out on foot they would not get far.

Jack got up behind Andrew, who was still firing, and shouted down to Caitlin "Cat, I'm gonna assault! Get the kids back into the woods and hide!" She looked back up at him with wide desperate eyes, her head shaking slowly from side to side.

He turned back to Andrew. "I'm going right flanking, moving round to the right on the embankment. I'll try and get into position above the Hummers to shoot down on them. Ok?"

Andrew nodded, took a bead on the turret of the nearest Humvee, and kept up his deliberate rate of suppressive fire.

Jack pulled back into dead ground away from the roadblock and moved around to the right, just out of sight on the other side of the slope. He pushed back up till he emerged on the summit behind a tree, looking down at the roadblock.

Both gun turrets were facing down the road towards his vehicles and there were also a couple of guys in fire positions behind each Hummer. They were firing at his minivan and also into the surrounding woods, where they had not yet identified Andrews's position. Andrew was well in cover using the slope and the tree, with just the muzzle of his rifle exposed. Jack was happy with that.

Jack pulled back and moved down to the furthest Hummer; he pushed back up into a position where he could see the two guys behind it and also down into the turret. His position was elevated enough that he had an angle into the armored turret where the gunner was standing.

He brought his weapon up and opened rapid fire into the turret, striking the gunner in the back of the head and upper back; he then switched fire to the two at the back of the vehicle and shot them down, before switching fire again to the two at the back of the other Hummer.

As his buddy sprawled on the ground, one of the enemies realized what was going on, trying to spin and engage Jack. A last shout burst from the dying man as Jack unloaded the remaining rounds from his magazine into him.

The remaining turret gunner was alerted and tried to disengage the lever to spin the turret but was not fast enough to track onto Jack as he launched himself headlong down the slope, dropping his magazine and putting on a fresh one as he ran.

Jack ran to the rear of the hummer and the turret gunner could not track him, so he reached down and grabbed his M4 from inside the Humvee before standing up and trying to get an angle on Jack. Andrews's bullet took the gunner in the base of his skull as he leaned up over the armored turret side, leaving him draped over the rim.

Jack quickly checked the vehicles were clear and went to check the enemy bodies. He saw one of them crawling away from the rear Hummer, a blood trail on the road surface.

Jack walked up to him, "Hey asshole!" he called and the guy rolled over onto his back, a handgun in his hand. Jack put his foot on the man's wrist, trapping the pistol to the road, and pointed his M4 down at him.

He could see the man was not dressed in army uniform, but in the blue tactical uniform of the FEMA Homeland Corps. The man's ID badge was laying on his body armor where he had it hung around his neck. He was maybe mid-thirties, fat with his belly protruding from under his tactical vest, a goatee grown over his double chins.

"Who are you?" Jack said to him.

"Go to hell." whispered the thug with false bravado.

"Really?" said Jack, as he raised the rifle to point at the guy's head. He saw the bravado evaporate, to be replaced by fear filling the man's eyes.

"No, no, please." whispered the Regime thug who had just tried to murder Jack's family, just before the 5.56mm round hit him in the face. His head was raised as he pleaded and the bullet went in through his eye, exiting out the back of his skull in a mess of brains as it smacked into the asphalt.

Jack went to check the rest of the enemy before calling Andrew down.

They stripped the bodies and vehicles of useful weapons and ammunition. They had a collection by now. It appeared to be a National Guard roadblock run by the DHS agent. The National Guard guys were all basically kids, none of them wearing combat patches on their right arms. It was a tragedy that they had been used in this way.

Jack had sent Andrew back to call for Caitlin and the kids and they extricated the Suburban. It had not been badly hit, but the minivan had been shot up badly, the engine block riddled with bullets and both front tires flattened. Jack considered taking a Hummer but decided that it would not only be too high profile, but also probably had a tracker on it.

They loaded what they could into the Suburban and continued on their way, threading through the roadblock and on down the road. Jack was again concerned that a call could have gone out and he worried about a quick reaction force (QRF) or airborne reaction force (ARF). Rather than try and outrun any aerial surveillance he headed down the road for a few miles until they spotted what looked like a vacant run-down farm back through the trees.

Jack approached it cautiously in case anyone was in residence, but there was no one around and they pulled the Suburban and trailer into an old barn round the back. It looked like the farm had been looted and then abandoned. Jack had a good look round as a clearance patrol while Andrew stood guard, before they relaxed. They took it in turns to stand watch while they prepared to stay the night.

Shortly after they had taken cover in the barn, they heard the sounds of a helicopter flying down the road towards the roadblock. Andrew went to look out but Jack stopped him. A few minutes later, the helicopter returned, did a circuit over the farm, and continued down the road.

Later, they heard the engines of Humvees down on the road as a recovery party drove down to the roadblock.

The derelict farm escaped their notice.

Late that night, Jack was on watch. He was doing a circuit out the back of the barn, getting a bit of fresh air, when it all came crashing in on him. The violence of the last couple of days coupled with the danger to his family, his responsibility to keep them safe and his fear for them.

Images of his combat deployments to Afghanistan and Iraq flashed up, superimposed over the dead of the last days. He tried to fight it, but the tears welled up and he could not fight back the sobs.

He heard a soft noise from the barn as Caitlin quietly slid from her sleeping bag. She came up behind him and put her arms around him; he turned and lowered his head to her neck as he cried it out.

So much for being a tough guy.

But it was not the first time since he had been home that the tears had come unwarranted, triggered by some unknown thing.

They set out early the next morning for the final twenty miles of their journey, Caitlin driving so that Jack could maximize his tactical options and use of his weapon. They did not come across any Regime patrols. It was clear from the response times the day before that the Regime forces in this sector were spread thin. They had to patrol and cover large distances.

Although the Regime had at its disposal what was left of Americas impressive military, with all the technology and equipment that entailed, in Jack's estimation it would be a mistake to think them all-seeing. True, if the 'eye of Mordor' was turned on to you then you were in trouble, but it was in the cracks, gaps, frictions and inefficiencies that people like the Berengers survived.

Jack thought that they probably concentrated operations in certain key sectors, probably the more urban ones, only occasionally venturing out into the sticks. It was probably a patrol like that which they had encountered yesterday. The urban areas were where most of the violence and gang activity was concentrated anyway, and they had seen evidence of it decreasing as they got further out into the rural areas.

Jack did worry about aerial surveillance the most, from UAV drones, helicopters and even satellites. In particular he worried about thermal imaging (TI) from those assets.

He had seen the damage that attack helicopters could do in Afghanistan and he did not want to be on the receiving end. There were possible counter measures, and he was going to have to seriously think about how to approach the problem.

Chapter Four

As they were rolling along the winding rural back roads that morning, they didn't see too many refugee camps beside the road. However, at one point they passed a man sat straddling a motorbike, back off the road on a dirt trail.

The man was sitting casually astride the bike and seemed to pay a little too much attention to the Suburban with the trailer as they passed him. Jack turned around in his seat and as the guy was dwindling behind them he saw him take out what looked like a walkie-talkie and speak into it.

"OK, stand-to everyone, I think we're gonna have some trouble." said Jack.

Caitlin looked across at him, worried. "What is it?" she asked.

"Guy on the bike that we passed, he paid us too much attention, and I think he radioed ahead."

As they came around a bend about a mile later, they saw a green pickup pull out behind them from the cover of a side trail and some trees. They had not seen it as they passed, but it was now several hundred meters behind them. Caitlin instinctively sped up but Jack told her to hold it steady, to just keep going at a safe speed.

Andrew was looking back and passed the information that there were at least four armed men in the vehicle, two in the cab and the other two in the back. The pickup started to accelerate towards them. Jack knew that trying to outrun them could well end up in disaster, and maybe there was another vehicle up ahead acting as a cut-off group.

"Ok, round this next bend, slow it down enough so I can get out," he said. "Andrew, protect the car in case of more trouble ahead, and in case these guys roll through me. Stop round the corner and I will rejoin you there."

Caitlin nodded and as they curved round the bend, temporarily out of sight of the chasing vehicle, she slowed the car down. Jack opened the door and rolled out onto the verge. As soon as he was gone, she sped up again and continued round the corner, stopping so Andrew could get out and pull security.

Jack rolled into the ditch and came up on one knee with his weapon pointed back down the road. He was barely in a fire position when the pickup accelerated around the corner towards him. He could see the two men in the back holding rifles at the high port, and the passenger had a rifle up and pointed forwards through the windshield.

Jack acquired a sight picture and opened fire rapidly into the windshield of the approaching car, his main target the driver.

The impacts of his rounds left starburst shapes across the windshield as they smashed through it on their way through the pickup, exiting out the back.

The passenger brought his weapon to bear and returned fire towards Jack through the glass. The vehicle was now about seventy five meters away. There was a spray of blood as the driver was hit and the vehicle veered across the road, suddenly without power, coming to a bumping halt in the ditch.

Jack switched fire onto the passenger; they both traded fire before Jack's rounds hit home, thus killing the two occupants in the front seats.

As the pickup sat half in the ditch, the two guys leapt out of the back of the truck bed: one to Jacks right, taking up a fire position on the vehicle behind the angle of the hood, the other bursting out to the left, sprinting across the road into the opposite ditch.

As the rounds from the guy behind the hood starting to crack past Jack, he dropped from his knee into a prone position, using the ditch for maximum cover. Taking aim through his ACOG, Jack shot the man through the head, watching it snap back as he dropped behind the hood, one arm flailing limply off the hood as he went down.

Jack rapidly switched fire to the other man in the ditch, killing him with several shots to the torso. He wasn't wearing any armor. Jack scanned back over the scene of the killing, as his weapon sight passed over the downed assailants he fired a couple of extra rounds into each, to make sure they were not coming after him. Then scanning the scene for a moment more, he saw no other threats and sprinted back around the bend to rejoin his family.

"Let's roll!" he called out as he came round the corner to see the parked vehicle with Andrew standing guard, "let's move!" He really did not want to continue forward, in case the bandits had any more buddies ahead, but he also did not want to drive back past the scene.

However, it was not prudent to carry on ahead into a potential ambush that the pickup may have been driving them towards, so they turned around and headed back down the road a ways, to where they could take an alternative side road.

As they passed the ambush site, Jack and Andrew vigilantly scanned the bodies for movement, weapons trained through the open windows of the Suburban. Caitlin had put a DVD in the roof mounted player to distract Sarah and Connor, so they never even noticed.

Once they were past, they brought their weapons back inside to resume a low profile posture.

Luckily they did not encounter any more hostile vehicles as they exited the area.

They drove down the road towards Bill and Cindy's farm. It was situated off a rural road out in the countryside. They arrived at the turning, which was a small lay-by with the gate to the farm driveway set back from the road; there was a small gravel area where they could park.

They could see the farm building set back several hundred meters away on a rise, behind a screen of trees and nestled in a cluster of barns and outbuildings. The gate was of metal construction and it was locked shut with a chain and padlock. There was no sign of anyone.

Jack decided not to park in the obvious place and had Caitlin drive on a little way to a place where they could get the car off the road onto the verge and in the cover of some trees. He told Andrew to pull security, everyone else to stay in the car and he climbed out, slinging his rifle on his back.

He walked cautiously along the road for the fifty meters back to the gate and stood, staring up to the farm. Beside the driveway, which curled up to the farm buildings, was a ditch with a hedgerow on the outside of it. Fifty meters back the hedgerow merged with a copse of trees before exiting on the far side and continuing alongside the driveway up to the farm.

Nothing.

He waited.

How to get their attention in the farm?

He was getting nervous, his family sitting there in the car just down the road. He was about to turn back to the car when he caught the glint of an optic from up near the farm buildings.

Crap!

He instinctively crouched and half turned to shout to Andrew when a soldier stood up from the edge of the small copse. Jack threw himself into cover, reaching back for his rifle, and was just pulling it forward when he saw that the soldier's weapon was held down by his side.

"Whoa there, Jack, steady there!" called the unknown soldier as he started to walk forwards, grinning. Jack paused, and stood up slowly. No shots rang out. The soldier approached, and Jack still did not know him.

"How do you know my name?" asked Jack, feeling a little dumb, as the man approached. He was a big guy, fully geared up in the old style woodland BDUs, with a tactical vest and AR15 style rifle. Jack realized that although he looked like a soldier, he did not look like an active duty army soldier. He also looked well trained and switched on.

"Bill told me, on the landline. You must have seen him watching you through his binoculars. I'm Jim," said the soldier as he extended his hand, which Jack took, "welcome to the farm."

Jack called the family forward in the car as Jim unlocked the gate, explaining that they had an observation post (OP) in the copse covering the entry gate, keeping it low profile. They had a field telephone run up to the farm, which was how they were able to alert Bill, who had recognized Jack through the binoculars and given the all clear.

They walked up to the OP position, Caitlin following in the car, and when they got on top of it they saw that it was a concealed foxhole with overhead protection, camouflaged in the trees. There was another man still in the OP, covering his sectors, who nodded to Jack as he approached.

There was an ATV concealed at the rear of the copse; Jim told Jack to follow in the car as he led the way up to the farm on the ATV. He drove round the back to one of the barns and gestured for Caitlin to drive in and park.

There were several other vehicles in the barn. Jim took them round to the back door of the farm building where they bumped into Bill, who had a huge grin on his face. He grabbed Jack in a bear hug, only letting him go to grab hold of Caitlin and the kids.

"Damn it Jack, it's good to see you. I was worried about you and the family."

Bill was older than Jack by about ten years. Jack had served under him as a young lieutenant when Bill was a Major in the Ranger Battalion. Bill had mentored Jack and they had kept in touch after Bill left the service.

Bill hustled them into the kitchen where they found Cindy. She broke off the coffee she was making on the wood stove to launch herself into a hug fest with Caitlin and the kids. Jack and Bill sat down at the kitchen table and Jack suddenly felt relieved yet extremely tired all at the same time.

They all sat around the kitchen table, drank coffee, ate, and talked for a long time. Jack was determined to make it clear to Bill that he did not want to impose on him. He explained what had happened at their house, to Cindy's huge shock, and how they had decided to head to the farm simply as a first stop and somewhere to aim for as they bugged out. Bill and Cindy would not hear of it, and told them they were welcome at the farm for as long as they needed.

It soon became apparent from the comings and goings in and out of the kitchen, and from what they could see outside of the kitchen windows, that there were quite a few more people at the farm, most of them moving about in some form of camouflage clothing.

After a while, the kids started to drop off to sleep, including Andrew, and Cindy helped Caitlin put them to bed in a spare room. Then they sat around and talked.

As it got dark outside Cindy lit some lamps. Bill began to explain that he was part of a Resistance movement, fighting against the excesses of the Regime, the destruction of liberty and the loss of the Constitution. The time for political solutions was long gone, and the only option left for them was to fight to restore the Republic.

One of the key things that had concerned Bill in his operational planning was the potential for reprisals against the families of Resistance fighters. It was plain that the Regime respected no law or morality and there was no separation of fighters from their families or the public at large. It was a form of total war, against the American people.

Regime forces would simply wipe out a man's family if they discovered he was a Resistance fighter. It was brutal and nihilistic and entirely in line with national socialist tyrannies throughout the ages. It was a game of kill lists, lethal raids and reprisals by the Regime. Truly, the Regime had the monopoly of terror and was exploiting it to reinforce their agenda of fear.)

Bill explained that since before the collapse he had been working covertly with his Resistance cell on a couple of secret hidden locations in the hills and forests to the west of the Shenandoah Valley. They had found several locations that were well hidden in small valleys, ravines or draws in the forested hills. Each location could only be accessed by hiking trail at a distance from a single forest road or track.

They had selected the best location and taken small excavators up there and over time had dug reinforced bunkers into the sides of the draw, creating underground living spaces in the hollows.

They had named it Camp Zulu.

(The idea was that this hidden place would be a refuge for the families and loved ones of those engaging in the Resistance fight.) Bill hoped to expand the number of bases as time went on. The fighters could live there from time to time, and visit, but operations would not be conducted from those bases.

Instead, each base would be for the families of a certain Resistance company and that company would rotate through providing security and defensive forces for that base, while operating elsewhere. Each location, in addition to the underground living spaces, would have a well sited network of fighting positions dug in around it.

Not everyone in the network would move there. Bill and Cindy would stay on their farm, as would many others, because they needed to maintain the network outside of the forests for intelligence gathering and passage of information. Bill had a ham radio and other communications equipment in his barn for this purpose.

(One of the reasons for the underground bunkers was concealment primarily not from naked eye observation, but from aerial TI surveillance.)If there were small signs of the bases, this would not be the end of the world, although best avoided if possible; the reason was that the woods and forests were by no means empty; they were filled with the camps and campfires of those that had fled the cities, each group trying to grub an existence out there in the trees. So a small amount of visible sign was acceptable, just not the presence of an organized camp and large numbers.

"Jack, I want you to join us at Camp Zulu," said Bill.

Jack glanced over at Caitlin and replied. "My absolute priority is my family. I get what you are doing and I admire it. We've seen the way it is first hand over the last couple of days, so I understand the need. But I'm not ready to leave my family; I have to be there to protect them."

Bill grinned, "I thought you would say that. What I want to do is offer you all a place at Zulu. I'd do that anyway Jack, for the kids' sake. But I want you to train my guys."

Jack looked at him quizzically, "You mean, just a training role, based out of Camp Zulu?"

"Right, Zulu is also planned as the only training location; it's a dual location, families plus those rotating through training. It's very well hidden with some good backwoods real estate. I could use your expertise."

Jack looked over at Caitlin, "What do you think Hon, do you want some time to talk about it?"

She looked him in the eye, "Actually, no, it sounds like a plan. We need a safe place, and there isn't a better offer out there. If you agree to just a training role, then I'm happy. I've been worried enough about you over the last couple of days."

"Ok, it's a deal," he smiled at Caitlin and reached out to shake Bills hand, "we'll do it."

"Ok guys," said Bill, "that's great, we have a convoy heading up there the day after tomorrow, so rest up here and we can prepare to get you up there."

Jack spent some time in discussion with Bill before their departure and they went over the scope of the Resistance plan.

One of the primary concerns was operational security, OPSEC, and the fear of betrayal by infiltrators. Bill had been working on that and he explained in broad terms that he had set up his networks separated by cut-outs. He had been working on an intelligence gathering and collating network based amongst the population.

One of the key strengths was that this was a local Resistance movement, spread across communities in the region, based in the surrounding area. As such it was based in, amongst and from, the population. This meant that it was easier to vet participants.

It also meant that the fighters were often local, with the addition of some vetted outsiders, so the community was broadly supportive of them. One of the priorities was to retain the support of the population and avoid reprisals against families and communities. This was the main reason for moving the loved ones of the active fighters out of the communities and into safe hidden locations.

However, those safe locations were primarily designed for the families of active fighters and there was a whole support network based around those who remained in place in their farms, villages and small communities.

Those going to the hidden camps would be taking as much in the way of supplies that they could, but they would be supplemented by the community from the producers that continued to operate on the small farms in the region. There would be no forced tithe or tax, which is why the goodwill of the population was paramount.

Those remaining in place in their homes would not be active in any Resistance fighting. They would produce food, and act as the eyes and ears, the sensors, for the intelligence gathering operation.

Not everyone was involved, and OPSEC was paramount, but there were enough Patriots spread around through the communities, in the contested zones where

Regime control was weaker, to allow the network to function. Clearly, the plan was well thought and already in place, but it was in the early stages of implementation and needed development.

There would no doubt be glitches.

One of the great weaknesses of the Regime was corruption, based in part on how the progressives had infiltrated the fabric of the country before the collapse, and the moral bankruptcy of the Regime that continued into this civil war.

It also came out of the tedious and crippling bureaucratic system that had pervaded the country before the collapse; the stifling bureaucracy of rules and regulations that had acted as a layer of control because it was so tedious to navigate and so easy to fall foul of.

The corruption allowed a black market and barter economy to thrive. There was an interaction across the lines in the gray areas of the corruption and greed of the Regime bureaucrats. It was in those gray areas and gaps that the Resistance movement saw its chances and was also able to procure items, information and supplies that were scarce.

Fuel was an example. It was scarce and closely guarded; a coupon system used to allocate supplies to those the Regime considered needed it, mainly the security apparatus. Corruption circumvented this, allowing bureaucrats at many levels to procure fuel as they required. Occasionally, a tanker truck would go missing in the chaos of the contested sectors, a bureaucrat compensated in some way for the favor.

As part of the discussion, Bill told Jack where he believed the enemy forces situation currently stood. His farm was located in the country south west of Warrenton, which made it about thirty five miles south west of Manassas and roughly central to the area of operations.

The two primary Regime zones were DC to the north east and Richmond to the south. DC was clearly the center of the Regimes power base and operations were ongoing to subsume the surrounding urban areas into the pacified zone; as such, Manassas was currently being 'pacified' by Regime forces.

The Regime was also conducting ongoing route clearance and convoy supply operations along the main supply routes (MSRs) in the region; the I-95 joining DC and Richmond, with the I-66 heading out west from DC and the I-64 similarly from Richmond. The I-66 and I-64 joined up with the I-81 that ran north-south through the Shenandoah Valley and was also an MSR.

The Regime was operating patrols on this route, the I-81, which bisected the forested terrain of the Shenandoah ridge to the east and the George Washington National Forest to the west. It was in these forests that the hidden camp and the training base were located.

In the areas to the west of Manassas and Richmond, and particularly in the Shenandoah Valley and the surrounding rural areas, the regime presence was currently not strong enough to effectively lock down the area.

It was the intent to begin to train and develop an effective armed Resistance, initially operating to disrupt regime operations in the Shenandoah Valley. The intent would be to start slowly, conducting harassment operations to deny use of the I-81 and the valley, before expanding the scope and area of operations.

Bill was determined to keep his Resistance organization safe from electronic warfare, tracking and interception. He, and several others in the region, did have ham radios that were primarily used for listening in to events and news as they were passed on the network; there were multiple Resistance movements across the country and they were not centrally coordinated, but rather fragmented organizations of individuals, communities, militias and ad hoc groups in all shapes in sizes.

The primary means of communication within Bills organization was a mixture of dead drops, 'runners' and caches. It would make the tempo of operations slower, but keeping it low tech would limit surveillance and tracking by Regime assets.

Both Bill and Jack had served in Afghanistan and they well remembered how the electronic warfare assets would listen in to ICOM chatter on enemy networks in real time as attacks were taking place. The Resistance did possess VHF 'walkie-talkie' type radios and there was a place for them, but mainly the focus would be on being 'old school' and low tech.

Bill also had a satellite system that he could use while the internet was locked down to transmit messages to the internet that remained outside of Regime control

Supply would largely be conducted by a 'quartermaster' system using cut-outs, dead drops and caches. Caches would be identified with a marker system to allow the location to be passed on and found by subsequent users.

(In simple terms, directions would be given to go to a certain location and identify the primary marker. This could be something such as an identifiable tree or fence corner, for example. From the primary marker the searcher would look for the described secondary and tertiary markers, leading to the location of the cache, hidden or buried in waterproof containers.)

For other situations, a policy of hiding in plain sight could be adopted. For example, discreet farmers markets had grown up since the collapse, bartering in goods. It was a simple thing for a covert Resistance team to show up at a market and 'barter' for supplies, that would then be driven away in plain sight.

One of Jack's concerns was the co-location of a training camp in the same place as where the families were to be in hiding at Camp Zulu. They developed the concept further in discussion together. It was agreed that Zulu remain as a well hidden 'family only' camp.

They would establish another training camp separated from Zulu. Bill had some ideas based on an abandoned farm he had come across while conducting his initial reconnaissance. It was in the same forested area as Zulu, up on the high ground, and it had a farm house, some outbuildings and a large barn type building that would be good for a training location. It was about five miles away from Zulu, the only route between the two being a small trail.

Although many of those that would be trained at this new camp would be the fighters whose families were at Zulu, this plan to separate the locations worked better because it kept the activity away from Zulu. This would also create a firewall between any new recruits, potential spies however well vetted, and the families.

They agreed that Jack would take over the establishment and running of this training camp once he had settled his family at Zulu. They agreed to call the camp, 'Victor Foxtrot', which stood for Valley Forge, a name which they considered appropriate.

Bill had recruited a group of volunteer fighters that was about three platoons strong at this point and which he hoped to continue to recruit to get it up to strong Company strength. The concept was to hide this force out at the training camp in the wooded hills and train over the winter, beginning operations in the spring once training was complete.

Bill and Jack both realized that they were fighting an irregular Resistance campaign and the Regime had the upper hand in terms of surveillance assets and firepower, and they would have to organize and operate accordingly.

The broad concept was to train up a force based on a basic cell structure that could come together to coalesce into larger formations in order to allow the Company to concentrate force as appropriate. A system of dispersal and cell level small team IED operations, infiltration, and also concentration of force into larger groupings when necessary

The Company would begin to conduct operations as soon as they were ready, but in a most careful way. Strategically, they would aim to harass, disrupt and dislocate Regime operations with the initial aim of preventing the pacification of the sector.

If they could establish that, they would increase the pressure on the Regime safe zones to demonstrate the weakness of the Regimes legitimacy as the provider of 'safety and security'. This would be accompanied by an information operations campaign in order to attempt to wake up the people and generate support for the Patriot cause.

The focus of the Company training would be on small unit insurgency operations, attacking the Regime where it was weak. Force on force pitched battles were to be avoided. The Company would be trained to operate as small teams but with the ability to mass up to Company level in order to concentrate overwhelming force against key targets as necessary.

The big focus was on counter-surveillance, avoiding detection.

This would mean surprise attacks from ambush positions in order to temporarily overwhelm damage and destroy the enemy, before exfiltration to fight again another day. This would mean that both team members and leaders in the unit would have to develop an aggressive and independent way of thinking that would allow them to conduct operations as a small group, or come together and mass as a larger team.

Bill told Jack that the group he had so far was a somewhat eclectic bunch, a mixed bag of loyal Patriots, some of whom were better prepared than others. Many were veterans, others were not. They had all volunteered and were willing to put the required effort in. He had a core platoon sized group, of just less than thirty fighters, that he had been working with for some time, and they would be the baseline for the new unit.

Jacks role was to be as a lead trainer. Jim was also going with them along with the latest bunch of recruits and family members who were with them at the farm.

Jim Fisher had been a Special Forces NCO, an '18C' special operations engineer, an expert at explosives and demolitions. Jim had deserted before joining up with Bill. He would be Jack's second in command of training, effectively his 'First Sergeant', and would also be responsible for running the training for the IED specialists.

Jim came across as very competent and professional, an imposing figure with a relaxed manner, backed by just the suspicion of a potential for violence.

Bill also told Jack about Major John Cassidy, who was the company commander. He was currently up at Camp Zulu overseeing the final build and preparations. He was an active duty engineer officer who had deserted and still insisted on using his rank. He liked to stand on ceremony, Bill told him, but he was a good man. Jack would be working with him getting the Company ready, and supporting him with continuing training, in particular of any new recruits coming through.

Because of the cut-out system and the lack of communications, Bill would be sending Jack up with a letter of introduction for Major Cassidy, explaining the plans and arrangements.

Chapter Five

They left the next morning as part of a convoy taking personnel and supplies up to Camp Zulu. They had about sixty miles to travel as the crow flies, along country roads, and this meant that they needed to break the journey. It would not do to be in a hurry and run into trouble.

There was a safe farm on the plateau just over the Shenandoah ridge and that was where they were aiming for, before resting overnight and making the final journey across the valley and into the forests to the west.

Jack was pleased by the way the move was run. The convoy itself was six vehicles including their Suburban, mainly SUVs, pickups and a minibus. Running interference ahead of the convoy were two other vehicles. One was an old beat up Chevy pickup and the other an old Ford sedan.

Both vehicles contained old married farming couples, volunteers, looking entirely natural in the environment. They were equipped with handheld VHF radios that they were only to use in an emergency, to warn the convoy. They rotated ahead of the convoy, taking it in turns to run point and check that the route ahead was clear of security force patrols and checkpoints. If they hit one, they would just pass through it and alert the convoy, who would take another direction with the remaining recce car.

The journey itself was uneventful; they stayed the night and headed out the next morning for the wooded hills, crossing the I-81 in the center of the Shenandoah Valley after the route had been cleared by the recce cars.

They wound up into the hills, the roads getting smaller, until they came to a parking area. Here, the recce cars left them and they waited, the new recruits pulling security around the convoy.

After a while, they were approached by a pickup truck with forest ranger markings; recognition signals were passed prior to the link up. Jack was impressed by all this; it was an example of the cut-out process at work.

The convoy moved further into the wooded hills and diverted from the asphalt road onto a fire trail which they followed for a couple of miles before coming to a concealed parking area in a natural bowl, cut back amongst the trees.

Oddly, under a camouflaged net at the back of the bowl, was a fuel tanker truck. There were a couple of other rugged looking pickups parked under nets and everyone gathered round the guide for a brief.

"Ok, welcome," he said. "I'm Grant, your guide. We go on foot from here; it's a couple of miles on a hiking trail. We have four ATVs with trailers and a couple of gators for the heavy gear and they will make a couple of trips as necessary. Leave your keys in the cars: once we have all the gear at the camp, we will move the extra vehicles out to satellite laagers to reduce our footprint."

It was about a three mile hike on a small trail through the woods. It was slow going with the various family members struggling under their packs. Some gear had been loaded on ATV trailers and had gone ahead, what remained was under a guard force by the vehicles, ready for the ATVs to shuttle back up to the camp.

There were a lot of supplies to carry in; most of the families arriving here were preppers and had brought their salvaged food stocks with them, mainly in five gallon buckets, as well as equipment. What was useful was brought to the camp, and the rights of the families over their property were respected.

Bill had been clear that although he expected people would fall into a teamwork mentality and begin to meld and rely on each other at the camp, it was not a commune and people's property rights were to be respected.

Jack noticed that they were mainly heading uphill until they were contouring along several hundred feet below the crest of a minor ridge, heading south down the eastern side of the valley, the ridge to their left.

He had a chance to talk a little with Grant as they walked. It turned out that he was a forest Ranger who had been employed in the surrounding National Forest. As such, Grant had an intimate knowledge of the area and had been instrumental in helping Bill find the various locations. Such local knowledge had been essential in the scouting missions that Bill had led, in order to find the location for Zulu and the well hidden abandoned farm that would become the training base.

They passed a well camouflaged bunker on the left of the trail, dug in with overhead protection.

The faces of two sentries were visible in the shadowed interior, the muzzle of a machine-gun protruding out and facing down the track the way they had come. A little way further there was an identical bunker on the right of the track, well sited to provide depth and mutual support.

They came to the edge of a draw, in fact it was more like a ravine, and the trail went off the edge and cut left diagonally down the face of the steep drop. They followed the trail down and found themselves at the bottom of the draw, in a place where it opened out to form a bowl.

The sides of the draw were quite steep and high, but not rocky or cliff like. There was an area of flattish ground in the central area where the draw opened out in a bowl like fashion, with a creek gurgling through the center of the feature. As Jack looked around him, he could see the wood framed entrances to multiple bunkers dug cave-like into the banks of the draw.

In the central area, which was dotted with trees, were several open sided roofed areas, created out of timber and boards and covered with a layer of dirt with tree litter strewn around on top of them. One appeared to be an open kitchen area, another maybe a meeting area or schoolhouse.

Between the entrances to the bunkers, these various structures and the trees was a combination of similarly roofed covered walkways. Camouflage nets, held up on poles and wooden frames, covered other areas and the gaps in general.

It struck Jack in an instant that this was a wonderfully planned and protected base. As they had been coming down the slope into the draw the effect of the roofs and camo nets had been to create a false floor, or canopy, above the ground of the open area. The effect of the camouflage netting was enhanced by the falling leaves, catching on top and adding another layer of obscuration of the ground below.

He needed to look more at the defensive plan, but from what he had seen the camp itself had been planned with an eye for avoiding aerial surveillance, both visual and thermal. The living bunkers looked deep and expansive and the areas outside were covered either with the roofs or thermally resistant camouflage nets, all of which would cut down thermal and visual signature.

What would make it succeed or fail was the discipline and patterns of life of those living within the base, and the defensive plan.

The guide told them to dump their gear and led them to the meeting area, where there were a series of benches under the roofed area, facing a lectern. The meeting area looked like it was also used for schooling and maybe religious services. They each grabbed seats on the bench and waited, the families huddled in shoulder to shoulder.

Jack noticed that under a camo net tucked up in the draw were parked a couple of the small tracked JCB type vehicles, the ones with a backhoe attachment, which must have been used to help the digging of the bunkers. They were small enough to get up the trail without doing too much damage and thus leaving too much sign.

A few minutes later Major Cassidy appeared. He was slightly built, average height, balding with glasses. He had an efficient but somewhat pedantic manner about him. He was dressed in old style woodland BDUs, self-styled with his rank and name tags visible.

After the introductions, Major Cassidy handed them off to Paul Granger, who was described as the camp administrator. They headed out for a tour of the base and to be allocated accommodation, prior to stowing their gear.

Major Cassidy had arranged with Jack to meet up again to discuss tactics and training, once he was settled. In the kitchen area Caitlin met and struck an instant friendship with Gayle, who was a matronly type coordinating the activities of a group of ladies, working hard over a mixture of propane ranges and wood fueled rocket stoves, laid out on tables.

Gayle was running the place with cheerful enthusiasm while driving them like a Sergeant Major.

One of the dug-out bunkers was a storeroom for group supplies; it had the doorway section of a shipping container somehow fixed into the wooden entrance to the cavern, securing the supplies behind. Clearly, it would not have been possible to get a whole shipping container up the trail, but they had cut, transported and welded the doorway part. A lot of effort and thought had gone into the building of the base.

Downstream of the base, within the secure perimeter but away from the stream itself, was a series of porta-john latrines that had been strapped to the back of an ATV trailer and driven up the trail. They had been modified by painting the usual blue color green. The floor of the receptacle part which usually contained the blue liquid, which was usually pumped out, had been cut out.

The latrines were placed over long drop latrine holes with lime liberally tossed in; the idea being that the holes would be filled in and the latrines moved to new sites as necessary. Alcohol gel dispensers were filled and fixed to the latrines – hygiene was imperative and it would not do to spread germs or disease.

For washing, just upstream of the latrine areas were separate male and female areas, privacy provided by a mix of plywood panels and cloth partitions attached to pickets to form enclosures. Within the two enclosures were tables and a supply of plastic washbowls. Hot water was available from the kitchen area most of the time and it could be collected in a bowl and taken to the wash area.

In each area was also a couple of camping shower tents with attachment hooks for hanging up the solar showers that were available. Failing summer, hot water could also be used to fill these solar shower bags. The latrine and washing areas were entirely covered by camo netting and there was a covered walkway down to the area from the kitchen site.

The accommodation bunkers were shored up with timber, it was like being in a mine passage, and there were rough plywood partitions inside that divided up family areas with cot beds, a table and a few chairs. There were lockers and shelves for the stowing of personal gear.

There was not a great deal of privacy; Jack could see where other families had done a bit of rough carpentry or hung blankets to help with this. It was obvious that there were some generators in the base and there were some electrical cables with lights strung throughout the dugouts, but they were not running now. Fuel was obviously a concern and would be rationed. There was a mix of candles and propane lamps dotted around to provide light.

The Berengers were allocated an area and started to move their gear into it.

Jack found Major Cassidy over in the operations center bunker at his desk. They shook hands and Major Cassidy gestured to Jack to take a seat across the desk from him.

"So Captain Berenger, it's good to have you on board," he said. "We need to get the training operation going so we can hit back. I have a core of veterans organized into two squads that we should be able to put into action soon."

"Roger that Sir," said Jack, alarm bells going off. "It's been a while since I was called Captain," he said with a smile.

"Yes well, it's important that we maintain standards and discipline," retorted Major Cassidy.

Jack agreed that this was so, but he could not help feeling that Major Cassidy was standing on ceremony a little too much. Cassidy went on to describe the defensive situation at the base, and let Jack know that he would take him and Jim around later on a tour of the positions. It was apparent that they had enough fighters to maintain a basic defense of the base, while training the Company to conduct insurgency operations.

There were three defensive positions; the first was the two bunkers they had passed on the way in, there were two more bunkers where the trail continued on the other side of the draw, and also a listening/observation post above the camp up on the ridge above.

There were enough fighters allocated to Zulu to rotate through these positions and keep them permanently manned, but no more, and as yet there were limited personnel available for clearance patrols. The burden of manning three defensive positions around the base was manpower intensive.

They discussed the idea of operating an area defense, but it was manpower prohibitive at this point. An area defense would involve not simply manning the sentry positions surrounding the base, but conducting a reactive defense based on detecting the location, direction and size of approaching enemy threats. This would come down to establishing observation posts, OPs, pushed out to observe possible enemy routes in to the base.

There were primarily three routes in – the trail running through the base on both the north and south sides, and also from the ridge above following the draw downwards to Zulu.

To mount an area defense, each route would require a prepared defensive or ambush location that would be manned following triggering by the outlying OP positions. This would make it a combination of an area and a mobile defense. It was certainly true that in this situation 'he who defended everywhere defended nowhere.'

But such a plan would have to wait on manpower.

Major Cassidy read the letter from Bill and seemed happy enough with establishing the training base over the ridge at the farm, about five miles away to the south east. He wasn't going to interfere too much with Jack's training plans.

The fighters that would remain at Zulu manning the static defensive positions were mainly the older, injured, or less experienced 'home guard', while the younger, fitter, more experienced or recent veteran types would be moved out to the training base.

The plan was that any further recruits, unless they were coming with families, would not be moved through Camp Zulu, but directly to the training base from the other side of the ridge, in order to maintain OPSEC. The fighters with families at Zulu could be relied upon to keep their mouths shut about the location, and would be briefed on the importance of this.

They would establish a light trail through the trees to link the two bases, running it into the main trail where it met the sentry bunkers on the south side of the base.

Major Cassidy was the operational commander for the Resistance region, or at least he was within the organization that Bill had created. It meant that he called the shots. He explained to Jack that in the light of Bill's letter he planned to run operations initially from Victor Foxtrot. He was going to hand off the administration and running of Zulu to Paul Granger. He was keen to get operations running, though Jack got the feeling that he was perhaps not too keen to be directly involved himself.

Jack was increasingly getting the feeling that although Cassidy was a professional and well educated former officer, he tended to stand on doctrine and ceremony and was perhaps a little too conventional in his outlook for Jacks liking. He did however make headway with him over training and the model for the Company. Jack wasn't going out on operations anyway, so his job was to best prepare the fighters and hand them back to Major Cassidy ready to go.

They did discuss the logistical requirements for the new training base. It was now October and they were heading into a winter in the mountains. Weapons and equipment had been procured and cached and would be moved to the new training site, as well as an administrator and staff to keep the place running around the training requirements.

They had plenty of weapons, ammunition, equipment and items such as body armor available. It had either been brought in by the fighters themselves, many who were deserting veterans, captured or profiteered on the back of the looting, or 'procured' via bureaucratic corruption.

Cassidy explained the he would make available a truckload of military body armor and various pouches and ancillaries that had been diverted from its destination. It was all in the UCP, or universal camouflage pattern, used in the army ACU uniforms, but they had also acquired plenty of camo spray paint in flat camouflage tones to spray it up and make it unrecognizable.

They agreed that Jack and Jim would move up to Victor Foxtrot in a week once the stores had been moved into place, in order to get the training in motion.

The next week for Jack was divided between his family and planning. He was helping to settle Caitlin and the kids into their new home in the bunker while also making logistical arrangements with Jim to get Victor Foxtrot up and running.

Jim was an invaluable help with this, not only because of his experience as an NCO and thus the ability to take a lot of the burden away from Jack. He was also single, with no family to distract him at Zulu.

Jim apparently had a teenage son and an ex-wife living down in Texas, but Jim had not been able to do anything about it when the collapse happened and the relationship with his ex was a sore point anyway. Jack got a partial story, something about her being unfaithful while Jim had been away on yet another deployment, and Jack almost felt sorry for the other guy when he visualized having Jim coming after him.

The population at Zulu was about a hundred and fifty souls, including the guard force, family members and the kids. The intent was to keep life going at the base in as normal and constructive a way as possible.

The meeting area was used as a schoolhouse and for religious ceremonies on Sundays. The women had started to specialize in roles that they had skills at. Some of the mothers ran daycare for the younger kids, so that others could work. There was much to do, from cooking, food preparation, schooling, child care, nursing, equipment and clothing repair, carpentry, store management etc.

It was not an all-female force at Zulu; some of the older and perhaps less fit males fell into roles there, and a few of them were carpenters, mechanics and handymen. Jack also discovered that some of the volunteers that he would be training were female. Having served in a Ranger

Battalion, having females in an infantry role was new to him, so he was going to have to figure that one out.

One of the key things amidst the hustle and bustle of Zulu was OPSEC. It would not do, for instance, to have wild teenagers ranging out through the woods, or kids running wild around the camp. The signature of the base to any overhead surveillance assets had to be managed. This meant keeping people under the cover of walkways and nets, and any parties that went out would have to be small and managed.

Jack and Caitlin were having a spat over what to do with Andrew. She wanted him to stay at Zulu, but Jack wanted to take him up to Victor Foxtrot with him. His reasoning was that although Andrew, like himself, would not deploy on operations, he needed to learn. If he spent time at the training base he could assimilate the training and be trained for when he became an adult. He had already proved himself in the firefights he had been involved in.

Caitlin was having none of it.

Unfortunately for Jack, he had not yet figured out that although he thought he was in charge of his family, he was not. Caitlin was. In the end, they came to a compromise where Andrew would base himself at Zulu, where he could be supervised by Caitlin, but that Jack would be allowed to take him up for visits to Victor Foxtrot to see some of the training.

Jack had got the use of a mountain bike from one of his new neighbors at the base, who had brought it in and would not be using it. He would be able to use it to make the trip between the two bases in breaks in the training, to see the family.

Chapter Six

Victor Foxtrot was up and ready. It was now late October and fall was progressing, temperatures falling. Major Cassidy had moved into the farmhouse and turned it into his headquarters along with a small staff.

The barn had turned out to be a large warehouse type affair of steel and aluminum construction with a concrete floor. It was ideal for conducting training classes, and provided weather protection and concealment from aerial observation. Jack had the building divided up using plywood partitions, creating a sleeping area with rows of cot beds, a large open training area, several smaller classrooms and a stores area.

They kept ammunition and explosives in one of the separate outbuildings. Another outbuilding was turned into a field kitchen. Latrine and hygiene areas were built back in the wood line behind the barn.

Jack had been working with Jim on the training program. They had the advantage that they would be effectively overwintering at Victor Foxtrot and thus had considerable time available. Weather and temperature conditions over the winter would make it harder to operate against the enemy, though not totally impractical.

The fact was that although they had supplies, they were limited, and there was no central heating. Conditions would be harsh, in the same way they used to be harsh in the old days before modern conveniences. They had to factor this in.

This meant that although they had the advantage of time, and were planning a long three or four month training program, they had to pace the volunteers. They were arranging for wood burning stoves to be put into the barn, to keep the worst of the chill away, and they were creating a dry room in one of the outhouses where wet clothing could be hung out to dry.

If they were going to push the volunteers, they would have to do so with full consideration to the weather, their calorie intake, and the need to recover in the conditions.

They were not planning on a physical training program: the training base was itself in a tactical environment, without the benefit of being separated from the theater of conflict, and thus it was impractical to go out running in the local area. Army style PT in formation and all that would have to be foregone. Physical conditioning would be conducted simply as a part of the tactical training.

They also didn't have the excess calories available and did not want to exhaust the fighters.

Jack and Jim were in agreement that they would make it plain to the volunteers that this was not like the sort of training or selection course that they may have been used to, or heard about, in the army. There was no badge collecting here.

The fact was that the course would be hard, but the purpose would be to effectively train the volunteers as fighters in small unit and insurgency tactics, from team to company level. It would not be Ranger School or Special Forces Selection, but it would be realistic, challenging, and it would produce fails and voluntary withdrawals. The training course was not set up with the express aim of doing this, but naturally not all personnel would be suited to the role.

The plan was that those who did not make the grade would be dealt with delicately and kept on side, being given duties more suited to their abilities. Some would be rotated back to the guard force at Zulu, closer to their families.

The basic organizational concept was based around four man teams, each team split into two pairs. In each team, one pair would be the IED specialists, the other pair would be a cover team selected for their ability to shoot well. The volunteers would be selected for their talents and allocated to specialties as appropriate. This would facilitate the deployment and infiltration of these small four man teams to conduct independent operations.

At the next level up, the teams would become fire teams, two fire teams to a squad, making an eight man squad. An additional squad leader could be added as the ninth man if one was available. Three of those squads would make a platoon, with a headquarters element added.

At the company level, Jack also intended to create a fire support platoon, within which he hoped to have machine-gun and mortar squads. He would work the details out as the personnel and equipment became available.

Their first challenge would be to identify who exactly they had to train. This would involve interviewing everyone. From this, they would make initial allocations into teams. It would also allow them to identify those with experience and potential leaders.

There was an element of identifying potential instructors also, so that they could 'train the trainer' and spread the burden – there was no way that as they got up to company level operations they could run the whole program themselves, monitoring everyone. So there would be a phased element to it, as they 'trained the trainers' and allowed these instructors to work with new recruits as they were phased in.

The allocation of teams and leaders would be reviewed, amended and reorganized as necessary. No doubt there would be problems and personality clashes as time went on. Some would be solved; others would result in reorganization and even removal of personnel.

If teams were working, then the priority would be to keep them together to maintain small unit integrity.

Teams would not be reorganized simply for the sake of it, only if personality clashes or leadership failures needed to be addressed.

However, again they were adamant that they must deal with people in a fair manner and not squash too many egos – they did not want disaffected fighters informing or defecting to the Regime. In fact, Jim was adamant that if he got the feeling someone was really bad news, he would take care of them himself. Given the safety issues at stake, Jack did not raise too much complaint about this.

Over the next few days, the fighters already recruited by Bill started to arrive in small groups, transported in by the Resistance movement network utilizing multiple routes and modes of transport. Some came up the trail from Zulu, just as Jack and Jim had. Others arrived in small convoys; still more had been dropped off a distance away and hiked in through the woods with a guide.

There was a hard core group that filtered in as the first arrivals. They were the original platoon sized group, three squads and a headquarters element that had been working with Bill as an ad hoc militia grouping since before the collapse.

This group was mostly veterans and had been training together for a while. Jack was hoping that this group would provide him with a solid cadre of instructors. The success of this would depend on how malleable they were to his training ideas, and the leaving of any excessive egos out of the training camp.

Since the collapse, with the wild living out in the woods, personal grooming had taken a backseat. The groups that were showing up looked like mountain men, with beards and hair growing in, often cut off raggedly at the collar. They turned up in a variety of outfits and clothing.

Jack and Jim had discussed this and were not planning on doing much about it. It had the potential to turn into a sore point with Major Cassidy, but they were an irregular force fighting an insurgency style conflict, so uniforms and being 'dress right dress' was not what it was about.

They had agreed that the focus would be on strong self-discipline within an organization of leaders appointed into command tasks; some permanent, others temporarily allocated a command role for specific missions when groups came together. Leadership roles would be merit based and could be taken away for poor performance or if the team lost faith in an individual.

It would be trial by ordeal and fire for all of them. Given that there was no pay or career advancement involved, they hoped to foster a culture of excellence based on personal motivation rather than organizational politics.

As for the uniform thing, clothing was to be policed for serviceability and alternatives provided if personnel did not have it. Acceptable clothing included military or outdoor clothing in military or hunting camouflage, as well as drab and earth tone colors. No blue jeans, they did not work well when wet.

Clothing had to be serviceable and workable in the outdoors environment, and the right color. More mainstream civilian clothing would be retained for use in necessary covert or close reconnaissance operations.

Boots were a key factor, and if personnel turned up without suitable footwear then it had to be sourced for them. They would be out working through the winter and good footwear, layers of warm clothing, waterproof gear and changes of socks were essential.

In terms of tactical gear, the focus was not on being uniform or identical, but rather that each fighter had the correct equipment in some format, depending what could be sourced or foraged. Everyone that did not have it already was issued body armor, including ballistic plates, and the necessary tactical pouches for carrying magazines and equipment. The extra supply came from the purloined truck that Major Cassidy had produced.

The minimum personal protection allowed was a plate carrier, with the preference being for a full set of soft armor with plates. Helmets were also issued, but their use was to be reserved for conventional set-piece operations, when they happened, as well as defensive tasks.

Each fighter had to show that he had magazine pouches for a minimum of eight thirty round magazines on his tactical vest or battle belt. He also had to carry an IFAK (Individual First Aid Kit) as well as an additional CAT (combat application tourniquet) on his vest. He had to have a rucksack, daypack and water source. If he was deficient any gear, it was sourced or reallocated to bring everyone up to standard.

The rest of the fighters' personal load, such as sleeping and outdoors gear and all the various ancillaries was either provided by the fighters themselves or found from other sources. Some gear was donated from Zulu where those static there had no need for it.

It caused a little consternation, but Jack and Jim decided on a specific weapons policy. The aim was ultimately for everyone to run a personal rifle that fired 5.56mm NATO. The preference was for M4 style weapons. The idea was that this was the ammunition that the Regime was using and it would make ammunition resupply and reallocation easier.

Inter-operability was the key. 7.62mm NATO was also useful, because it was used in the Regime 240 machine-guns. They already had a number of captured M4, SAW and 240 weapon systems, as well as sniper rifles, and these would be allocated as required from the central armory. This meant that AK type weapons, utilizing the 7.62 x 39mm short round, were out in the long run.

The Regime military mostly used military 5.56mm 62 grain ammunition for their M4 rifles. Those fighters with AR15 style weapons, many of which appeared on the surface identical to the M4 but were not chambered for 5.56mm, could only use .223 ammunition.

As far as Jack and Jim knew, 5.56 rifles could successfully use .223 ammunition, but the other way around could cause problems to varying degrees. Even if it simply caused stoppages, it was an issue in combat. There was a limited supply of this .223 ammunition in the hands of the Resistance, just what the fighters had personally stored, and any looted resupply from Regime units would be 5.56mm.

This posed a problem, and just as with the AK style rifles, Jack simply couldn't tell the guys to dump their AR15's. The compromise was that captured M4's were handed out, as many as they had, and those left with AK or AR15 rifles, using either the 7.62mm short or .223 ammunition, would continue to run those rifles until suitable replacements could be found as operations were conducted.

Jack had been standing outside the barn talking to a group of the arriving original platoon. They were a wild looking bunch but he was getting a good feeling off them. He was just thinking that his worries about problem egos were ill founded and it looked like the training should go smoothly. The group was dispersing to go to the accommodation area.

The shout came from his left, "Hey, Berenger you douche, you owe me twenty bucks!"

Jack turned and saw a wiry man dressed in filthy outdoor clothes, a pair of intense blue eyes staring at him out of a heavily bearded face. Jack stared at him intently, and then the recognition dawned.

"Caleb! What the hell! Get off my farm before I kick your ass!" This grabbed the attention of the group, who were turning back in anticipation.

Jack advanced on Caleb, who put his hands up. Suddenly, Jim appeared from the flank and was on Caleb, grabbing him by the scruff of the neck.

"Wait, wait!" called Jack, "I'll let you beat him later, it's just Caleb. We're buddies."

Jim let him go, a little reluctantly, and Jack and Caleb shook hands.

"Jim, this is Caleb Jackson, we went through Ranger School together. He's an asshole, but don't worry about it," Jack grinned. Turning back to Caleb, "What's the deal buddy?"

"I'm the platoon leader of this sorry bunch," said Caleb, "good to see you man."

The atmosphere had visibly relaxed and the onlookers started to disperse. Jack, Jim and Caleb went to grab a coffee and catch up on the porch of the farm building. They spent several hours sitting around catching up and discussing the tactical readiness of Caleb's platoon, as well as the training program. Caleb had been a lieutenant in a light infantry Battalion.

"Hey you!" came the forceful female shout from over by the barn.

What now?

Jack looked up.

"Oh no," said Caleb, shrinking into his chair.

Advancing across the farmyard was a healthy looking young woman dressed in boots, BDU pants and a tight thermal base layer top, red hair streaming out behind her. She was fixed on Jim, and it did not look like it was going to go down well for him. Jim was looking confused, which was a first for Jack.

She halted at the bottom of the porch steps, "Which of you sorry assed cowboys are responsible for organizing the female accommodation?"

Jack and Jim shared a look, understanding dawning. *Oops.*

Jim stood up. The woman put her hands on her hips, and smiled at him.

Jim went red.

Jack stood up.

"Who are you," said Jack.

"THAT, is Megan," said Caleb, grinning.

Megan shot Caleb a look. "I'm Megan, I'm your paramedic."

"Ok," Jack said, "Megan, my apologies. I'm Jack Berenger, I'm running the training here. We overlooked the female accommodation. What do you need?"

"Look, it's not a big deal, but you just need to partition an area off. We don't want to be changing in there with the guys."

"Ok," said Jack, "give us a minute to figure this out."

"No problem," she said with a smile, before giving Jim a look and walking away.

"So, you met Megan," Caleb chortled.

Jim was still looking a little embarrassed.

"She's not short on character, I'll tell you that. She was a civilian paramedic and a flight medic in the army reserves. She knows her stuff, and don't mess with her, she'll bust your balls."

"Well," said Jack, "that was our little 'Xena, Warrior Princess' moment for the day. Jim, what the hell were we thinking? What are we going to do with the females?"

"Boss, it's bigger than that," said Jim. "We can partition off a sleeping area, but what about all the extra-curricular shenanigans that will end up going on?"

"Yea," said Caleb with a grin, "maybe you need to ban the wearing of thermal base layers then?"

Jack gave him a look, "Ok, let's fix this."

They sat and discussed it. It was relatively simple to partition an area for the females to sleep in, and they called over one of the carpenters and asked him to get on to it immediately.

The issue was bigger.

The solution they came up with was that the females would go through the training exactly the same as the guys. If they made the grade, with the same standards applied, they would be deployed in the teams with the men. If they fell short, they would be employed in other roles, just like the guys.

It was apparent that a good portion of the females were medics, and they would be useful in a medical role at base.

The 'fraternization' issue was bigger. They needed more time to figure it out, but they came up with a short term conclusion that it was not really going to pose a problem. If couples got together, that was fine, so long as it was discrete, at appropriate times, and did not get in the way of training.

If it ended up affecting training or operations, then a solution would be contrived, usually moving the involved people around as best as possible. If people got up to anything that was considered unseemly, like having sex at inappropriate times and places, it would be dealt with accordingly.

Common sense seemed to be the best solution.

It looked like out of the projected one hundred and twenty strong fighting company that they would train after all the recruits were in, around forty of those would be females. It was a new thing for Jack and Jim, but they would incorporate the females into areas they were qualified for, showed aptitude at, and could handle just as their male counterparts were expected to do.

One of Jacks pet projects involved what he was calling the 'thermal poncho'. He had a bunch of the ladies back at Zulu working on the creation of them based on a prototype that he had designed.

He had taken an old style BDU camouflage poncho; on the bottom side he had placed a mylar thermal space blanket, one of the green ones so it remained tactical. On the top side, the side that faced up when the poncho was used as a shelter, he had laid a swathe of drab colored cloth. Onto this cloth he had sewn strips of burlap and camouflage cloth.

109

The poncho on its own would have been a better waterproof shelter, but he was concerned by the shine of the plastic waterproof material. The cloth laid over it would get wet but it would appear more natural. The sewn in pieces of cloth created a ghillie suit effect, although a lot less densely packed; to sew on massive amounts of cloth like a ghillie suit would have created a huge and unwieldy item, particularly when wet.

He could have used something like the army poncho liner instead of the poncho, which would have reduced the shine effect but he wanted the thermal poncho to actually work as a rain tarp that the fighters could use when sleeping out, and thus be waterproof. The poncho also added strength to the whole thing, as well as having the eyeholes to string it up.

The effect was that the mylar blanket blocked the heat signature from the person underneath, the poncho allowed it to be strung up and kept the rain off, and the cloth on the topside gave it more of a natural surface appearance through optics.

What was also important about this thermal masking concept was the clearance between the blanket and the person underneath; if the person touched the blanket, body heat would transfer and heat up the blanket, thus eventually showing the thermal signature.

Jack hoped that the standard use of these thermal ponchos when conducting operations out in the woods should allow for thermal screening.

Jack intended for the fighters to develop a standard operating procedure so that for all halts of more than a few minutes, and tactical positions, they would always put up the poncho between pairs of fighters, however much of a chore it became.

He wanted them to carry it at all times as part of their personal equipment, rolled up like a bedroll. They would also carry tent pegs and paracord or bungees pre-attached to the poncho eye-holes. Using this set-up, and sometimes a couple of cut sticks, they would always be able to string it up, whether off trees or from the cut 'tent poles'.

(Thus when they overnighted in a patrol base, or laid in ambush, or whatever they were doing, they should be able to conceal themselves from aerial surveillance. The ponchos themselves were also well camouflaged, with the ghillie suit effect, from visual surveillance, so in that sense they were an excellent camouflage asset.)

Jack and Jim had discussed the concept and design of the thermal ponchos at some length and agreed it was a good plan and design. If feedback were to come from the fighters that the design could or should be improved, they were happy to make the modifications.

One of the problems they had was a lack of thermal imaging gear to actually test the ponchos, so they would have to rely for the moment on their theoretical design, in the knowledge that at least they had considered the thermal threat and taken steps to counter it.

Now that they had the fighters actually arriving at the base and getting settled in, administrated and equipped to standard, they were able to start selecting their training cadre and allocating teams. They took the initial training cadre from the original platoon, which in the end resulted in them taking a squad of guys away from Caleb, who had to reorganize his remaining fighters into two squads.

The initial few days of the training effort revolved around training conferences with the new cadre and the building of facilities. This included the building of a twenty five meter and one hundred meter rifle range back in the woods. They identified suitable outdoors areas where they could run tactical training in the trees, which were providing less and less cover every day as the leaves fell.

They also found another abandoned group of farm buildings a couple of miles away through the woods and decided that they would use it as a training site. It was suitable for an objective for various types of training, such as recon patrols, attacks, defensive planning and also as a basic urban operations site, for room clearing and urban assault.

However, once they began the training, it would be crawl, walk, run and they would start with the basics. It did not matter that some were veterans and others were at different levels of training; it was key to get everyone on the same page and up to standard together.

They planned a program which started at the basics of shooting, field-craft, navigation and tactics and moved up from there. The shooting started at the basic marksmanship principles and evolved into combat shooting in multiple positions. The tactics started at individual field-craft and moved on to larger formations; team, squad and platoon. In addition they included movement and administration in the field.

They had to cover it all, because they were effectively training a light infantry company to conduct irregular warfare from team up to company level, so they needed to be good at what they did. Once they mastered the basics of combat shooting in parallel with the field-craft, the intent was to meld the two and begin to learn fire and movement, starting at individual level and building up.

On top of these skills would be built the other operations of war, from patrolling through offensive and defensive operations.

Once the basics were mastered, at the same time as they moved on to train in the conventional infantry tactics, they would also begin lessons on the small team insurgency aspect, including role based training for those chosen as the IED specialists and the sharpshooters.

It was to be a hard school, exhausting and practically oriented, not simply for the sake of selection and trimming numbers but to ensure that the fighters were up to standard.

They would have to manage the volunteers as the approaching winter and basic diet took a hold. They could not be out all day, every day; they had to plan for warming classes back in the barn classrooms and rest periods.

However, there would be a time and a place, as the skills and training built, for field training exercises, full rehearsals for what was to come.

Jack had been keeping up a close dialogue with Major Cassidy throughout his work to set up the training site. The Major kept out of his way, and was mainly involved with planning in his tactical operations room, or TOC, inside the farmhouse.

Jack had a notion that they needed to separate the training and operations functions, for operational security reasons, and had been trying to inoculate the Major to the notion of eventually moving his TOC to an alternate site, perhaps on the other side of the valley on the plateau. It wasn't urgent anyway, because while the training was in its early stages there were no ongoing operations anyway.

The security of the training base was the responsibility of the operations room and they had established a covert observation and sentry post overlooking the one entry gate. The gate accessed a long dirt drive up to the farm though the trees, feeding off a back country road. There was a field telephone run back to the operations room. The sentry post could be approached in cover so that sentry exchanges could not be observed from the road. It kept the place low key but ensured they had security.

They also ran an air sentry with a couple of fighters placed in a position of observation to watch the skies and horizons for approaching aircraft. They had a field telephone and also an air horn to sound a 'take cover' alarm if necessary.

Major Cassidy always addressed Jack by the formal Captain Berenger. Jack and Jim were not standing on ceremony with the Company, first names were fine, and the only titles were those of the position the person filled, such as squad leader. It was working fine, and if it did not, then those responsible for bucking the system would be moved out to another role. Self-motivation and discipline was the basis, with good teams and leaders in place to reinforce the motivation of the individual.

Given the nature of the fight that was ahead, it was crucial in Jack's opinion that they ran effective 'mission command'. This meant that the teams would be given a mission, with a 'reason why' and their commander's intent. This was made even more crucial given the handicap caused by the lack of, or slowness of, communications that they would be operating under.

The theory with mission command was that when the situation changed on the ground without a higher commander to immediately refer to, the teams would be able to make an informed decision about what course of action to take.

It was also important in the light of that approach, to allow people to command, and operate effectively, within their own sphere. This also meant that people's strengths and weakness were extremely important, and should be taken advantage of to strengthen the overall effort.

115

An example of this was Gayle, the lady running the field kitchen back at Zulu. It was her thing, she had created a great team, it wasn't broke, so don't fix it.

A messenger found Jack and asked him to report to Major Cassidy in the TOC, which he did. Cassidy always liked him to salute when he entered the office, so he did to keep him happy.

"Captain Berenger, I need Lieutenant Jackson and his two available squads for a mission. I have an Op Order for him. They will leave in four days. Please make it happen."

Jack was nonplussed, "Wait – what? Come again?"

"A mission: We have credible reports of a regular Homeland Corps convoy. They run to and fro from a training base they have up near Front Royal. They run this convoy every couple of weeks with newly graduated recruits back into DC."

"Uh huh," grunted Jack.

"The next convoy is coming up. We are going to hit them where the I-66 runs through the defile in the State Park east of Front Royal."

"Surely not?"

"What?" said Major Cassidy.

"Well," Jack gathered his thoughts, "it's too much too soon. We need to start off asymmetric, using the small IED teams, before building to larger concentrated operations on our own terms at opportune moments.

Hitting the Interstate with a platoon ambush now is too high profile."

"Really," said Major Cassidy, "now is not the time for cold feet. It's not as if you are going out with them, is it?"

Jack bit down on his retort.

Jumped up little prick.

"So, Major, you are determined to go ahead with it?"

"Yes."

"Right then. I'll get Caleb."

The patrol left four days later. Caleb led them as the patrol leader. Jim had given them a crash course in some of the explosive devices they had already created.

Jim had been building a metal shop but he had not so far got around to milling any of the copper cones that were required to create the off-route mines that he planned, based on the design of the 'explosively formed penetrator' mines, or EFPs, used so prevalently in Iraq.

Instead, Jim supplied them with improvised claymores with command wire triggers. They also had some procured AT-4 anti-armor missiles, the one shot type in the plastic tubes that slung on a man's back. That was their only way to stop armored vehicles at this point. They also had four SAW 5.56mm 'squad automatic weapons', one for each of the four teams in their patrol.

They had spent the last four days going through orders, rehearsals and refining their 'actions on' drills. They had already worked extensively together so their team drills and battle discipline were good. Jack spent a long time sitting down with Caleb going over the ambush plan. It was the best they could come up with given the weapons available.

There were no thermal ponchos available for the patrol to take; they had not been produced yet.

Chapter Seven

The patrol moved from Victor Foxtrot to their drop-off point in several covert vans. From the outside, the vans looked just like contractor work vehicles. They did not go in a convoy, but split the patrol up and infiltrated by a couple of routes in teams. Once together at the discrete drop, the patrol reformed in cover and moved off into the woods.

The plan was for a different pick up location, for which every man had the location description of the markers to the dead drop. A guide would return to check the dead drop at a certain time each day starting in several days. If the dead letter box was active, he would bring the vehicles to exfiltrate the team.

It was a eighteen man patrol. Caleb was the team leader and he had with him 'Doc' Oliver as the medic, making a small two man headquarters element. Under him were two squads of eight men.

Alpha Squad was led by Rob Olson, a former Army Ranger who had separated from active duty with combat fatigue after too many deployments. He had needed a rest.

Bravo Squad was under Vince Chavez, a deserter from the 82nd Airborne, formerly a career light infantry platoon sergeant. Olson was a single man, but Chavez's family shared the dugout with Caitlin and the kids back at Zulu.

The patrol was out for a week before they accomplished their mission.

They had patrolled cross country using the terrain and forests to remain concealed. They approached the 1-66 objective area from the south and went into all round defense in an objective rally point (ORP).

Caleb went forward with a security team to recon the ambush site. He planned a linear ambush using a cut where the road passed through between some wooded embankments. He found a spot where the woods curved back in to the road on each side of the cut. This would allow him to place his cut-off groups closer to the road, which was essential to his plan.

The left side cut-off group position had a great view of the road to the west where the convoy was expected to arrive from.

He had Bravo Squad split into two teams, four men occupying each of the cut-off positions on the left and right flanks of the ambush. Alpha Squad was the kill group and lay in the tree line along the top of the embankment, some seventy five meters back from the road.

By night, they laid the command wires for the improvised claymores down to the road, some of them fed through a drainage culvert to the wide median between the eastbound and westbound lanes of the 1-66.

He laid out a series of improvised claymores along the near side of the road, aimed to fire into the kill zone. He also set up claymores in the median, angled to sweep the grassy area with ball bearings. The median itself formed a grassy depression between the east and westbound lanes, some twenty meters wide, sloping inwards to a central drainage ditch. It would provide some cover from the fire of his kill group up on the embankment.

Doc lay to the rear of the kill group, providing rear protection and a casualty collection point.

From Intel received, Caleb expected a mixture of armored and unarmored vehicles to form the convoy. Probably a lead, middle and rear armored Humvee, with a mix of other vehicles, including a couple of LMTV trucks and a bus. He did not have enough explosives to blow a crater in the road, nor did he have any off route mines to conclusively destroy the lead armored vehicle.

His solution to stopping the convoy was to wire up a couple of trees near to the right, or eastern, cut-off group with demolitions charges to bring them down over the road ahead of the convoy.

Each cut-off group had two AT-4 rockets and one SAW. From their position closer to the road they would

121

have enfilade fire up and down the road, which meant more of a head on or rear end angled shot into the convoy than the kill group would have.

The sectors of fire of the two cut-off groups were de-conflicted so that they did not fire towards each other, but rather at an angle into the kill zone.

There were another two AT-4s in the kill group. The remaining two SAWs were situated at each end of the kill group.

The Intel said that the convoy usually left Front Royal at dawn. That morning, Caleb got the signal from his left cut-off group an hour after dawn. He was controlling the triggers to the various demolition charges and claymores that they had, with the labeled triggers laid out in front of him.

The ambush would be initiated by the firing of the demolitions on the trees.

Caleb lay in the tree line as the convoy crept up the curve of the road at a steady convoy speed from the west. All his men were silent in position, ready with their weapons.

The convoy did in fact have the three Humvees, as well as three LMTV trucks and a central bus containing the main body of the newly trained regime storm troopers, the blue shirts.

As the convoy reached the middle of the killing area Caleb sprung the ambush by firing the clacker on the tree demolitions; there was a loud concussion, severing and kicking out the bases of the two trees. They didn't sway and fall like they would if they had been cut; they simply went smashing down across the roadway.

As the convoy came to a halt, the kill group erupted in a fury of small arms fire as they poured rounds down into the vehicles. Caleb hit the next clacker, firing the array of six improvised claymores down by the roadway, at the bottom of the cut. The six brutal detonations hurled shipyard confetti into the convoy, ripping into the LMTVs and in particular tearing through the sides of the bus and wreaking carnage inside.

In the two cut-off groups, the team leaders directed two men to fire the AT4s as their other man provided covering fire with the SAW. Each cut-off team targeted a Humvee at the front or rear of the columns, respectively, and having two AT-4s meant there was less chance of missing.

At each end of the ambush the rockets streaked into the escorting Humvees at about fifty meters range. The HEAT round on the warheads detonated on the armored Humvees, melting the copper cone inside the warheads and sending a stream of molten metal into the vehicles, killing all inside.

The central armored Humvee was destroyed by AT-4s fired from up at the kill group, the first one clipping over the top of the vehicle and detonating in the median while the other smacked into the rear armored door and killed everyone inside.

The kill group continued to pour an ambush weight of fire into the trucks and the bus. The new Homeland

Corps personnel were fully trained and armed and some had got out of the vehicles and were fighting back. A number had got out of the bus and from some of the LMTVs, and they were taking cover on the other side of the roadway, in the median and behind some of the vehicles.

There was desultory fire coming back towards the kill group, but nothing too effective.

Caleb waited until he thought that most of the enemy was taking cover in the median. He had sited the claymores at an angle to sweep the area of cover where the verge met the roadway. He fired the claymores, the blast and shrapnel smashing into and flensing the remaining enemy.

After assessing the situation for a moment more, Caleb grabbed his whistle and blew a long blast: 'ceasefire, watch and shoot'.

The shooting stopped, the order being passed verbally now down the line, and the kill group searched the roadway with their optics for any enemy movement. A few shots rang out here and there, enemy movement ended.

Caleb got up on one knee and blew the whistle in a series of short blasts, followed by voice, "Fight Through, Fight Through!"

As they had rehearsed, the kill group got up and skirmished forward down towards the killing area, moving as an extended line in buddy pairs under the control of the squad leader.

The idea was to fight through, sweeping the killing area and ensuring there was no enemy left. The cut-off groups provided flank protection while this happened.

The squad reached the road with Caleb in the center of the formation; they double-tapped any enemy bodies they saw. They all got the same treatment, whether they looked dead or were trying to crawl away wounded.

Teams went into each vehicle, finishing off any bodies they saw. The bus was a charnel house. Once they had finished with the vehicles and the bodies that had taken cover behind them, they skirmished up to the edge of the road where they could observe the windrow of bodies that had attempted to take cover there.

The kill group went static, a fusillade of fire rang out as they made sure the enemy was dead, and then Caleb gave the signal to withdraw. They skirmished back up to the top of the embankment.

Once there, Caleb gave the order to withdraw. The cut-off groups peeled in back behind the kill group, checked in with him and then moved back to where Doc was waiting. Following them, the kill group peeled in to the center and moved back to the RV.

They all grabbed their rucks, which had been laid out in order, and the squad leaders got accountability. All present, no injuries. Caleb gave the order to move and they set out at a rapid patrol pace in single file through the woods.

As the ambush had been sprung, the convoy commander in the center Humvee had managed to hit the panic button on the 'blue force tracker' navigation system, which utilized a satellite transponder to send an automated alert with their location to the Regional Tactical Operations Center (RTOC), located at the DHS Fusion Center in Richmond, Virginia.

Tyrone Woods was the Director of the Richmond Fusion Center. He was a political appointee, placed in charge of the region's security by the Regime leadership. At the time when the alert came in, Director Woods was not in the RTOC, and after he received the call he hurried into work, driven by his security detail in a convoy of armored SUVs.

Woods was a veteran activist, a political bruiser, who had grown up in the gutter political environment of Chicago. He was adept at vote rigging and intimidation and exhibited naked unbridled ambition. This all made him a valuable asset to the Regime. He was a rabid racist, Muslim and communist; he hated white Americans. He saw them as the very evil at the heart of everything that was wrong with America.

In fact, at the heart of it he hated America and wanted to be part of its destruction, bringing in the new order.

Woods was big on the injustices of slavery, and it was slavery that was at the root of his hatred. He railed against the injustices of slavery and the heritage of white western imperialism and colonialism. America was the new empire, subjugating the Islamic and third worlds.

America was the 'Great Satan'.

He in fact had never been a slave, neither had his ancestors. In fact, his father had emigrated from Nigeria after his number had come up in the green card lottery. It was a little ironic, but Woods did not know that his father's tribe in Nigeria had historically been responsible for capturing and selling into slavery many of the original people who had been shipped over to the American Colonies.

Woods hated the white majority in America. He wanted to see them broken and enslaved. He hated what he saw as the gun owning, constitution hugging ways of white Americans; their pickup trucks and Patriotism. He had no truck with the achievements and traditions of America, he wanted to see it all wiped clean. Such was the motivation of this racist, communist, 'progressive' bully.

By the time Director Woods arrived at the RTOC an unmanned drone was in the air, surveying the destruction of the ambush site. The burning vehicles and the bodies of the slain blue shirts were all too evident on the TV screens.

Woods was incandescent.

"Find who did this. Use the drones. Bring in the hunter-killer troops. I want them dead. Kill them all."

The patrol had accomplished their mission, after lying in position overnight to ambush the convoy, and they moved rapidly away before continuing to patrol out on their route through the fall forest, headed south to their pick up point.

The previous afternoon, they had identified a suitable patrol base on the map so that they could rest up and administrate themselves before continuing the extraction.

As they moved towards the area of the identified patrol base, the patrol was not following a trail, but instead they were 'hand railing' a small creek, keeping it a hundred meters to their right as they moved.

The patrol leader, Caleb, signaled for a hasty ambush and they broke track, moving off left at ninety degrees to their trail and then peeling back into a line covering the route they had come. They had not seen any evidence of a Regime tracker, but they took precautions all the same.

Once they had been in the hasty ambush for a few minutes, observing their back trail, Caleb took a small party away and found a suitable patrol base in the deep cover of the trees. A buddy pair returned to the ambush party and led them into the occupation of the base.

Caleb had decided to occupy in a linear formation, with the two squads parallel to each other in two lines, Alpha to the south side and Bravo to the north, headquarters between the two squads. There were two sentry posts, one at each end of the line, each squad responsible for one of the posts.

The patrol occupied the base in buddy pairs, with four pairs per squad. As part of the work phase of the occupation each pair dug a 'shell scrape', a shallow twelve inches deep rectangular hole large enough for two men to sleep in with their rucks. Each pair faced out of the patrol base with interlocking sectors of fire allocated by the patrol leader.

A track plan was cleared behind the scrapes, with communications cord strung between the trees to allow for hand rail movement at night. A latrine was dug under the watchful eye of one of the sentry positions and each time it was used the fighter would pile a little dirt back in over his leavings, to cover it up and reduce smell.

Once the work phase was complete, the patrol went into routine. They were on hard routine after the ambush and this close to the enemy and there was no cooking on open flame. Weapons were battle cleaned and food was eaten cold, unless heated using the flameless MRE heater packs. Socks were changed and feet powdered.

Following evening stand-to, in the dark, ponchos were put up over the scrapes. Throughout the night the sentry rotation went on. There were always two sentries at night per sentry position. Each man was woken ten minutes before his duty and he would quietly and without use of light put all his gear away in his ruck, save taking down the poncho.

All gear not in use was always stowed, in case of the need for rapid movement.

In the night it started to rain but by morning the rain had stopped. It was fall, and it was cold out there in the woods with a hint of the coming winter. The rain didn't help, and it continued to drip down out of the trees long after the rain itself had stopped.

Prior to dawn, the sentries woke the patrol for stand to. In the cold pre-dawn the fighters crawled out of their bags and packed their gear away. They took down the ponchos and removed excessive warm clothing, donning their tactical vests arrayed with their ammunition pouches.

It was cold, and some of them shivered uncontrollably as they adjusted to the temperature outside of their sleeping bags. The worst part was putting on their cold sweat-damp helmets with wet chinstraps. Before dawn the patrol was silent, laid in their scrapes covering their sectors.

There was a light mist on the forest floor, with the rain dripping down out of the trees. Yes, they were cold wet and hungry, but that did not impact their morale. They would bitch and moan, but if they weren't moaning, that was when you had to worry.

They were hardened fighters, with a deep motivation unaffected by the temporary hardships of their situation. Their morale was born of self-discipline, coming from a hard place deep inside, unbreakable.

The sky began to lighten but the dawn was delayed in the deep woods. The fighters shivered in their scrapes and waited for the end of stand-to.

Bravo Squad was covering the sectors to the north, where they had come from the previous day. Loud in the silence came the snap of a twig and they tensed, staring into the lightening forest. Slowly the silhouettes of a squad sized skirmish line came into view, maybe fifty meters away, as they came on through the woods.

The hunter-killer force did not know exactly where the Resistance fighters were, but they knew they were in these woods somewhere. As the enemy closed to twenty five meters the Bravo leader, Chavez, opened fire by shooting a silhouette in the chest, which was immediately followed by the rest of his squad opening fire.

The gunfire was harsh in the silence of the dawn and several of the enemy skirmish line were immediately hit.

The Regime troops were well drilled and immediately went to ground and started to return fire, the harsh orders of their squad leader competing with the screams of one of his men who had been badly wounded.

The firing increased to a crescendo and fire control orders were ringing out on both sides. The enemy managed to bring a SAW into action on the left flank and high velocity rounds went cracking through the trees in both directions.

Luckily for the patrol, they were in hard cover in their scrapes and most of the rounds were passing overhead; they were also able to take advantage of the shock effect their initial weight of fire had on the Regime skirmish line. Some of the enemy had been hit, most were well drilled veterans, but a few had frozen in cover and were not yet responding to calls for rapid fire from the Regime squad leader.

131

Caleb was assessing the situation. Alpha Squad was still covering the rear, to the south, in case of an enemy flanking attack. Having been 'bumped' by the enemy it was now paramount for the patrol to bug out and extract to the Emergency RV. Caleb was reading the battle and listening to the sounds of the firefight.

The ground was generally flat but to the left, north west, of Bravo Squad was a small depression where the ground sloped away in the beginnings of a draw that ran down to the right flank of the Regime force. It was not a significant feature really, the very beginnings of a creek, but he could anticipate how the enemy platoon leader would see it.

Caleb could hear the shouted orders from the remainder of the enemy platoon behind the point squad that was currently engaged. He gave orders for Alpha Squad to move up to the left of Bravo Squad.

Bravo gave rapid fire and threw smoke while Alpha peeled out from their scrapes and back on to line covering the small draw.

Normally the patrol would have bugged out with their rucks but the situation was too serious, so they just grabbed their daypacks. From now on, if they got out of this fix, it would be 'travel light, freeze at night'.

Alpha peeled in to the left of Bravo, getting on line, both squads facing north.

Caleb had Doc Oliver observe to the south, just in case. However, he was soon confirmed as correct in his assessment; the Regime commander had identified the depression and rapidly moved a second squad up to the patrols left, to try and flank and roll up the patrol.

As the enemy flanking squad moved through the trees, jogging in a squad wedge formation, they ran into a hail of fire from Alpha on the left side and rapidly took cover, returning sporadic fire from positions behind trees as they tried to regain their balance. .

The situation was now the two squads of the patrol facing two Regime squads. The patrol had taken the initiative and inflicted casualties on the enemy. The Regime platoon leader was organizing his reserve squad and relaying the situation back to his company commander to the rear.

The enemy was gaining momentum, the pressure was going to build, but they would be unable to bring down indirect fire while the two forces were so close.

Caleb gave shouted orders for his two squads to prepare to break contact. The drill was for each squad to fire and move as fire teams, keeping both squads roughly on line as they moved south back away from the enemy. If they stayed in place, the enemy would roll them up from the flank.

They threw smoke to the front, and on orders the whole patrol started a rapid weight of fire to knock the enemy back before beginning to bound back, fire and maneuvering south, away from the enemy.

The patrol only had the ammunition they carried, so they slowed the rate of fire to deliberate whenever rapid fire was not called for; they aimed at positively identified enemy or fired steadily into cover where they knew the enemy to be.

The Regime platoon leader had by now deployed one of his 240 gun teams up to his left flank and the gunner brought the 7.62mm machine-gun into action just after the patrol had completed its first couple of bounds back. The deep staccato beat of the gun rang out and the rounds cracked through the trees, tearing off chunks of wood and felling leaves and branches.

Bravo was conducting fire and movement back and as one of the guys bounded, zigzagging in a short rush, he was hit in the rear ballistic plate and thrown off balance into a face plant, winded. He rolled over and got up, adrenaline pushing him to finish the bound.

Another fighter was hit in the thigh as he ran; his leg kicked out from under him as the round smashed his femur and tore open his femoral artery. He went to the ground with bright red arterial blood pumping out of the wound. As his buddy was running back, he grabbed the downed fighters harness and dragged the wounded man with him on his rush back, the leg bouncing agonizingly on the ground, until he could get him into cover behind a tree.

The fighter grabbed the wounded man's CAT tourniquet and whipped it onto the leg over the BDU pants, right up in the groin 'high and tight'. He cinched the windlass down mercilessly until the bleeding stopped. The rest of his team had paused to cover this and the fighter pulled the wounded man up onto his back in a Hawes carry, running back and continuing the move north, covered by the rest of the squad as they bounded back.

Doc joined the wounded group and they moved south looking for a suitable rally point as the squads continued to skirmish back in teams. Caleb maintained a position between the two squads as they moved.

They continued in this way for about three hundred meters. As they were about halfway they had heard the 'whop whop whop' of helicopters passing overhead, but they could not get a good view through the tree canopy. The Regime platoon was just starting to regain its balance and cautiously move forward by bounding over-watch.

The patrol had temporarily broken contact and on reaching the medic and the wounded man Caleb called "Rally, Rally, Rally!"

The squads got into an all-round defensive position and leaders checked on their fighters. The lightweight stretcher was broken out. Chavez organized Bravo Squad, who took charge of moving their casualty, four men at a time carrying the stretcher, the remainder providing security and ready to changeover as necessary.

Caleb did a quick map check and they continued to move off south, with Alpha split into front and rear security teams to cover the casualty evacuation in the center.

As they moved south they came to a fire break that had once been used as a vehicle track. Rather than cross it or walk on it, they veered off to the south east and hand railed the feature, keeping it about seventy five meters to their right. The patrol was moving at a fast walk, the two teams of Alpha to the front and rear, with Bravo in the center carrying the stretcher with the wounded man.

Olson's team was on point, strung out in single file. Phillips, Gibbs and McCarthy formed the rest of the team, with Phillips walking point. Caleb moved a little behind Olson's front team and they all moved in a single file through the trees.

There was something nagging at Caleb. It suddenly hit him with a realization.

The helicopters!

They had passed over headed south, following the contact with the Regime platoon to the north. They sounded like the big Chinook CH-47s with the front and rear props. He had a pretty good idea that they were facing a Regime hunter-killer company, probably based off one of the old Ranger Companies from before this all started.

Hand railing the feature, which was an obvious egress route from the patrol base, meant that the patrol walked into one of the flank protection/cut-off groups belonging to the airborne reaction force platoon's hasty ambush.

The Regime platoon had been landed by the helicopters in a clearing just off the trail to the south east in response to the sweep platoon making contact with the rebel patrol base. They were to act as a blocking force (or cut-off group) across the patrols expected line of exfiltration.

They had expected the patrol to move along the track, and as such the main kill group was oriented in a line facing south west to cover the track. Their right hand cut-off group was a fire team sized component and they had also been concentrating on the track, where they expected the enemy to come from the north west.

Caleb heard the shout of 'Contact Front!' from the lead team just as a fusillade of firing went off at the head of the patrol. The lead team had the drop on the cut-off group and had walked pretty much on top of them, Phillips opening fire at a range of fifteen meters as he saw them. As Phillips fired on rapid the other three in his team stepped left and right to create an angle of fire, Olson as the second man now able to fire at the enemy past Phillips.

As Phillips and Olson bounded back, they were covered by Gibbs and McCarthy, who had pushed out left and right. The team ended up roughly on line, forming two buddy pairs to fight back together.

Olson took control of them and they began to buddy move back, firing as they went, having hit at least three of the enemy cut-off group. Celeb moved back and Bravo, the stretcher squad, also moved rapidly back ahead of him while the rear team from Alpha moved ahead of them as security and to establish a rally point.

The main kill group of the new Regime platoon was trying to move out of their ambush position in order to maneuver on the patrol, but before they could do so the lead team managed to break contact in the trees.

The patrol moved back several hundred meters in a north easterly direction to a rally point and the patrol leader got them into a wedge formation, each squad forming a side of the wedge in a hasty ambush position so that each of the squads faced the last known direction of one of the two enemy platoons: Alpha to the south west, Bravo to the north west. Some of the guys provided rear protection.

It was effectively a hasty triangular ambush with the third side missing, just covered to the rear by a couple of guys.

Doc was working on the casualty in the center. The team leaders got around and checked on the men, redistributing ammunition and 'bombing up' their empty magazines during the lull.

Caleb was running out of options. He was still pretty close to the enemy and with the confusion in the woods it would be hard for the enemy to bring in indirect fire. He was doing a map estimate, assessing the situation, and reckoned that their best bet would be to head off the high ground in an easterly direction, getting into one of the draws or ravines that ran down off the ridge, then exfiltrating from the current trap.

As Caleb was about to give the order to move out they were contacted again by the Regime platoon following up from the south. From their static ambush position the patrol were able to hit the enemy lead squad with accurate effective fire, forcing them to go to ground.

However, shortly after they were contacted by the original Regime platoon moving down from the north west.

Then a worrying thing happened: having fixed their position, the enemy pulled back.

The helicopters must have dropped off an 81mm mortar squad and shortly after the mortar rounds came screaming in on their position with concussive detonations: 'crump, crump, crump'.

Some of the rounds hit the trees, effectively air bursting and sending both shrapnel and wood splinters down onto the patrol. The fighters were hugging whatever cover they could find as the rounds impacted around them. Luckily, indirect fire is an area weapon and none of the patrol was hit in the first barrage. They were however, effectively suppressed.

It was either dig in and die in place, or get the hell out of there.

Caleb gave the preparatory order: on his order, rally three hundred meters east of their location. He waited for a lull in the fire and gave the order; the patrol 'bomb burst' out of their positions and ran like mad men out of the killing area, Bravo team sprinting with the stretcher.

As they ran, one of the fighters was hit with shrapnel in the upper back, puncturing his lung. He stumbled, caught himself and kept running, aided by a buddy. They made it the three hundred meters and were out of the impact area of the incoming mortars. Caleb called the rally point and the patrol got into yet another defensive position.

They got into an all-round defensive formation. Doc was working on the new casualty and he slapped an occlusive dressing on the sucking chest wound. The casualty was starting to suffer progressive respiratory distress, indicating a tension pneumothorax, so Doc put in a needle chest decompression in his upper chest slightly below the collar bone, which alleviated the symptoms. Given the exigent circumstances it allowed the fighter to keep moving.

The patrol got themselves back into formation and started to move rapidly away east towards where the ground fell away down the steep sided ridge into the valley.

As they moved, one of the fighters noticed the sound of a distant helicopter engine and passed it on up the line. They reached a place where at some point the trees had been felled and it was an area of thinner brush and tree growth extending about a hundred meters before the forest started again on the edge of the slope down. It was a linear danger area but they did not really have much choice but to keep going.

As they headed across out of the forest canopy in their patrol formation, the gunner in the Apache attack helicopter picked them up on his thermal imager. He had been tracking what he thought was the hunted patrol for a few minutes, but given the close combat in the woods he had been unable to clearly identify the patrol from his own forces. The pilot maneuvered on station in order to give the gunner the best shot.

The Hydra 70 rocket burst in the air before it hit the patrol, sending ninety six flechette darts into the center of the patrol where the stretcher party was jogging along.

The casualty on the stretcher as well as four others surrounding him, including Doc and Chavez, disintegrated into a red mist under the impact of the darts.

As the patrol roiled from the shock Caleb screamed: 'RUN!"

Meanwhile the Apache gunner switched to 30mm cannon. The cannon aimed where he looked, slaved to the sight in his helmet, and he decided to roll up the patrol from the rear.

The burst of 30mm M789 HEDP cannon rounds exploded around the rear security team as they were running for the tree line. The gunner chased them all the way with the cannon rounds exploding around the rear team. Three of them didn't make the tree line.

Caleb had lost half his patrol, with just half of both squads left. They kept running into the trees. The Apache could still see and track them, but there was a little more cover from the FLIR thermal imager in the trees and some of the explosions from the 30mm rounds were absorbed.

There was no way they could go back to recover the downed members of the patrol. It was something they had learned since the civil war began: the old rule of 'never leave a fallen comrade' just never worked any more when you were on the run and didn't have the overwhelming force and assets to get them back. Sometimes fighters went down and there was nothing you could do for them.

The patrol ran into a ravine and followed it as it steepened down towards the valley. In an area of the ravine with steep overhanging sides and good tree cover they went static. The Apache had struggled to continue to follow their move and despite continued circling was unable to find the patrol while they were both in the ravine and under the tree cover.

After a time of searching, the Apache had to return to base to refuel, and luckily the exigencies and scarcities of the collapse situation meant there was no back-up to replace it on station.

In the Fusion Center RTOC, Tyrone Woods was sitting in his command chair. He had been watching the live feed 'kill cam' footage from the Apache, and following the action from the footage provided by an overhead drone. He was raging inside, while concurrently turned on by his power to reach out and kill the 'redneck terrorists' as they scuttled on the ground below his cameras.

"Track them. Get me that Apache back on station. I want them all dead," he announced to the RTOC.

A young Ranger liaison officer from the hunter-killer company, a Lieutenant Jefferson, approached him. Jefferson was a West Point Graduate, a college football star quarterback. He was an ambitious and rising young officer.

"Sir, if we capture rather than kill, we could exploit the intelligence…" He was cut off in mid-sentence as Director Woods came out of his chair, grasping him by the collar of his ACU uniform jacket.

"Listen to me," he shouted, "I said kill them, every last one!" The spittle flew into Lieutenant Jefferson's face as he tried to recoil, shock plain in his expression. Director Woods let go his grip and pushed him away.

"Listen you fuckers," he announced to the RTOC, "No one ambushes and kills my guys in my area, you hear me! Those blue shirts are the vanguard of the revolution! If you are not killing these insurgent vermin, you are terrorists just like them. If I hear another word of complaint from any of you terrorist sympathizers, I will send the offender to the camps for reeducation!"

With that, he stormed out.

After a while of listening watch, the patrol determined that the Apache had gone. There was still the problem of the dismounted hunter-killer company.

The patrol packed up their gear and started to head down into the valley to the west. They followed the steep ravine down, jog-walking as best they could, occasionally slipping in the steeper areas.

Then they heard the baying of the tracker dogs from up on the ridge.

Caleb called a halt and gathered the team around, "Ok, we are gonna split. First into two teams, then split again into pairs. Head away from each other and keep altering your course. We will RV at the pickup point as per the orders. Ok?

They nodded, the stress was apparent on their faces.

"Ok," said Caleb, "I'll call the first split. We are gonna move fast. Let's go."

They took off back down the ravine again, in formation and spread out. They heard the beat of a CH-47 pass over top of them, headed east towards the valley. The patrol emerged on the lower slopes of the ridge, still in the trees, and kept jogging downhill.

"Watch for hasty ambushes, they will try and get ahead of us," called Caleb, breathing heavily, "Split now."

"Roger that," called Olson. "Alpha with me!" He led them off to the right as Caleb continued on with the remainder of Bravo.

A couple of kilometers later, the teams spit again into two man buddy teams, preparing to exfiltrate back to the pickup point. As Olson sent Phillips and Gibbs in one direction, he paused with McCarthy and removed a pre-prepared improvised claymore from the top of his daypack. He rapidly emplaced it, sited covering their back trail and armed to be triggered by a tripwire.

As the hunter-killer dog teams emerged from the ravine they soon found the place where the patrol had split. They also split, following the two directions. Once they had the line of travel, they called it in to the RTOC, located at the Fusion Center in Richmond, which responded by directing the CH-47s to drop troops ahead of the line into hasty ambush positions.

The helicopters made multiple dummy landings to confuse the pursued and make it harder for them to predict the location of the hasty ambushes.

Once in the valley bottom, the fighters found that the trees thinned out and there were more fields, areas of farmland for grazing. The pairs tried their best to make changes to their direction to make pursuit more difficult.

Around twenty minutes after Olson had split his team, he and McCarthy were jogging through some trees when they heard the distant sound of the claymore detonating. Olson grinned.

That'll give 'em pause for thought.

One of the pairs from Bravo team got complacent and started to try and head due south along a creek in the valley bottom. It was a predictable route and a hasty ambush had been placed in a tree line overlooking the line of the creek.

The pair was walking in the shallow creek, hoping to throw off the dogs, when the squad ambush opened fire on them from seventy five meters. They were not initially hit in the fire, which was heavy on quantity and not so much on accuracy.

The pair dove for cover in the creek bed and tried to use it for cover to crawl back out to the north.

The hunter-killer squad was static in the tree line, shooting the area of the creek to pieces, but not hitting the two men low crawling along below the creek bank.

Suddenly a CH-47 roared into the air above the pair, directed by the contact report from the Regime squad. The Chinook went into a right hand circuit above the two fighters and the door gunner in the front right window opened fire with his chain gun.

The creek around the two men erupted in gouts of flying water as the rounds struck home into the rocks and mud of the creek bed.

One of the men was hit and lay still. The other scrambled for the creek bank and tried to return fire. He stood, leaning against the bank as he fired rapidly into the huge body of the looming helicopter. As he did so, he was hit by a burst of fire from a SAW gunner laying in the tree line, killed instantly.

Four days later, two vans arrived back at Victor Foxtrot containing the survivors of the patrol; Caleb, Olson and six others. They were cold, wet, exhausted and starving after escape and evading back to the pick-up point.

Jack was waiting with Jim and Megan as the driver opened the side door of one of the vans and Caleb got out. The exhaustion was plain in his face.

"Hey," said Caleb.

"Hey," said Jack, "this is all of you?"

Caleb looked haunted, "Yea."

"Oh no." said Jack, before turning to Jim and Megan. "Let's get them warm, dry and fed pronto. Megan, give them a medical checkup. Ok?"

"Roger that, Boss," said Jim as Megan nodded, concern filling her face.

Jack turned to Caleb, "As soon as you are able, I need a report on this."

Jack strode through the door of Major Cassidy's office, the door flying open before banging back off the wall. The Major looked up, startled. Jack's jaw was clenched.

"What the hell, Captain?" said Cassidy.

Jack stood in front of the desk, looking at him, scorn written over his face.

Ok, much as I want to rip his head off, don't do it. Watch the temper, Jack, get a grip.

"Ok Cassidy, the ambush was a success. But we lost ten good men. I warned you, wrong time, wrong place. Was it worth it?"

Realizing Jack wasn't going to come over the desk at him, Major Cassidy recovered some of his cunning. "It was unfortunate, Captain, but it was collateral damage. The mission was a success."

"Collateral damage!" Jack roared, about to forget his attempt to hold his temper back. He realized in a flash that this is why he had left the army: He could only tolerate authority if he respected the senior officer. And too many were not deserving of that respect.

"Those were good men, the cream of our experience," Jack said, "That was not collateral damage. That was negligence. I am giving you a week to get your crap and get reassigned, or I will beat your sorry ass you useless pile of shit."

Jack turned on his heel and strode out, leaving Major Cassidy ashen faced at his desk.

Dealt with that well then - so much for keeping the temper in check.

Jim was outside. He raised an eyebrow at Jack. "Hey Rocky, let's get a brew," he said with a grin, before leading Jack away.

They found a spot to drink some coffee. Jack was still hopping mad but starting to calm down, feeling a little ashamed of his outburst.

"Look Boss," said Jim, "don't worry about it. The guy is a prick and he had it coming, it was only a matter of time. It wouldn't do for him to remain in charge of this circus." Jim fixed Jack with a look, "Thing is, they need a combat leader."

Jack looked at him. Jim fixed his gaze, a wry smile at the corner of his mouth.

Caitlin was going to kill him.

Four days later, Bill arrived at Victor Foxtrot. He had received a message from Major Cassidy and with the backwards communication and transport systems it had taken a few days to turn around and make the trip.

He took Jack aside and questioned him on the situation: the ambush, Major Cassidy, Jack's role, all in detail. After that, he took some time to run his investigation.

Later that day, Bill pulled Jack aside, looking serious. "Ok, it's a royal mess. It seems plain that my faith in Major Cassidy was misplaced. He's more of an administrative officer than a combat leader, I think. But the situation is not helped by you kicking doors in."

"Hey Bill, I'm sorry, but the man is an ass and I warned him about the mission. We lost some good people."

"I know, I know. I get it." Bill playfully punched Jack on the arm, "I just forgot what you are like!" he said with a grin. "Look," Bill continued, "I'm taking Cassidy with me. I have another role for him. But that leaves me short here."

Jack looked at him.

Bill continued "I know we had a deal, and it still stands. However, if you'll do it I want to make you the operational commander here, responsible for this Company."

Jack thought for a moment.

"Look, I'll do it. It was a hard enough training these guys and knowing I would not be going on operations with them. But I have to speak to Caitlin."

That's gonna be the hard part.

"Ok, head down and see her tonight. I will wait around here for a couple of days for your answer."

Later, Bill got Jack together with Jim and briefed them about what he had heard on the network so far. Apparently Texas was leading a group of southern States in a move to secede. There was also talk of an attempt to create an independent 'free zone' in the area of the 'American Redoubt' around Idaho and Wyoming.

Bill had heard that the group of southern States, led by Texas, was becoming known as the 'Southern Federation'. He didn't have clear details, but apparently as the Federation had emerged there had been a lot of internecine fighting, betrayal, defections and just plain murder as allegiances were sorted out.

The National Guard units in the region remained under their respective State control, but the active duty army units in the area had been obliged by the circumstances to figure out their loyalties, with massive defections of active duty troops based in Texas and the south to the Federation forces, not without bloodshed.

Jim commented that for any sort of insurgency to work against the Regime, it had to have the right ground. It had to be in some combination of forests, mountains, hills, swamps or similar slow going back country. If you tried to operate in the deserts or the great plains, that was tank country, mobile warfare country, and you would be cut down by the more conventional and armored Regime forces.

This led them on to the attack helicopter threat. Bill let them know that MANPADs, which were shoulder fired surface to air missiles, were simply not available. The Regime was keeping a tight lid on them, not needing them to counter any threat themselves, and knowing the threat they posed to the Regime's air superiority.

None of the Regime ground troops carried them: they did not need them to counter a threat and there was too much risk of them falling into Resistance hands. Jack reasoned that they may ultimately get hold of them through an allied group, such as from Texas if they could link up networks at some point.

They gave Bill their shopping list. In the absence of MANPADs, they wanted heavier caliber machine-guns, such as 240s and .50cals, along with the tripods to mount them on. They also wanted Barrett .50 Cal sniper rifles and 81mm mortars to equip their mortar squads with. They needed the ammunition to operate these weapon systems, which would have to fall off the back of a truck somewhere.

Once the training progressed to the right point, these weapons systems would allow them to equip a dedicated fire support platoon.

Bill already had access to a lot of these weapon systems, stolen or looted and stashed away. Some he would have to procure, as well as the additional ammunition, through his network.

Jack took a trip down to Zulu that night. As he entered the dugout, softly lit with lanterns, he passed the partitioned section where Chavez's family lived. He caught a glimpse of a Catholic shrine with a group of candles around it in the niche, and heard the soft sobbing of a woman.

I need to go see her, in a little bit.

Jasper came running out from his family area, wagging his tail and trying to lick Jack's face.

"Down Jasper, down," he laughed.

At the sound of his voice, Sarah and Connor came running out to him, "Daddy, Daddy!" and he picked them up in his arms.

As Jack walked past the wooden partition into the family area, Caitlin looked up from what she was doing at the table at him, smiled, and then sensed his mood and her face changed.

"Hi Hon," she said, "What's the matter?"

'Hey, I missed you. And you guys too!' he said, turning to the two kids with a smile. "Bill was here," he continued, "Major Cassidy is gone."

She looked at him, her mind working.

"So, honey, I was thinking…" he started.

She made the connection in a flash.

"Oh no. No you don't Jack Berenger, that wasn't the deal."

"Hon, they need me."

"We need you," she replied.

"I know, I'm sorry, I promise I'll be careful, but this is something I have to do."

"Damn it Jack, there is nothing truer than that I know you. I should have guessed. This is just typical."

Jack stood there like a klutz, both kids in his arms. "Look Hon, I'm sorry."

She turned back to the table, "It's FINE, don't worry about it.

Clearly it wasn't fine.

"Fine," he said.

"Fine," she said, face to the desk.

"Come on kids, let's go for a walk."

Later, the kids were sleeping and he was sitting at the table in their partitioned area when she came up behind him, put her arms around his neck, and her cheek onto his.

"I'm sorry Hon, I love you," Jack said.

"I love you too. Just don't get hurt."

Chapter Eight

Come early January, the training was progressing well. Bill had sent the support weapons they had requested and they had begun to train a fourth platoon as a fire support element. They had two mortar squads with three barrels each. There were two machine-gun squads who had a choice of 240 or .50cal weapons depending on the task at hand. They also had several men trained up as .50cal Barrett rifle shooters.

Luckily amongst the veterans that had been recruited they had some with relevant experience, either as machine-gunners or mortar men. This made the training process smoother and allowed them to identify trainers for these specialist weapons.

The training had been pretty tough through the winter, the harsh cold and wet was a constant challenge, exacerbated by barely adequate rations. As they had anticipated, some of those being trained had fallen off the course, either voluntarily withdrawing or being told they would be better elsewhere. A steady flow of new recruits had allowed them to reach the desired four platoon Company strength.

About fifty percent of the women had not made it through the training, finding jobs elsewhere within the organization but leaving a hard core behind, spread across the platoons. Some of the women, although not allocated to the fighting Company, had been kept as covert assets to be used by the IED cells or for covert recon tasks.

They had begun to deploy the four man IED/shooter teams. These teams would be taken out of the training for a week at a time, given IEDs and an area to operate in, to include several miles of road. They would deploy and conduct harassing IED operations on the routes used by Regime convoys and patrols, attempting to disrupt Regime movement through the Shenandoah Valley.

Jim had his metal shop up and running and was creating the off-route mines, otherwise known as explosively formed penetrators or EFPs. These were set at the side of the road and angled for a shot into a passing vehicle. The explosives behind the copper cone would detonate and shoot an 'incoherent spray' of molten metal at the target, burning through the armor with the molten slugs.

It was a related process to the way a HEAT warhead or RPG worked, but with the difference that the EFP was set off the road away from the vehicle, whereas the RPG warhead detonated on the side of the vehicle and used the Monroe effect to fire a molten jet, or stream, through the armor.

The EFP was unstoppable by the Regime armored vehicles but the vital factor was accurate targeting. It had to fire at the right time and strike the enemy vehicle in the right place. The thing about EFPs was that, for example, one could strike through the cab of a vehicle, but leave everyone in the back unharmed. This is why they were often deployed as a targeted array of multiple devices in the Middle East, for maximum damage.

Jim designed the initiation system straight from the briefs he had received and the examples he had seen of recovered devices while on deployment. The device would be triggered when a vehicle broke the beam of an infra-red (IR) 'tripwire' set across the road. The distance between this trip beam and the EFP itself determined where on the vehicle the device would hit.

In order to avoid striking the wrong vehicle, or civilians for instance, the beam would be turned on by an observer using a remote device, from a distance. The Regime troops had not so far been deployed with electronic counter measure (ECM) equipment to disrupt such attacks, but as the IED campaign continued no doubt they would.

The ECM protection created a bubble around the convoy within which the remote controlled devices would not work. This meant that for the EFP, timing was critical: it was to be switched on when the convoy was imminent, but not too late so the ECM would counter attempts to turn it on with the remote device. Initially, there were failures due to experimentation and inexperience.

The EFP was the key device that they deployed with. It had the advantage of being a hybrid of a remote controlled IED, but at the same time it was victim operated and the detonation was tied to the placement of the IR beam.

When the IED team deployed, it was more of a covert operation than the more conventional side of the Resistance operations they were training for. They shed most of their overt irregular fighter garb and went as low profile as possible, equipment and battle belts with jackets and such.

The teams would select a kill site within their allocated area of operations using whatever intelligence they had supplemented by their own recon. The two IED specialists would covertly place and camouflage the EFP by the side of the route and fall back to an OP where they could over-watch the device. The two shooters would usually be deployed in a separate location in order to provide early warning and cover for the withdrawal.

The teams took to taking the thermal ponchos on these OP missions with them, because they could set up and lay in the OP under the ponchos and avoid any aerial surveillance. As the campaign progressed through the month of January they started to see more and more 'top cover' flights by helicopters equipped with FLIR, forward looking infra-red. Sometimes these would be AH (attack helicopters: Apaches), sometimes even just police surveillance helicopters. The Regime intent was to conduct a route clearance ahead of any convoys utilizing their FLIR equipment.

Through the Resistance network and also from previous missions into the valley, the Company was building up a database of information on the valley, patterns of the Regime convoys and patrols, and also useful places to lie up. There were places that were known to be available, such as barns and sheds on the land of sympathizers, convenient wooded copses and the like, where IED teams could lie up while out on mission.

Along with the lay-up points, sometimes co-located or in separate areas, was a network of caches for food supplies that would be checked and refilled routinely by local sympathizers. This was working well for the Resistance, and maintaining the support of the people in the valley was essential.

Jack knew that if the attention of the Regime really began to focus on the valley, with detailed surveillance and Intel gathering assets, then some of this network would be exposed to reprisals.

For now, the Regime was not trying to occupy the valley, but rather use the I-81 as a main supply route and also conduct occasional patrols. So far there was no forward operating base (FOB) in the valley in order to establish a permanent presence. It would likely be coming, as the Regime spread its influence out of the zones. Pushing back against that was the mission of the Company.

It was only a matter of time before the Regime had to push into the rural areas and start to take control of food production, for its long term survival. That was probably why the rural patrols and traffic control points, outside of the zones, had not so far insisted on the RFID chip, or the whole DHS registration that those in the FEMA zones had to do.

The Regime was motivated to leave the farmers, the producers, alive. And they knew that the time was coming as the Regime gathered strength, when they would push out and try to gain further control of the contested sectors.

Sometimes the IED operations would be a success, other times the devices would not even be initiated if the enemy failed to appear, and the ambush would be collapsed, the IED recovered and returned to Victor Foxtrot. With about thirty percent of missions resulting in a successful kill on a regime vehicle, the operations were gathering attention and the Regime focus on the valley was increasing.

They lost a team early on, caught withdrawing from the contact point after successfully destroying an MRAP. (The MRAP was the successor to the armored Humvee, bigger and heavier.) The team was moving back though a wood line when an Apache was called on station. It effortlessly picked them up on thermal and tracked them, first destroying the IED pair and then sniffing out and snuffing out the cover team.

It was increasingly apparent that the possession by the Regime of the Apache was a huge force multiplier and the Resistance would have to do something about it. They had developed the thermal ponchos, which had been proven to work well when static. Good use of ground and cover, as well as alert air sentries, was another factor that helped them.

They had discussed the use of smoke for any set piece attacks they were to plan. The idea was that the presence of hot smoke particles in the atmosphere interfered with the thermal imagers employed by the helicopters. If they could get set up upwind of an objective, it would be possible to light fires and allow the hot smoke to drift over the objective area. They had planned for this and prepared some half oil drums that they could burn diesel fuel in. A collection of old tires, thrown on top, would really get some nasty hot acrid smoke going.

They really felt strongly that although the IED plan was working well to harass the enemy while the training reached its conclusion, they wanted to hit back at the Apaches. They had noticed that they seemed to fly mostly in pairs, sometimes alone if there was a resource issue.

Now that the fire support platoon was equipped with the machine-guns and Barrett sniper rifles, Jack felt it was time to plan something, and he enlisted Caleb as his key volunteer. Caleb had strong reason to want to get back at the Apaches.

Jim had established a couple of vehicle laager points under camouflage netting spread around the area of Victor Foxtrot. He had trained a couple of welders to help with his metal shop and the IED production, and also used them to modify vehicles. Now that they had the fire support platoon up and running, under training right now, they had been working on some ideas that Jim had come up with.

They had acquired three large dump trucks, the multi-axle type with the large metal high box rear. These were big heavy trucks with a huge weight capacity. Jim had his guys weld additional plate steel around the inside of the truck bed, and sandbag the floor. They also welded steel plate to the cab doors, removing the windshield and welding a steel plate across, with a rectangular viewing port to see through. This resulted in a cab and truck bed resistant to high velocity rounds.

They set the trucks up to receive two mortar barrels each, baseplates buried under sandbags in the bed of the truck, along with gear and ammunition to operate them. If utilized in this way, it would give the six-barrel mortar squad the potential to be mobile and dispersed.

While they were about it, they also rigged the trucks to run as machine-gun carriers. They did this by mounting receivers at various points along the front and sides of the truck bed, in place of pintle mounts, which allowed the machine-guns to be slotted in rapidly and mounted on the sides of the dump trucks.

They also worked on acquiring and setting up some heavy pick-up trucks as 'technicals'; these were gun trucks.

Rather than using the tripods which came with the 240 and .50cal machine-guns, for deployment in the ground role, they welded in pintle mounts that were set up to receive either the 240 or .50cal machine-guns. This would allow the pickups to be deployed against ground targets, but having a pintle mount also allowed use in an air defense role.

They used heavy pick-up trucks for this purpose; they had ten of them for the machine-gun sections. They had acquired some dual rear axle trucks for use with the .50cals. Jim knew from experience that firing these machine-guns in the back of a truck could cause some heavy rocking on the suspension. Thus the .50cal trucks were designed to be heavy duty with solid dual rear axles and a reinforced pintle mount built off a strong frame.

As well as the technicals, they also had a few ATVs and gators. Using either the trucks or the gators would allow them to utilize options for deployment of the fire support platoon. They could go entirely mobile in the dump trucks and technicals. Or they could go lighter and move into position using either the technicals or the Gators, but stopping short in the vehicles and moving forward to set up the guns in either the light role or tripod mounted sustained fire (SF) role.

The technicals, unlike the dump trucks, were not armored. This reduced survivability from enemy fire and thus their deployment had to be considered. It was best to deploy the technicals from cover, even a 'hull down' position, or at long range out of the reach of enemy small arms. Either that, or use the technicals as simply transport vehicles, dismounting the guns onto their tripods in cover to engage the enemy.

It was certainly true that all their weapon systems, including the .50cals and the 81mm mortars, could be man-packed in. They practiced as such with heavy carries through the woods on field training exercises. The key thing was ammunition quantities and resupply. Using even a single ATV to accompany a mortar or machine-gun section allowed an exponentially larger supply of ammunition.

If absolute stealth was not required while moving into position, ATVs could be brought up to just short of the fire support position, and then when the attack went 'noisy' they could bring ammo resupply up to the firing positions.

Come early February, they had been observing the Regime tactics of often flying surveillance or Apache attack helicopter top cover over many of the convoy moves along the highways. Jack and Caleb had been looking for some suitable ground to mount an ambush and they thought they had found it.

At the town of Lexington at the southern end of the valley was the junction between the I-81 and the I-64. The I-64 ran out to the west and went through the lower part of the George Washington National Forest, cross graining the ridges of the hills which made up the western boundary of the Shenandoah Valley. Victor Foxtrot was further north in those hills, shrouded deep in the wooded ridges.

Jack was going to be personally in charge of this mission. He planned a multi-weapon shoot using 240 and .50cal machine-guns, as well as a couple of Barrett .50s. The idea was to try and bag one or a couple of Apaches. He took with him an IED team, a kill group from the machine-gun sections with four 240s and four .50cals, as well as two Barrett sharpshooters.

He also took Caleb and one other fighter from his platoon, Sam, in a technical with a mounted 240. Sam had been the one hit in the plate by the 7.62mm round while breaking contact from the hunter-killer force. As well as this group, he also took a man with a video camera.

They drove cautiously south through the web of rural roads, firebreaks and forest trails until they came to a position north of the I-64. Jack had identified where a small side valley opened up north of the road, with spurs of wooded high ground to the east and west of it. Running north up the valley along the banks of a winding creek was an asphalt road, partially obscured in places by the tree cover.

Jack had the machine-gun kill group set up in a defilade position on the spur to the west of the valley, looking to the north east. They dug shallow 'shell scrapes' to increase their protection and covered the position and the tripod mounted machine-guns with thermal ponchos. The way they were oriented put them out of view of the I-64 south of them in the main east-west valley.

In a position on the small road in the side valley a few hundred meters north of the I-64 waited Caleb and Sam in the technical. They waited under a thermal poncho beside the vehicle, which was hidden amongst some trees.

Down by the I-64 itself the IED team set up an ambush utilizing an array of EFP devices in a daisy chain. Their positions overlooking the highway were camouflaged by the thermal ponchos. They had also dug shallow 'shell scrapes' for cover.

Once the ambush was set, they all went into routine, waiting. They ate rations cold and drank water, moving covertly back to the rear of the positions to defecate in cat holes that they dug.

Two days later, they heard the beat of helicopters approaching from the east, from the Shenandoah Valley. They were moving slowly, providing top cover for a convoy down on the road. There were two Apache attack helicopters, sniffing and searching along the route. The ambush team hunkered down under the thermal ponchos.

The supply convoy passed under the position of the IED team and they initiated the ambush; the daisy chain was largely effective due to predictable spacing between vehicles and several convoy vehicles were left immobilized in the road. The convoy stopped and started to return fire from turret guns, attempting to gain fire superiority into likely positions of cover. The IED team did not move; they just hunkered down in place.

As soon as the IEDs went off, Caleb was in the vehicle, Sam manning the 240 on the back. The two

Apaches had swung around in response to the contact. As they came into view around the shoulder of the spur, Sam opened fire with the 240. The Apache pilot picked up the stream of tracer headed his way, notified the gunner, and started towards the technical.

Sam screamed for Caleb to go and he took off north up the road like a rally driver, Sam still firing the 240. The Apache followed them, trying to acquire the target as the pickup flew round the bends and disappeared under the tree cover, emerging intermittently. The gunner was engaging with 30mm explosive cannon rounds but could not quite get them on target, the explosions of the rounds chasing the pickup along the road.

Caleb's mad drive drew the Apache north into the valley. The second Apache was flying a circuit at higher altitude, passing over the top of the ambush position each time round. The engaged Apache was flying slowly in pursuit of Caleb, sniffing and worrying its prey, trying to get the kill shot.

A burst of 30mm cannon fire from the Apache chased the pickup up the road, finding the back of the truck and creeping into the truck bed. A round detonated in front of Sam, killing him instantly, and sending shrapnel through into the cab, narrowly missing Caleb. He went round a bend and brought the truck to a slewing stop, in the same motion opening the door and sprinting out into the creek, taking cover in the water under the bank.

The Apache went into a hover, preparing to finish off the truck and then sniff out Caleb under the bank. At that moment, Jack gave the order and the kill group opened fire at the hovering Apache below them in the valley. It was a range of five hundred meters. Jack had the kill group split into two, with two 240s, two .50cals and one Barrett .50 designated for each chopper.

The ammunition in the machine-gun belts was loaded as standard with one in five rounds being tracer. The idea in an air defense role was to create a cone of fire that the aircraft would fly into, using the tracers to see where your fire was going. In this case, the Apache was stationary and the gunners were able to walk their long bursts of fire onto it. They opened up with a massive weight of fire, 7.62 and .50cal rounds smashing into the hovering Apache.

The Apache is a very well protected attack helicopter designed to withstand small arms fire, with critical areas protected up to either 12.7mm or 23mm rounds depending. It is also over engineered to have redundancy, for example the twin engines and larger parts than are necessary, such as the drive trains. However, nothing is invulnerable, and the machine is only as strong as the human component.

As the Apache hovered there, the gunner in the front seat was engaging the pickup while the pilot in the rear seat flew the aircraft. He had never come under effective ground fire before. Suddenly, the airframe was rocked to the right by the impact of the striking rounds, many of them finding their way into the airframe. The Barrett gunner was hitting the cockpit canopy to the pilots left by his head with .50cal rounds, impacting the canopy but not penetrating.

The pilot panicked, lost altitude and tried to bank away to the right, but the controls felt sluggish – some vulnerability had obviously been hit by the incoming rounds. He tried to bank away but lost control as the aircraft was driven towards the ground by the impacting machine-gun fire. The aircraft accelerated around in a wide turn towards the spur on the far side of the valley, engine screaming with the pilot's effort to pull it up. Before the pilot could exert control and pull it out of the low turn, the helicopter smashed into the trees, crashing through them into the side of the spur.

Reacting to the initial contact, the second Apache was above the kill group when they opened fire. It flew out over the valley and spun to acquire the target. Just then, the second part of the kill group opened fire, forcing the Apache to fly in a cone of machine-gun fire and tracer rounds.

This pilot did not make the mistake of hovering, he kept moving while the gunner acquired the target, but they were both distracted by the volume of fire they were being subjected to. They were only five hundred yards away from the kill group, really too close for a killing machine that often operated up to seven kilometers away from the target.

Although the cockpit was protected against .50cal fire, it did not prevent the impact of the rounds into the laminated glass and the starburst effect as the massive weight of fire hit. This also had a psychological effect on the gunner, who was trying to engage and saturate the area where the kill group was with 2.75 inch rockets. The distraction saved the lives of Jack's ambush team, as the rockets burst around them, scattering up the hillside, leaving them unharmed in the shallow scrapes.

Facing the volume of fire from the kill group, both groups having now switched fire onto the second helicopter, the pilot decided discretion was the better form of valor and withdrew. He banked away, his aircraft surrounded by a hail of flying tracer, to limp back to base. The Apache had certainly shown its survivability, but not without damage.

Jack knew that the crew of the downed helicopter were likely alive, given the designed crash survivability of the Apache. But he could not afford to hang around. An airborne reaction force was likely to be on the way and the ground convoy was probably going to be tasked to deploy into the valley to recover the crew and secure the crash site.

There was no need for radio silence any more so he gave the order over the radio to withdraw. The IED team pulled back and Caleb headed out on foot to join them at the ORP, carrying Sam's body over his shoulders in a fireman's carry. Down in the valley Caleb had been closer to the crash and dearly wanted to go over there to finish them, but he also knew it was not practical.

Jack's group dismounted the guns from their tripods, policed up their gear, and commenced the hump out to the ORP, moving as fast as they could under the heavy load. Once all the various elements were back at the vehicles, they mounted up and moved north away from the objective area.

Every so often, they would move the vehicles into cover, turn the engines off, and listen out for the sounds of helicopters. It was soon plain that they were not being pursued.

They had lost one man, but they had taken down an Apache and damaged another such that it had withdrawn from the battlefield. That was a major coup in Jacks mind and the team was exultant as they drove along.

Jack had a look at the video camera footage. It was good; the cameraman had captured all the action. The footage would be sent to Bill, who would distribute copies throughout the network, and also upload it to what remained of the internet.

It was invaluable psychological operations footage.

Jack also knew that the ambush was probably a one off, partially successful due to the unexpected nature of the attack. The Apaches were used to being unopposed, kings of the battlefield, invulnerable in the sky as they wreaked death and destruction on those below. They would adapt their TTPs to this current threat, no doubt.

In the absence of any type of surface to air missiles, Jack was going to have to come up with another way to neutralize the Apache threat in the valley.

Kill the beast in its lair, perhaps.

Following the Apache ambush the Company continued IED operations on the valley. The patrol reports for these operations, as well as the reconnaissance patrols they put out, corroborated by input from Bill's network, were telling them that there was an increase in Regime patrol activity in the valley and surrounding areas. Clearly the success of the IED campaign and the downing of the Apache had caught the attention of the powers that be in DC.

Jack considered this interesting, and it perhaps heralded a slight change in the focus of their operations. As part of the reports, there were indications that a Regime battle group may be earmarked for deployment into the valley, to turn it into its own 'AO' or area of operations.

When he had originally discussed strategy with Bill, the intent had been to begin small in the valley, training and getting up to speed, starting with the IED operations and concentrating force up company level when appropriate.

Now, it may be the case that the Regime would come to them. If so, the idea would be to avoid discovery of their various bases while turning the valley into a crucible of death for the Regime forces. Jack felt that he would have to bleed them in the valley, while avoiding a two way attrition battle that would leave the Resistance reeling.

From reports that Jack had seen, they were not the only Resistance outfit around, not even in the area. The difference was the investment they had put into training, equipment and personnel. In fact, as they had trained over the winter Jack had put specific criteria back to the network, to be passed to those vetting new recruits, specifying what he wanted. He wanted quality over quantity.

The old argument over the twenty million hunters in America was interesting. Jack wanted trainable potential. He either wanted veterans with experience who were not too set in their ways or egocentric, or he wanted those with similar skillsets who were able to be trained how he needed them. So far it had worked out well. The wrong sort of veteran was worse than the right type of newbie.

There was certainly a lot of Resistance activity in Virginia and further afield. Some of it was low level 'enthusiastic amateurs' of the hunter variety, other activity was better organized and prosecuted by former militia or veteran organizations.

The success of his Company in the valley was a case of the tallest poppy syndrome as measured against the surrounding area. The problem was that his selection and training process would now likely lead to the age old 'selection destruction cycle'. It was therefore paramount that they rose to the occasion and met this new Regime focus in an effective way.

Chapter Nine

It was late February when they got word from Bill. The Regime was sending an armored battle group into the valley. The specific intelligence suggested that this force was going to initially conduct 'clearance and re-education' operations on the town of Harrisonburg, which sat central to the valley.

This translated to a clearance and reprisal operation to use Harrisonburg as an example 'to encourage the others'. This operation had been brought on by the success of the Resistance in the Shenandoah Valley and the perceived need for the Regime to crack down on it.

It appeared that due to the presence in Harrisonburg of a local militia unit, the Regime had put two and two together and made ten. The actual militia unit in question had formed as a local defense force to protect the town against marauders following the collapse. They still ran checkpoints and controlled access into the town. The

Regime had conducted aerial surveillance and believed that this force was the one responsible for the IED attacks.

Bills message stated that he expected the attack to happen within two weeks, possibly as soon as a week. He had already notified the network in Harrisonburg and urged the remaining population to evacuate. The mission that he gave to Jack was to conduct urban delay and attrition operations within the town in order to inflict maximum possible casualties on the Regime battle group.

Jack launched into his battle procedure which varied a little from what he had learned 'doctrinally' while serving. He had a general idea of what he intended to do, so he called in his various 'heads of sheds', the chain of command, and gave them the verbal 'warning order' concerning the Intel he had received and the mission. He told them that they would be required to move rapidly to Harrisonburg to concentrate force as a fighting company.

His intent was to attrite the Regime battle group as it conducted its move into the town. But he did not intend to get dug in to a casualty intensive defense of the town. There would be no Alamo. His concept was for a mobile defense, falling back from the outer edges of the town in the face of the advancing Regime forces, hitting them at every opportunity but remaining light on their feet to minimize Resistance casualties.

Once he had outlined his concept he threw it open to the floor and effectively chaired a brainstorming session in order to extract the best ideas from the team leadership. They sat for several hours, thinking through the plan, and at the end of it they had a good workable concept that crucially had buy in from everyone. They had all had their say, and they all had all contributed their input. Some ideas had been put to the side, others adopted, but all could see the pros and cons and the 'why'.

Jack dismissed the leadership to start passing out the warning order to initiate movement. He sat with Jim and refined the plan, both of them looking at the operational concept and the practical logistics. Once they were done, they passed out the time of the orders group.

Jim headed out to see to the ammo, vehicles and logistics of the operation. Andrew was visiting and Jack had him help construct a scale model of the town of Harrisonburg in the briefing area. They showed a general representation of the town, with the main roads and key features represented and labeled.

Later that night, Jack gave his verbal orders. He had arranged a seating plan around the briefing area for the whole Company, with the fighters sat clustered in their various elements, as organized for the coming task. This was a case of the Company coming together to concentrate force for a company sized operation.

Caleb's platoon was designated as 1st Platoon. Jack had designated the other two infantry platoons as the 2nd and 3rd Platoons, with the mortar and machine-gun squads designated to the fire support platoon.

Jack gave verbal orders. It was important that the Company in its entirety sat to hear them. It ensured that they were all on the same page and fully understood the mission. It was a chance for Jack to apply his leadership and inspire them with the plan. It was also an opportunity for questions and clarification.

Jack followed the standard process. He covered the situation, going over what he knew of Intel on the enemy and also friendly forces. He outlined the task organization of the Company for this mission, which corroborated with the seating plan.

Next was the mission, which was the task they would complete along with a unifying purpose, which allowed the exercise of mission command – if the situation changed, the fighters knew the 'why' of the mission, and could therefore adapt in the absence of specific orders.

Next was the concept of the operation, including his intent and scheme of maneuver. Jack had the Company organized into three maneuver platoons that would conduct the delaying operation, falling back through the town, as well as the fire support element. The mortar squads would deploy in the three dump trucks to provide a mobile base of indirect fire, while the machine-gun squads would man the technicals, primarily in an air defense role.

There were small groups designated for ancillary tasks; for instance there was a 'smoke team' responsible for the burning of the drum and tire fires, and also select buildings, in order to mask the battlefield with thermal smoke.

The broad concept was to fight back to the north west from the I-81, towards the old quarter of the town, before dispersing and exfiltrating back into the hills and forests to the west. The I-81 ran through the center of the valley from the north east to south west. It ran through Harrisonburg, cutting off a small portion to the south east, which part Jack was not concerned with.

It was approximately three kilometers from the 1-81 to the center of the town. Closest to the interstate it was mainly residential housing with small shopping areas, before the main commercial district in the center of town, characterized by taller and more solidly built buildings. Out beyond the town center to the north west were a series of industrial complexes, including several very tall granary buildings.

Jack had made an assumption that to move the battle group through the valley to Harrisonburg, the Regime would likely use the I-81, and would therefore likely plan to begin their clearance from a position along it. It was important that the defense remained flexible, maintaining OPs to give early warning and allow the defensive forces and ambushes to react to the direction of enemy approach.

Each platoon would therefore operate independently but under Jacks coordination, providing its own OPs and recon teams, organizing into squads to provide a mobile area defense to fall back through the allocated sectors via a series of phase lines.

The mortars would be operating in their mobile fire bases from multiple positions to the north west of the town, guided by the mortar fire controllers (MFCs) allocated to high points, likely concealed on top of the granaries to give them over-watch of the battlefield.

The air defense technicals would be similarly organized, but further forward and coordinated by fire controllers. The idea was that the technicals would remain concealed and dispersed as much as possible, moving out from cover when there was a target to engage.

Given the wind direction, the fires would be set mainly out to the western edge of town to provide best thermal cover to the activity on the ground. Finally, Jack would locate his Company headquarters central to the action in the buildings of the town center. He had a group of key players, including his communications guys and a mortar and machine-gun fire controller.

They had given some thought to the use of radios and it would certainly be a lot easier to coordinate the battle with them. They had considered the possibility of the Regime using electronic warfare to jam the radios, but they concluded, based on their own deployed experience, that the Regime would more likely view their radios as a source of Intel and direction finding.

As such, the Company would use the radios to coordinate fires and movement as necessary, minimizing as much as possible; employing veiled speech and codes rather than communicating in plain language.

It was knowledge of the technology available to the Regime that was behind the thermal screening smoke, because armored vehicles as well as aircraft were equipped with thermal imagers. The intent of the smoke was to degrade the advantage that this technology would have, and to mitigate Regime aerial FLIR surveillance.

180

Also mortar locating radar was a concern. In order to avoid counter-battery fire vectored in by such radar locating systems, it was essential that the mortar firing points were mobile. Having them split into three squads in three dump trucks allowed them to essentially conduct fire and movement, one truck moving while the others continued to engage targets.

Following the concept of the operation, Jack handed over to Jim to cover service support, which was the nitty-gritty of logistics and administration. Following that, Jim handed over to Ned, a recent recruit and communications expert, to cover command and signal, which was basically the communications plan, codes, and location of the chain of command, including command succession in case of casualties.

After this detail, some of which was mind numbing to the less experienced members of the Company, Jack stood back up.

"Ok, listen up everyone, put your notebooks down, and listen in to my summary of execution. This is going to be an urban defensive battle, dirty nasty dangerous stuff. We will be facing a full battle group. It is imperative that you keep your mission in mind and keep nimble and light on your feet. There will be no 'Alamos' here. Do not stand and die. Hit, run, hit again. Ok, now we've had the detail of the plan, here it is in plain speech."

Jack launched into a simple verbal summary of what he intended to happen, painting the picture of the coming battle. He looked them in the eye and threw his soul into it.

When he was done, and had asked for any questions, he looked around at the team for feedback. Some were hard to read, but most looked inspired. He looked over at Jim, who nodded assuredly.

"Good job Boss," said Jim as they walked back to the office afterward. "Now let's get this show on the road."

They were planning to move out for Harrisonburg the following night. It was important to get there as early as possible to prepare the area for defense, before the enemy arrived. It was a busy time, and although he could have headed back to Zulu to see Caitlin and the kids, he felt that it was not appropriate; all hands were to the grindstone getting the operation ready, and no-one else had the opportunity of home leave. Jack took Andrew for a walk around the training base.

"Dad, I want to come with you."

Jack looked at him, "No way Andy, no chance."

Andrew looked crestfallen.

"Look," Jack continued, "it's simply too dangerous this time. When you turn eighteen, I will try and get you out on some operations."

"But Dad, I'm old enough, I'm sixteen!"

"Look Andy, what I need you to do for me is go back to Zulu tomorrow. I'm not going to get a chance to see Mom and the babies. Give them my love and keep them safe for me. Ok?"

"Ok."

Jack put an arm around Andrews shoulders, gave him a squeeze, and then they walked on in the darkness, each in his silence.

The Company infiltrated in small vehicle packets by various routes into the north western outskirts of Harrisonburg. They consolidated into a forward operating base inside a large warehouse belonging to the dominant grain company in the area. It gave them a covered assembly area out of view of aerial observation.

Jim had some people marshaling and organizing the arriving vehicles, and placing the various fighting elements into administrative areas in different parts of the warehouse.

Megan and her aid station arrived in a couple of discrete vans decked out as mobile ambulances, towing a couple of gators on trailers. The gators would be used for casualty evacuation back to the aid station, once the casualties could be pulled back from the fighting. Megan was a force of nature; she had taken and molded a team of medics, both for the aid station and field medics to deploy with the platoons.

Jim allocated her a permanent area because this warehouse would be the home for the aid station for the duration of the battle, unless exigent circumstances forced relocation. Jack watched the interaction between Jim and Megan, it always made him grin. There was definitely a chemical reaction there, but neither of them would admit to it, and pride made them bristle towards each other. The sooner they admitted it and got on with it, Jack thought, the better.

Once they were consolidated in the warehouse they pushed out an OP screen for security and bedded down for a couple of hours sleep. They were up with the dawn and Jack gathered the leaders around him. They were going on a recon into the town and it was going to be low key, for the benefit of any drones or spies that were in the area. It was civilian clothes, no rifles.

Leaving the warehouse under Jims command, Jack took his leadership team on a ground recon.

He had a pretty good idea from the map of where he would establish his defensive sectors and phase lines, but it was vital to get out on a confirmatory recon. There was no Regime presence in the town; they were waiting on the coming operation to establish one. The only recent activity appeared to be convoys running through on the I-81, and Jack had historically had IED teams targeting the stretch of road as it ran past the town.

They noticed that the town really seemed deserted; it appeared that the warnings from Bill's network had been heeded. They ran into a checkpoint run by a local militia unit that had stayed behind. It seemed more of an ad hoc citizen's force, armed mainly with hunting rifles and the odd AR-15 and AK, than an organized militia.

They pulled up to the checkpoint and Jack had to explain that they were a Resistance company operating in the valley and they had come to conduct operations in the town for a short period of time.

One of the local men went to get his leader. He came back with a grizzled looking character with a Vietnam Veteran ball cap on.

"Good morning sir, how are you?" said Jack.

"Well, who do we have here?" replied the man.

"Sir, we are a Resistance company, we've been conducting anti-Regime operations around here, based out of the hills west of here?

The man peered at him "You the fellas that shot down that Apache?"

"Yes, that's us."

"Well hell yea! Let me shake your hand young man. Next time, just introduce yourselves right; you're known round here as the Mountain Men."

Jack grinned, "The Mountain Men?"

"That's right, you're the ones been living up in the forests and coming down to blow up those Regime convoys. And you brought down that Apache."

"That's us."

"Ok, how can I help?"

Jack explained to him that he could help with a tour of the town. He also explained that it would be best if the militia evacuated for the next few days, and apologized that it was likely the town was going to get chewed up some.

It turned out that the militia was in fact an ad hoc force that had come together from the local community after the collapse. They had protected the town from the evacuating hordes as they poured south down the I-81, manning roadblocks to prevent them accessing the town. It was the same up and down the valley.

That night back in the warehouse Jack gave confirmatory orders, issuing the sectors and phase line information. The three maneuver platoons were to deploy that night and infiltrate on foot to the south east, occupying their initial lay-up positions in identified buildings.

The OPs for the mortar and air defense controllers would also deploy up onto the grain silos, to set up concealed positions under thermal ponchos. The mortar dump trucks and air defense technicals would wait in the warehouse until the time came to deploy them.

Once in their lay up positions, the initial job of the maneuver platoons would be to create their routes and rat runs, preparing the buildings for a mobile defense falling back through successive positions. This was easier to do closer to the town center, when enemy options were easier to identify. Further out towards the I-81 it was a case of establishing OP positions that would identify enemy approach routes. Once the approach was identified, assets could be switched to it, establishing hasty ambushes in pre-identified locations.

As the platoons fell back, fighting by squads, towards the center of town, their defensive measures would be more thorough. The buildings were also more substantial towards the center of town. It was important for the squads to aim to move through and under buildings as much as possible, keeping out of view. Not only were the streets and open areas in an urban conflict kill zones, but there was the additional threat from aerial observation and attack.

The platoons were equipped with their usual squad level weapons as well as AT-4 anti-armor rockets and an assortment of IEDs. They had victim operated EFPs that they could rapidly set up in advance of enemy movement, and also ones on command wires for observed command detonation. They also had an assortment of improvised claymores and pipe bomb devices, some of them set up as booby traps.

Jack had identified three likely access routes into the city center, each of them originating from the I-81. There was State Route 11, which would amount to an enemy right flanking thrust from the north east. The main direct route in was the 33 from the east, and from the south west was the 11 again, forming a left flanking option for the Regime commander.

The fighters worked for three days to prepare the defense of the town. They created obstacles, laid booby traps, reconnoitered ambush sites, cleared routes back through buildings and smashed 'mouse-holes' to crawl through. They located and identified successive firing positions to allow the squads to leapfrog back past each other while providing covering fire. They identified hide positions for their integral sharpshooters to fire from, creating a multitude of shoot options onto the likely approaches of the enemy.

They had trained all this over the winter, using the training farm complex buildings. They had worked both urban and rural offense and defense. Jack had been thorough, and they had undergone an intense period of training. The 'mountain men' were ready as they ever would be.

On the fifth day, dawn broke to the scene of the Regime armored battle group drawn up on the I-81 where it bisected the town. The OPs had picked them up the night before as they rumbled down from the north. They had laagered up on the interstate, established security, and readied for the morning assault.

They were a mix of armored vehicles, M1 Abrams main battle tanks (MBTs), Bradley armored fighting vehicles (AFVs) and even some MRAP and armored Humvees. The three fighting companies were based around the Abrams and the Bradley but there were also a multitude of ancillary and support elements, from an APC mounted mortar platoon to an EOD detachment in large wheeled armored personnel carriers (APCs), looking like they came straight from Iraq.

With the dawn, Jake had the fires lit. There was no sign of Regime aircraft yet, but there was the assumed presence of unseen drones overhead. With the drum and tire fires lit, and multiple buildings fired on the western edge of town, soon an acrid black smoke was drifting over the town, obscuring both thermal imaging and the naked eye.

Shortly after, the Regime leviathan uncoiled itself from where it lay on the I-81, resolving itself into three armored columns as the Regime commander revealed his hand. Leaving a headquarters and security element back on the interstate, he was sending 'thunder runs' down each of the three routes that Jake had identified, in order to rapidly carve up the town, before conducting a detailed house to house clearance. The objective was the town center.

The U.S. Military had forgotten many lessons of general warfare while engaging in the 'global war on terror' since 9/11. They had learned many lessons pertinent to the conflicts in Iraq and Afghanistan. Some of these lessons would do them no service. As the three columns started to extend and sniff down the routes they would take into town, it was apparent that they were moving mounted. This meant that the infantry remained loaded into their AFVs. A general principle is that if armor is to operate in an urban environment, it must be protected by dismounted infantry.

As the Regime columns advanced, the OPs in front of the platoons picked up the routes they were taking. They relayed this in a quick series of code words and started to fall back to rejoin their elements. With this information, the platoons deployed from their separate squad areas, moving to the various pre-established hasty ambush positions astride the enemy approach routes.

Caleb's 1st Platoon was deployed in the central sector, responsible for the main route in on the 33, East Market Street, and ancillary side roads from the east. They were deployed forward in the largely residential area just west of the I-81. 2nd Platoon was deployed to the sector north and 3rd Platoon to the sector south of 1st Platoon.

2nd Platoon was commanded by a former Marine Gunnery Sergeant, Owen Westbrook. He was a craggy veteran, built of granite as far as Jack could make out. He made Jack think of old school Wild West gunfighters or Texas Rangers whenever he saw him. 3rd Platoon was led by a friend that Caleb had brought in, a young Ranger Captain called Alex Lambert that Jack had not met. He was a laconic character, but a human dynamo when required on operations.

Caleb's 1st Platoon had established a series of consecutive ambush positions, into which they were now deployed, with the intention of having the squads leapfrogging back past each other after hitting the enemy. Caleb had intentionally asked his squad leaders to (mix up the type and mechanism of their ambushes, in order to confuse the enemy and make countermeasures harder to adopt.)

Olson's squad was on point. They had deployed just to the west of the 33, not far from where it intersected the clover leaf at the I-81. They were concealed in a residential area using the side of a house to provide a defilade position, concealed from view from the armored column moving towards them from the right. Caleb was crouched there in cover with Phillips and Gibbs, both of them holding AT-4 anti-armor rockets, ready to fire. They were the kill team.

About two hundred yards to his west, again along the route of the 33, was his other team with both SAWs.

They were in a position to act as the cover group. Olson could hear the whine of the turbine engines of the Abrams, the roar of the Bradley engines, and the clatter of tracks on asphalt as the column approached from the right. The acrid black smoke was drifting over the town; he could taste it in the back of his throat, where it kept good company with the taste of fear.

He heard someone running behind him and turned to see McCarthy approaching. He had been on lookout. He was a young lad, only nineteen, enthusiastic but still a little wet behind the ears.

"Hey Rob," McCarthy said, breathing hard, "Yea, they're coming."

"No shit Sherlock," said Olson, dryly. He spat a stream of tobacco juice onto the sidewalk. "Get over there and pull security." He pointed with his chin back the way McCarthy had run from.

Turning to the two men, Olson said, "Ok, get ready."

Both men moved away from the wall and shouldered the AT-4s. They knelt next to each other, with Olson between them, facing the road but still with the corner of the building concealing them from the approaching column, providing that all important defilade position.

The roar of the engines and the clattering of the tracks grew louder as the first Abrams MBT came into view around the side of the house, its turret with its 120mm main armament swinging slowly from side to side as it scanned ahead.

There were a few scrubby bushes providing a bit of concealment between them and the road, then an embankment sloping down to the road itself, about forty meters away. Olson put his hands up on each man's shoulder.

As the MBT came level with him, he firmly squeezed each man's shoulder. They fired and the rockets streaked down together, impacting in a double explosion against the side of the tank's armor. The tank was dead in its tracks, but they did not even pause to look. They dropped the empty launchers and the team sprinted away along the sides of the houses.

As soon as the rockets were fired, the cover group opened up on the column with a stream of fire. They were in a good covered position and the idea was not so much to inflict damage on the armored column as to distract from the kill team as they ran. The lead tank was now burning, munitions starting to cook off inside. The vehicles behind started to push past and engage surrounding likely targets to gain fire superiority, hammering machine-gun fire out to their front and flanks.

As Olson reached the cover of retail store just beyond, running through the smashed doorway, he shouted into his radio to the cover team, "Move, move, move!" as he ran with his team through the aisles.

The cover team peeled out of their position just as the second MBT acquired them in its thermal sight and let loose a 120mm HESH round, impacting into their position moments after they had left it. Both teams were now sprinting back and they converged together before disappearing into a building and running back along a prepared route.

The Regime column pushed on until three hundred yards later they hit another ambush from Caleb's second squad. A hastily emplaced array of EFP devices were initiated by command wire. This time an MBT had a track ripped off to become a mobility, or 'M', kill and an AFV was destroyed, the squad inside torn apart by the spray of armor defeating molten metal from the EFP.

A similar effect was happening along all three of the enemy approach routes. As the columns pushed further into the town, the buildings became denser and better suited to urban defense. The troops were still sitting in the AFVs, the columns effectively blind to the hit and run ambush tactics used by the Resistance fighters.

As they were hit by the consecutively ambushing and falling back squads of the three platoons, the armored columns ground to a halt, the commanders confused by such organized resistance. They had not expected this, and certainly not to lose multiple armored vehicles when they were simply pushing into a town to extract reprisals on the civilian population.

The Regime battle group's operations order for this mission had included an 'enemy forces' paragraph laying the responsibility for the IED attacks in the valley on a Resistance group based out of Harrisonburg. The group was operating up and down the valley; evidence in the form of drone surveillance of militia activity and roadblocks in the town was used to back up the assertion that the center of resistance was located there.

The Regime commander called an 'operational pause' in order to adjust. They had to deal with the casualties and recover the damaged vehicles. In a change of tack, the infantry were ordered out of the vehicles to clear surrounding buildings and provide security for the armored vehicles. This was reported back to Jack, who called for mortar fire missions onto the enemy in the open.

The dump trucks moved out of the warehouse into prepared fire positions, where the coordinates were known, thus aiding quicker adjustment of fire. One truck with its two mortar barrels was allocated to each Regime advance route. The fire controllers coordinated the fire; once they had it on target they called for 'fire for effect'.

The mortar fire was devastating, whistling in to detonate high explosives in and around where the columns were stalled, smashing into the flimsy houses that the troops were trying to secure.

The Regime forces were quick to react with their mortar locating radar, and were able to bring in fast fire missions from their own mortars onto the vicinity of the dump trucks. As soon as rounds started to land, the dump trucks took off, protected by their armor from the worst of the shrapnel.

The mortar trucks moved to alternate locations and the game began again, before Jack called for a pause in fire to conserve ammunition; the desired result had been achieved, and the Regime columns were reeling from the blows.

As the Resistance mortar barrage ended, the dismounted Resistance platoons moved in closer again. They took up fire positions to cover multiple angles. They started to snipe at the dismounted troops and any vehicle commanders who were up in their hatches.

Chapter Ten

The Regime columns paused some five hundred meters after their start points. They were reeling from the initial ambushes and the mortar barrage and they continued with the operational pause in order to regroup. They were evolving to the situation, learning lessons long forgotten in the military education of the officers in charge. They prepared to advance the armored columns with dismounted infantry in support.

There was no question of the Regime pulling back. This was political. The battle group was accompanied by several combat camera teams and the Battle Group Commander had some pet Regime supporting journalists with him. They must push forward at any cost and seize the town from the rebels.

The Battle Group Commander was Lieutenant Colonel Vick Chester, a West Point graduate and career officer. He was a political man and careerist, not without intelligence and military acumen. It was essential for him to succeed here, if he was to make his way in the new Regime and find the advancement that he desired. He was adamant that he would conduct the operation with his own integral assets, and not call for outside support unless he absolutely had to.

The Battle Group had integral mortar and artillery fire support assets. As he gave the orders to prepare to continue the advance, Lt-Col Chester ordered indirect fire ahead of his maneuver elements. The problem for his fire controllers was the lack of an identifiable enemy location.

The Resistance fighters were highly mobile and tended to remain in the cover of buildings as much as they could. The Regime force's assumption was that any strongholds would be in the town center so they settled for a rolling barrage, starting in front of the columns and creeping up to the town center.

Jack watched the mortar and artillery barrages as they switched from target to target, moving steadily onwards towards his position of observation in the upper windows of an old apartment building. He knew that down on the ground the fighters would be hugging cover and hiding in basements as the high explosives rolled over them.

When contemplating his strategy, Jack had gone for the delaying withdrawal, but had foregone the idea of moving back to strongholds. Partly, they had not had time to effectively construct them, and also he did not want to be fixed in place. His intent was not to hold the town.

Caleb's platoon was sheltering in their various squads in the basements of several houses. The barrage rolled over them. It was noisy, violent and frightening, but it proved ineffective. Some of the modern houses in the outlying parts of town were so flimsily built that they were literally blown to pieces by the high explosive rounds. It just added to the cover and confusion.

As the barrage passed over top, they redeployed from the basements into fire positions to await the advance of the Regime columns. The Regime infantry started to move, patrolling in formation up the roads, including the side roads. With a roar of engines and belching exhaust smoke, the armored columns rolled forward again.

The Regime infantry was moving in the streets. Caleb's squads kept light, identifying enemy routes and moving through buildings to place explosives. They set hasty ambushes and started to hit the enemy infantry with improvised claymore and small arms fire. Out to the flanks, Caleb deployed several of his sharpshooter pairs to bring accurate crossfire onto the enemy squads.

If the Regime forces identified a firing point, they would move an Abrams or Bradley forward and use either the tanks main armament or the cannon on the Bradley to tear the building apart. All the while, they were facing incoming cross fire from multiple firing points. The Regime advance started to bog down again.

Caleb's teams were moving fast, hit and run, leapfrogging from position to position, mainly under cover of the buildings, sometimes sprinting across open areas out of sight of the enemy where possible.

The Regime infantry company opposing Caleb's platoon started to figure that the streets and open areas were killing grounds. They evolved again, and started to clear into buildings, adopting the approach of Caleb's fighters. They started to breach and enter buildings, with the intention of fighting down the streets using the buildings as fire positions to provide shelter and also cover the advance of the armor in the streets below.

Again they were not well served by the lessons in Iraq and Afghanistan. The basics of urban warfare had been forgotten, replaced by SWAT style breach and entry techniques that were more suited to dawn arrest and search raids. They targeted buildings and started to stack up by the doors, to breach and use them as entry points. As they stacked 'nuts to butts' they were vulnerable to flanking fire from Caleb's sharpshooters.

It was carnage.

The onslaught from all directions from Caleb's fighters was causing casualties among the Regime troops and bogging down the advance again. Fire was coming in from all directions and it started to cause a visceral reaction of terror and extreme violence from the embattled Regime forces. They started to fire wildly at any likely Resistance fire positions, in an attempt to gain 'fire superiority'. They used the armored vehicles to pummel the buildings around them, smashing them to pieces.

As Caleb's fighters withdrew in the face of this onslaught, they fired some of the buildings, adding to the confusion and the covering thermal smoke. In others they left booby traps. The Regime forces evolved again, and started to simply destroy buildings as they advanced.

The Regime infantry stuck to surviving buildings and the rubble, while the armored vehicles pummeled anywhere that was identified as a firing point. Mostly, Caleb's fighters skipped out before the tank rounds started impacting. The Regime armor was even starting to bulldoze through some of the buildings, smashing them and negating the need for the infantry to breach and clear them.

The battle had been raging for several hours now and the Regime forces had advanced somewhere around a kilometer. It was now around midday. Jack was keeping his mortar team in cover – he could not bring down fire because his fighters were so closely engaged with the Regime columns. The air defense technicals were still distributed around the north west side of town in covered positions.

Jim and his logistics party were using the gators to move ammunition forward and bring casualties back. They had established exchange and collection points for each of the platoons and Jim was organizing runs between the warehouse and the forward positions.

Jack had ordered more houses to be fired and the town was covered in a pall of thermal smoke, adding to that from the fighting in the front areas, and it was obscuring the surveillance of the drones overhead.

There was a steady trickle of casualties coming back. Many were wounded from flying shrapnel and debris. Urban fighting took a toll, there were so many hazards involved in fighting in such an environment. The fighters were a rough and tumble tough bunch, they had to be, and most of them fought on with the cuts, lacerations and minor wounds they received in the rubble and debris of the battleground.

Eye protection was priceless, as were protective gloves.

Jim was moving forward from the warehouse on his gator when the call went up for incoming enemy aircraft. Two A-10 tank busters came roaring in from the north. The air defense controller started calling out target indications and the technicals were pulling out from their covered positions.

The A-10 is a slow aircraft and the two of them came roaring in over the town to be met by streams of tracer fire as the gunners on the technicals tried to direct their machine-gun fire into the path of the oncoming aircraft.

The A-10s flew over, identifying targets, wheeled south of the town and came back over. One of them had seen Jim moving in his gator through the streets and roared towards him. The A-10 came in on a gun run, the sound of the burst from its chain gun was terrifying, like the sound of some primeval monster screaming in the sky. The rounds tore up the asphalt and caught Jim's gator, tossing it and throwing him clear to lay senseless in the rubble of the street.

As the A-10 pulled up from its gun run, the slow flying aircraft was caught by a burst of 7.62 rounds through the side. The pilot lost control and the aircraft went smashing down into the town, detonating in a fireball of flame and black smoke. The second A-10 pulled up with a swarm of tracer rounds whipping past it, banked out and took off for home. A ragged cheer went up from the rebel fighters below.

Jim sat up, his head spinning from the concussion. He was covered in dust and dirt, his BDUs and tactical vest as well as his face. He pushed himself up and staggered back towards the warehouse, bleeding profusely from a scalp wound, the blood mingling with the dirt to mask his face.

Megan turned to see Jim approaching the aid station. He looked in a bad way. She grabbed his arm and led him to a chair. "What happened to you?" she asked.

"Got blown up."

"Really, I never would have guessed. Let's take a look at you."

"Yea, just fix me up. I've got work to do. Couple of Motrin should do it."

"I'll be the judge of that, Jim Fisher." The gentleness of her fingers as she examined him belied her cold tone.

"Ok, you've got a concussion and a laceration to your head. Judging by your thick skull you should be ok, but you really need to rest."

"Yea, spare me the sarcasm, just put a band aid on it, give me a couple of painkillers, and I'll be on my way."

Megan cleaned and sutured his head wound, gently wiping some of the blood and grime from his face. "That ought to do it. You need to rest."

Jim stood up. "Thanks. See you later."

"I don't think so Jim, you need to rest and…."

Jim had taken her face in his hands and kissed her on the lips. She tried to pull back, her hands on his chest, and she pushed him off, looking flustered.

"Anything to shut you up Megan," he winked and walked off, a little unsteadily.

"Damn you Jim," she said to his back, a little unconvincingly, her face red.

In Caleb's sector, the fighters continued to fall back in the face of the ultra-violent firepower demonstration from the Regime armored Battle Group. They were not on the run; they were simply fire and maneuvering back, each element covering the other as they leapfrogged back through the buildings.

Caleb was using two squads, including Olson's, as maneuver elements working in tandem to cover each other as they hit the enemy and moved back. The third squad was divided up. Caleb had the two IED pairs working under his direction to set booby traps in the face of the advancing

Regime forces. The other two sharpshooter pairs were deployed independently to the flanks to harass the enemy with accurate small arms fire.

Caleb currently had each maneuver squad working back on each side of a street, consecutively covering each other as they attempted to stay ahead of the incoming MBT and AFV fire. The squads were running fire positions for small arms fire as well as versions of the anti-armor ambush using enfilade fire from defilade positions. It was trickier now that the Regime infantry were dismounted.

To add to the chaos, the IED pairs were hastily setting devices such as EFPs and improvised claymores and running command wires back to firing points. As the regime forces advanced, the Resistance fighters would detonate the devices, targeting vehicles and dismounted troops alike. It all added to the friction on the enemy, slowing their advance to a violent crawl.

Suddenly, there was a rapid situation change as a Regime squad went left flanking and inadvertently cut off the sharpshooter pair which was in a house. The Regime squad started to breach and enter the building, looking to occupy it as a fire base.

Trapped inside were Jenny and Carl. Jenny was one of the women who had graduated the training and been identified as a natural shooter. She was twenty two years old and a slim, athletic girl who had done well at the physical side of the training.

The Regime squad breached through one of the windows with grenades into the interior, followed up by a team rushing in. They cleared the ground floor and started up the stairs. Jenny and Carl were upstairs and had put out a distress call to Caleb. As the Regime team pushed up the stairs in a stack, weapons covering their advance, Carl engaged them from the upstairs hallway with his M4. Jenny was back behind him, supporting him from an upstairs doorway.

A firefight erupted as the squad pushed up the stairs under cover of automatic fire, tossing grenades into the hallway, pushing Carl back before hitting him with rifle fire and killing him.

Jenny was fighting from the doorway, popping out to engage the heavily armored troops. The sheer weight of fire that was returned to her pushed her back into the room, where she was forced to take cover as the rifle rounds smashed through the walls, filling the room with dust and noise.

Jenny crawled into the far corner and turned to face the door, raising her rifle. She heard the sounds of footfalls in the hallway and the shouted orders of the soldiers back down by the stairs. She fired through the wall to where she thought she heard the enemy soldier. She heard a scream as her rounds hit home, followed by the thud of a body hitting the ground.

Shortly after, a grenade rolled through the door, bouncing into the room. It detonated, sending shrapnel flying, some of it shredding into her legs.

Jenny screamed as the troops came rushing into the room. One of them shot her in the chest, the round stopped by her body armor plate as it knocked the wind out of her. They secured the room, dragging her weapons away, and the squad leader entered.

The velcro name tape on his armor said 'Gameros' and gave his rank as Staff Sergeant. He had been a gang banger in southern California before joining the army and 'making good'.

Gameros was a nasty piece of work.

"You fucking bitch, I'm gonna fuck you up good," he said as he came towards Jenny. He dragged her up and started to beat on her, ripping her helmet off to punch her in the face. "Me an' my boys gonna have some fun with you, bitch."

Gameros started to rip her body armor off. He produced a knife and started to cut open her clothes. He tore open her shirt and started to violently fondle her breasts, laughing. The squad stood around, the battle raging outside, as they laughed.

Gameros ripped open her pants and tore off her underwear, ignoring the bleeding lacerations on her thighs. Jenny was done screaming and fighting, she was sobbing in despair as all hope drained away.

The squad gathered; a couple in the room and the others outside in the hallway to watch. They neglected their security, lured in by the spectacle of Gameros and Jenny.

Olson had responded to Caleb's urgent call and brought his squad stealthily into the building, moving through the ground floor. He left one team downstairs to pull security while he took the other stealthily up the stairs.

Olson and his team stood shoulder to shoulder at the top of the stairs and unloaded a fury of fire down the hallway into the unsuspecting enemy.

They pushed forward down the hallway, taking the enemy completely by surprise, smashing them with 5.56mm rounds. As Olson rounded into the room, he caught sight of Gameros, holding Jenny, turned around to look at the doorway in shock. Olson shot him and pushed towards him, the rest of his team pushing into the room and gunning down the remainder of the Regime squad.

Olson pulled his knife and launched himself onto Gameros, stabbing and cutting, thrusting the knife through the rapist's neck into his jugular, a spray of blood pumping out as Olson continued to saw at his neck. Gameros's final screams were no different in sound from those of a butchered pig as the blood pumped out of his severed carotid.

Olson stood, blood dripping off him, calling to one of his men to get a blanket and wrap the sobbing Jenny in it. They stopped to collect the gear and weapons from the slain enemy, any equipment of value, in particular night vision goggles, before withdrawing. Gibbs carried Jenny in his arms.

They moved back into their positions ready to reengage the advancing Regime forces, while Gibbs and McCarthy carried Jenny back to the casualty collection point.

Jack was coordinating the battle from multiple vantage points in the town center. He would routinely move his tactical headquarters; firstly to get better views of the various sectors of the battle, secondly to make it harder for Regime electronic warfare assets to fix his position.

Ned was working the communications and part of his role during lulls in activity on the net was to put out disinformation. He found it amusing, using veiled speech in a way that Afghan fighters had done: phrases like "move the big thing up to destroy them" and "the time for the firestorm is here" etc.

Let the EW guys try and figure that stuff out.

The shelling was worse in the town center, the Regime forces assuming that was where the command nodes and main defenses were. Jack kept his guys off the roofs and several floors below the rooftops to be better protected while still able to see over the nearby rooftops to the battleground in the lower elevation residential areas.

There was an urgent call on the air defense net, a warning about fast movers from the north. Two fast jets came streaking down the valley at low level and buzzed the town, the sonic boom of their passage deafening. They were too fast for the technicals, which were just emerging from their concealed positions. Some tracer fire followed the jets as they streaked off to the south.

The two jets turned several kilometers to the south and came back on a bombing run. Jack screamed into his radio, "Take cover, all units cover now!" as they came in. This time the gunners on the technicals were ready and a stream of tracer fire was reaching out from the town to the two jets as they came in from the south. It was a valiant effort, but the jets were too fast.

The target was the town center and the main administrative buildings. The jets passed in sequence, both dropping five hundred pound bombs onto multi-level historical buildings in the town center.

The blast of the first bomb was huge. Jack and his tactical headquarters were lying on the floor taking cover. As the second bomb went off sending a massive concussive wave through the area, Jack looked over at Ned, to see him looking back at him wide-eyed, and noted that bizarrely Ned was not in contact with the floor, but appeared to be hovering in the air just above it.

Crazy.

As the jets passed on, Jack was up and looking out the window. The streets of the town center were choked in dust, a massive dirt and debris cloud reaching several hundred feet into the air and filling the chasm like streets with drifting dust.

The jets wheeled and came in for another pass, dropping two more bombs with similar effects. The massive amounts of dust they had created, adding to the general pall of smoke over the town, made visibility very hard and most of the technicals were unable to engage the fast jets. After their bomb drop, they came in for a couple of strafing gun runs, cannon rounds tearing into the town center, before roaring off back to the north.

Jack grabbed the radio and called for accountability. As the reports came in, he started to laugh. It was all a big dog and pony show, the jets were massively impressive, but without having accurate targeting information, they had done very little damage to the Resistance forces.

Jack got back on the radio and ordered the maneuver units to pull back to the second phase line. The platoons started to break contact and withdraw closer to the town center. This had the effect of moving them away from the Regime forces and it shrunk the perimeter around the town center.

Director Woods had given the executive order approving the mission in Harrisonburg, based on the Intel at hand and the advice from the military liaison staff at the Fusion Center RTOC. Woods himself had little understanding of military operations. What he did know was that he intended to ruthlessly wipe out any resistance in the Shenandoah Valley.

This was personal now, the Resistance struggle in the valley a direct challenge to his authority.

Woods had been sitting in his chair in the RTOC since dawn, watching the drone feeds on the monitors. He was frustrated. Most of the view had been obscured throughout the day by clouds of black smoke drifting across the monitors.

It was clear that the assaulting battle group was not making progress. It should have been a simple operation; drive into town, round up some militia, and execute them.

Woods had been on the radio with Lt-Col Chester a couple of times already during the day, urging him to push on and take the town. Lt-Col Chester was obstinate, assuring him that he could take the town, but so far failing to produce on that promise.

What Woods did not know, and failed to appreciate, was that he was not helping. He was interfering with the operation, harassing the commander, while using a 'long screwdriver' to interfere with the ground commander's train set.

It was now getting to evening time and the platoons moved into new positions for the coming night. Jack did not intend to hang around forever in the town and let the Regime forces fix him in place, so he planned to exfiltrate during the early hours of the morning.

The Regime forces felt the pressure of constant ambush, IED and small arms attack lift. As they started to relax and feel their way forward again, Jack ordered the mortar fire controllers to engage. The dump trucks pulled out to their positions again and brought down a rain of 81mm high explosives onto the Regime positions.

It had little effect on the armor, but a massive psychological impact on the dismounted infantry. The Regime mortar locating radar picked up the mortar trucks again and the counter battery fire began, so the trucks immediately moved and Jack called a ceasefire.

As night fell, the town was burning. The thick smoke cloud still covered the area and it had effectively put the drones out of the action as they circled in the sky above. The skyline was lit by the red glow of the fires dotted around. The Regime commander ordered another indirect fire barrage of the town center and the areas in front of his three armored columns. The Resistance fighters waited it out in positions of cover.

In the glowing darkness, as the armored columns felt their way forward, they moved into the net of the waiting fighters. The Regime forces had the advantage of greater amounts of night vision equipment, but it also made them clumsy, and the advantage was somewhat negated by the level of ambient light from the fires. The Resistance fighters moved within buildings and avoided the open, and they were able to creep close to the advancing columns and attack them with IEDs and anti-armor rockets.

The Regime advance ground to a halt again.

Lt-Col Chester was frustrated, trying to drive his men forward to the victory, but it was not working. The fighters were ghosts and with the obscuring smoke he did not have the advantage of drones to get 'eyes on' and survey the Regime forces locations. The artillery and close air support strikes had made no dent in the ferocious resistance they were encountering.

The Regime commander finally gave in to the need for additional assets in support. He prepared to call for support. He needed some way to flank the opposition and break the will of the Resistance. He had not been allocated any Apache support for this mission, simply the A-10s and fast jets in a close air support role.

Lt-Col Chester called over his XO and told him to make the call and request the regional airborne reaction force. This was the same hunter-killer force that had taken on Caleb's patrol, and came with Apache support. The XO got on the radio, turning to look at the map board.

Just then, the assigned Battle Group political officer appeared in the Lt-Col Chester's TOC, set up in a series of connected tents between APCs on the I-81. He was carrying a satellite phone and accompanied by the Battle Group second-in-command.

"Sir, you are needed on the phone," said the political officer.

"Not now, I'm busy," said Lt-Col Chester.

"Now sir, its Director Woods," insisted the political officer, holding out the phone.

Lt-Col Chester took the phone, "Colonel Chester."

"Yes, this is Director Woods. You are relieved of command effective immediately. You will surrender yourself into the custody of the political officer. Your second-in command will take over."

Before the Colonel could answer, the phone line went dead. Looking up in shock, Lt-Col Chester saw the political officer facing him, pistol drawn, with two Military Police coming into the TOC behind him.

"Come with me now sir."

The XO finished on the radio and turned back towards the commander. The answer had come back, the request was approved and the Ranger hunter-killer ARF was available. It came with two Apaches in support, the troops mounted in CH-47 Chinook helicopters.

The XO saw the commander being led from the TOC, wrists cuffed. The Battle Group second-in-command stepped up to him.

"I'm in command now, what's the update XO?"

"We have the ARF approved."

"Roger that. Have it logged that I ordered the request." The second-in-command stepped up to the map board and pointed. "Put them down here, in these fields."

Around midnight Jack put out the call to withdraw to phase line three, bringing in the noose a bit tighter round the town center and allowing his fighters some temporary breathing room. He was ready to call for the exfiltration as soon as the maneuver elements reported they were back at the phase line just outside the town center.

Shortly after, one of the OPs called in that they heard Chinooks approaching from the north. It was an unmistakable noise, the beat of the twin rotor choppers as they flew 'nap of the earth', contouring the ground. Jack put the word out for the mortars to move to fire positions and for the technicals to standby. He also called for the fires to be stoked with more tires, to keep the smoke pall thick.

The Chinooks skirted the north of the town and flew round to the west, landing in a field about one kilometer to the west of the town center, out beyond the huge grain warehouses. As they came in to land, they span round to show their rear to the town, touching down into the field in formation. The ramps were lowered and the hunter-killer force came running off the back, one platoon per Chinook, spreading out into dismounted formation.

As the Chinooks flared and touched down into the field, Jack called for mortar illumination and one of the barrels fired. The illum round popped and began to descend under its parachute, wobbling towards the ground. The OPs picked up the Chinooks and Jack called for fire, the MFC adjusting fire from all five barrels onto the landing zone, illuminated by the sixth barrel constantly firing illum rounds.

The rounds started to impact around the Chinooks and dismounting troops, a violent series of 'crumps' of impacting high explosives. The Chinooks disgorged their human cargo and started to lift off.

A mortar round burst in front of the center helicopter just as it was lifting off, shrapnel tearing into the crew in the cockpit, killing the pilot and causing the Chinook to crash nose first into the ground. The front rotor smashed into the ground, disintegrating, and the rear rotor continue to spin, pulling the helicopter over forwards until it crashed down on its back.

The dismounted troops started running towards the town, seeking to get out of the barrage in the open field and into cover. Five kilometers to the west, the two supporting Apaches were observing, hovering in the night sky. Their thermal imagers were degraded by the pall of hot smoke over the town, but one of them picked up the mortar truck firing the illum rounds. Two hellfire missiles streaked towards the truck, impacting and destroying it. Jack ordered the remaining two trucks to seek cover,

Jack ordered the force of technicals to move to the west, to fire support positions, in order to put up a suppressive screen of machine-gun fire to keep this new threat at arm's length.

Meanwhile, the Apaches were hunting, handicapped by the smoke over the town. They managed to pick up a few targets and engage them with a mix of 2.75 inch rockets and 30mm cannon. The effect was an area suppression barrage of explosive rounds, homing in around any targets they identified and engaged. Two technicals were spotted and taken out in this way. Another was destroyed by a hellfire missile.

The presence of the hunter-killer force of Rangers to his rear and the Apaches in the sky was a game changer for Jack. That was its intent, he realized. Jack sent out the code word to prepare to withdraw.

He figured that with the Apaches having a notional endurance on station time of around two and a half hours, he should wait for three hours, till around 0400hrs, before moving anyone. Hopefully by then the Apache's would have to go off station to refuel and rearm.

Jack had one of the technical crews go and grab a 60mm knee mortar from Jim at the warehouse, along with a supply of ammunition. They had not used these mortars much yet, but he figured that he needed to keep eyes on the advancing hunter-killer force to allow the guns to suppress them and prevent them closing with him from the west.

He had the light mortar team go mobile on foot, lobbing mortar illum up into the air routinely to light up the fields to the west and allow the technicals to keep the Rangers suppressed.

The Hunter-Killer Ranger force was trying to aggressively close with him from the west, and trying to maneuver, but they were out gunned by the 240 and .50cal guns mounted on the trucks. They were calling down artillery fire from the battle group to the east to try and suppress the technicals, but dispersed as the trucks were in a long ragged line they were not easily targeted.

What Jack didn't know was that that the company commander of the Ranger hunter-killer company was Captain Aaron Brookings. They had been friends back in Jacks active duty days. They had both served as company commanders on Jacks last combat tour to Afghanistan.

Aaron Brookings was an enlightened man, as were many others who served in the Special Operations community. There were many like him, who had the intelligence to question.

But Captain Brookings had little choice as did most of his men. There were many motivations for why these men continued to serve the Regime. Some of it was ignorance. Some of them just served as they always had, taking to these new domestic operations without complaint.

Others just did if for the money and security after the collapse, and still others such as Brookings did it because they had taken advantage of the Regimes security measures, moving their families onto military bases to protect them. Only later had it become apparent that this also gave the Regime security forces control over the fates of their families.))

Captain Brookings knew of at least one officer who had dissented and questioned unlawful orders. He was held to account by the political officer and his family moved to a FEMA camp. The officer himself was unrepentant and he disappeared into a reeducation facility.

As a result, despite his inner feelings, Captain Brookings worked ceaselessly to the best of his ability to ensure the wishes of his Regime masters were carried out.

At 0330hrs, Jack moved the two remaining dump trucks out to the west. They were undisturbed by hellfire missiles, so the assumption was that the Apaches had gone off station. Once in position, he moved half of the technicals up to positions where they could engage the armored Battle Group, still stalled to the east.

Jack did not need these technicals to get too close, he just needed them to be able to fire into the vicinity of the Regime forces to give the impression that his maneuver groups were still in place and simply trying a new tactic.

Jack now had the mortars in position to the north west, a screen of technicals to the west suppressing the hunter-killer force, and another screen presenting to the

Regime armored forces to the east. At 0400hrs he gave the order for the dismounted maneuver platoons to withdraw.

The platoons disengaged and moved back through a series of checkpoints to the warehouse, where they mounted up in vehicle packets. The aid station and ancillary support elements packed up also and headed out, moving to the north west and the security of the forested hills.

Jack gave the order to fire and the mortars engaged, before the three dump trucks moved in bounding over-watch back through a series of positions to avoid the counter battery fire. The technical screen to the east fired in the direction of the armored Regime forces, allowing the now mounted maneuver platoons to start moving out from the warehouse in a series of small packets on multiple different routes.

Once the warehouse was clear, the screening technicals started to move back by bounding over-watch and then peel out and move in small teams out to the north west. The dump trucks ceased fire and moved off.

As dawn broke, Jack was stood with Jim in the pass up to the hills, out to the north west. He looked back at the burning town, at the pall of smoke that still hung over it.

"Well," Jim said, "we certainly dropped the property values in that neighborhood."

Jack smiled grimly, "Ok, let's get back to the RV and get the butchers bill."

The plan had been for the elements to move back through a series of unique RVs, as they got further away from the town and safer into the hills they would begin to consolidate and join up with the other elements, before finally all coming together at a secure RV deep in the forested hills. They were avoiding moving back to Victor Foxtrot for the time being, in case they were being tracked.

When Jack made it to the final RV in the early afternoon, they went through the accountability process. After a full report, it turned out that from the Company of one hundred and twenty fighters, they had lost twelve fighters killed, six VSI (very seriously injured) who were still alive and being treated, eight missing in action and thirty one with injuries of varying severity that would need some form of medical treatment..

That was not to mention that most of the fighters had minor cuts and lacerations, as well as bruised and battered bodies, from the harsh nature of the fighting.

The use of body armor and helmets had limited the number of deaths, reducing penetrating injuries to the head and torso. Most of the wounds to the limbs were treated initially with a tourniquet and then later with some minor surgical intervention. The six VSI that had survived so far were all traumatic amputations of the limbs that had been correctly treated with tourniquets to prevent death from extremity bleeding.

The Company was exhausted but jubilant. The key thing now was to reorganize, treat the casualties, and move back to the base.

Chapter Eleven

Two days later, they were back at Victor Foxtrot, licking their wounds. Those with families at Zulu, Jack included, were desperate to go and see them, but there were a multitude of things that had to be done first. They had to run a thorough debrief and after action review (AAR), learning what lessons they could from the battle. They also had to do extensive weapons and equipment cleaning and repair.

Bodies had to heal, and Megan was busy with her medical staff doing what she could. Jack had put a call out to Bill on the network for a doctor or surgeon if possible, and as many antibiotics as they could muster. The troops were exhausted, and needed to heal. It was a time of consolidation, administration, and rest.

Following the full Company AAR in the barn, Jack got up and spoke to them. He told them how proud he was, and how well they had done. It had been a victory;

they had achieved the mission that they had set out to do, and had wreaked death and destruction on the Regime forces. He praised them for doing as he had asked, and remaining light on their feet, not getting sucked in to standing and slugging it out toe to toe with the Regime heavy armor and overwhelming numbers. He praised them for their initiative and their teamwork.

Once the work was done, he was able to grant 'home leave' in limited numbers, working in shifts. He got to head down to Zulu with the last group and see his family.

After he finished hugging Caitlin and the kids, he sat at the table in their subterranean home and felt the weight of it come crushing down on him; the loneliness and responsibility of command. When he was out there, in command, he had 'leaders legs' and always drove on to the goal. He was fully mission oriented, he always had been.

Sitting there now, drinking a coffee at the table with his wife, kids in his lap and Jasper at his feet, in their odd home, he felt the strangeness of the current situation and the responsibility he had taken on. He could never have envisaged that it would come to this, fighting his fellow countrymen, former comrades in arms, in full scale battles in the Shenandoah Valley.

Such was the nature of the fall of the United States, its slip into totalitarianism.

Caitlin did not push him for the details. She could see that he was exhausted and simply needed her support. She held his hand as they talked about the kids and life in

Zulu. Apparently Caitlin had naturally risen to a leadership and organizational position. To free her up during the day she had taken on a sitter, the sixteen year old daughter of one of the families. Her name was Vicky and she was lovely, according to Caitlin. Kind and responsible, she took pains to provide educational activities for the kids.

Apparently Andrew was also enamored, Caitlin told him, chuckling. Not that you would know it to see him, moping around and pretending that he didn't like the girl.

Teenagers, what could you do?

Temporarily released from the responsibility of command, Jack felt the crushing tiredness come over him like a physical weight. His eyes began to droop and he went and lay down on the cot. His head hit the pillow and he was out like a light.

The next day, Jack was back at Victor Foxtrot. As he headed over to the aid station to check on the casualties, a middle aged man walked out, wearing a white lab coat, stethoscope round his neck, and bifocals balanced on the end of his nose. Megan walked out behind him.

"Hey Jack," she said, "let me introduce you to Dr. Chris Davis, our new surgeon."

"Excellent, nice to meet you," said Jack, extending his hand.

"Happy to be here," said Dr. Davis.

"Did Bill send you?"

"Yes."

"What kind of surgeon are you?"

"I'm a vet."

"Great, where did you serve?"

"No Jack, I'm a veterinary surgeon."

Jack looked at him and grinned, "Seriously?"

Megan was smiling "Jack, he's done some excellent work with the wounded."

"Cool," Jack smiled, "happy to have you on board. Can I see them?"

"Sure," said Megan as they headed inside.

Jack pulled her to the side as they were doing the rounds, "How is Jim's concussion?"

"Oh, he'll be all right with that thick skull," she said, grinning.

Bill showed up himself two days later. Jack met him with Jim and Caleb. They shook hands and moved over to the operations room, where they sat around on plastic chairs drinking coffee. Bill was enthused by the 'Battle of Harrisonburg' as he was calling it.

"I know you guys took some casualties, and I am genuinely sorry for that. On the positive side, it was a great success, a huge blow for Regime credibility. Of course, the propaganda machine is spinning it that they won a huge battle and drove the insurgents out of Harrisonburg, but that's not what the people on the ground are seeing. The Regime got a butt kicking, and I am putting the word out on the network, including copies of some of the footage you took."

He went on to explain that the Apache footage had made its way as far as Texas, and people were sitting up and taking note. The Regime was not invincible, despite its overwhelming combat power.

However, word from informants in Bills network was pointing towards a consolidation of Regime efforts in the valley, as they tried to save face over such effective resistance this close to the Capital.

It appeared that Jack had been right, and Bill agreed with him. Now that the Regime was being drawn into the valley, it was their job to turn it into a crucible of destruction for the Regime forces.

"Keep your recon patrols out," Bill stated, "I expect some permanent FOBs to be placed here in the valley, and I would not be surprised if they start combing these hills for this base. Be alert."

Jack's current aims were twofold. Firstly, he needed to allow time for his fighters to rest and recover. Many of the walking wounded needed time; they would mostly all recover back to duty, but it would take some longer than others. Secondly, he needed to keep his eyes out in the valley and keep the pressure on the enemy.

Jack gave orders for the IED activity to continue in the valley. It was combined surveillance and opportunistic strike missions, and he started sending out two IED teams at a time to selected sectors to continue operations. Now they had concentrated force in Harrisonburg for the big battle, it was time to remain dispersed and lay low for a while.

Jack reactivated a small training cadre to take care of the new recruits he had asked for from Bill. He needed battle casualty replacements for those that had been lost or rendered combat incapable after the battle. Victor Foxtrot needed to remain operational as a training base, on a smaller scale than before. It would also be useful to have the training cadre for continuation training to prevent skill fade.

It was also an opportunity to employ some of the better guys who had been wounded and would not be able to return fully to the fight.

He had been long concerned about the security of Zulu. Its strength was in remaining covert, but the force protecting it was not his 'A' team. Now he had a fully trained company, blooded, he decided to allocate one of his maneuver platoons to defense of Zulu. One at a time, the platoons would rotate through this task, two weeks at a time, and it would be useful operational experience with training value for them.

Zulu was on the west slope of a ridge that ran roughly north-south. The trail from the southern side of Zulu's ravine was where the trail from Victor Foxtrot joined. That trail ran in a south easterly direction up and over the ridge to the valley where Victor Foxtrot was located. There were several further ridges and terrain features to the east of Victor Foxtrot that kept it concealed and away from the main Shenandoah Valley.

Jack had originally walked in to Zulu from the north, along the trail, and that seemed to him to be the most vulnerable direction to approach, given how the terrain was in the area. The valley that Zulu was on the side of opened up further as it ran to the north, down to where they had originally accessed the parking area with the fuel truck that had been concealed off an old fire road.

Jack ordered Caleb to take his platoon on the first shift. He trusted him most out of his platoon leaders to get the place set up right. Jack explained that he wanted a triangular patrol base, dug in with foxholes and concealed, upslope of the trail that ran into Zulu, covering the trail. He wanted this defensive position to be around three hundred meters north of the bunker sentry positions that protected the trail before it ran into Zulu.

The patrol base would be triangular, with two-man foxholes, a squad on each side. This configuration would provide excellent all round defense. One side of the triangle would face west to the trail, another looking north up the valley, with the third protecting the rear. The fighters would not have to live in the foxholes, they could set up shelters behind each one covered by thermal ponchos, but the triangular formation would act like a defensive rock if assailed by a larger force on all sides.

It was not to be merely a static defensive position. It was to be a patrol base, and the platoon would send out team or squad sized patrols into the surrounding area. There would always be two squads and a headquarters element in the patrol base.

This arrangement would add depth to the defense of Zulu, while allowing patrol surveillance and short term OPs to be sent out into the surrounding area, keeping the approach routes under observation.

They would call the patrol base Zulu Delta.

Caleb was enthusiastic about the new task. He was talking with Jack after receiving the brief, "So Jack, about the militia guys in Harrisonburg."

"Yes, what's up?"

"Well, they called us the mountain men. That's cool, but the guys came up with another name for the Company, for us."

"Yea, what's that?"

"Juggernauts. Jack's Juggernauts. We needed something to work with 'Jack', so that's it."

"Really?"

"Yep, the Company is yours, Jack. Some of these guys think the sun shines out of your ass. They named themselves in your honor, after we smashed up the Regime in Harrisonburg - like a juggernaut."

"Wow," said Jack, as Caleb walked away.

Following the return of the first rotation of IED teams into the valley after the battle, Jack was alerted to changes in Regime forces activity detailed in their patrol reports. It appeared that the battle group that had attacked Harrisonburg had settled near to the town. They were building a large forward operating base (FOB) just to the north east of the town, on the other side of the I-81.

It looked like this was going to be a location of their battle group headquarters and at least an armored company. They were walling in an area around two kilometers square with dirt berms, concertina wire and HESCO bastions; these were large wire and fabric boxes that were filled with dirt; stacked two-high they stood around eight feet tall.

They were also building small HESCO protected combat outposts (COPs) up and down the route of the I-81 through the valley, in an attempt to picket the route, dominating the valley and some of the main population centers.

There was some activity going on at the Bridgewater Airpark, which was located three kilometers west of the 1-81, some six kilometers south west of Harrisonburg and ten kilometers from the location of the new main FOB.

It was curious; they seemed to be walling in a large area of the airpark with HESCO walls. It included the airport buildings, hangers and a section of the runway as it ran behind the hangers, including a sizeable area of grassy field. But the HESCO walls were cutting off the main two thirds of the runway.

So they were not using it for fixed wing aircraft then?

Jack decided that he needed to develop more information on these two large FOBs. He tasked two squads with OP missions. This would entail establishing covert OP positions, with one squad overlooking each FOB location.

The reason for the squad size per OP was to allow longevity. He was going to put each squad in for a week. The numbers would allow them to run four men up in the OP itself, rotating through the observation and recording duties and a little rest, and the other four slightly back in a covert rest area, primarily resting, administering and pulling rear security. The two teams would change over routinely, usually every twenty four hours.

He allocated each squad an area of operations that included several likely suitable OP locations. They would be responsible for finding and establishing the exact location. Due to the lack of secure communications, the OPs would not be in radio contact. Instead, they used a dead letter drop system. Every second day, the OP would drop their log and report in a concealed dead drop, at a location away from the OP, to be picked up by a courier. If Jack decided to maintain the OPs, it was through this system that a relief team could be rotated through, by meeting at the dead letter drop.

To make the dead letter drop work, they had to take in a pair of couriers with them, so they could find a drop site that was in a suitable location to wherever the OP ended up being located. The couriers would then move away, returning every second day to pick up the reports and move them back through the network. These same couriers would also be able to guide in a relief OP team when the time came.

The dead drops also allowed a limited amount of resupply, such as water, if there was no source close to the selected OPs, which tended to be on high ground. The OP parties still had to carry a lot of gear in with them to stay in place for a week: food, water, binoculars, night vision, lots of batteries and of course the thermal ponchos and camouflage netting to conceal the OP positions.

Jack still tasked IED teams to go out on mission during this OP phase, but he set boundaries, areas of operation, that kept them away from the OPs, to minimize the chance of compromise.

Thus, with the patrol base down by Zulu, the OPs out in the valley, and the IED teams back on task, the Company entered a patrol phase of limited offensive operations. It was about information gathering. Jack wanted to see what the Regime was up to with the FOBs and the COPs. Once they had gathered enough information, he would be able to use it to plan further disruption operations.

Over the next few weeks, the information started to trickle back to the tactical operations center (TOC) at Victor Foxtrot. Jack ended up replacing the OP parties and leaving them in place to keep the enemy under surveillance. The IED teams had also had a few successes, with the targeting of patrols operating out of some of the COPs strung up and down the I-81. They had refined their techniques so that they were having better success with the IED ambushes and had not been spotted by Regime ground forces or aircraft top cover.

It appeared that the Harrisonburg FOB was indeed the battle group headquarters, housing an additional armored infantry company plus multiple support assets. Jack saw from some of the surveillance photos that it was now totally ringed by HESCOs, including several inner fortified compounds, and it reminded him of any number of FOBs he had seen in Iraq or Afghanistan.

No doubt the Company assigned to the FOB spent most of their time manning the bunkers and towers dotted along the HESCO perimeter, as well as the two entry control points. It was the usual story: cooks to feed the guards, and guards to guard the cooks.

The Bridgewater Airpark FOB was smaller. The vital point was that it appeared to be a FOB for an Apache squadron group, supporting operations up and down the valley. There was a guard force of two platoons of infantry, manning bunkers around the HESCO perimeter, with an OP on a central rooftop. They were equipped with MRAP armored vehicles, which looked like armored Humvees on growth hormones.

The Apaches had started to move in and it appeared that a squadron of eight of them was assigned to the FOB, along with their support organization. That was a significant force and it would have a huge impact on operations for the Resistance in the valley.

The strategy of the Regime forces in the valley was becoming apparent. They had placed the central FOB at Harrisonburg with the attack aviation support FOB at the Airpark. They had a series of COPs strung throughout the valley to protect the main supply route (MSR) of the I-81 and ancillary routes. They were conducting patrol operations in the valley to attempt to disrupt and dislocate insurgent attack operations onto the MSRs.

The Apaches were divided between surveillance and reconnaissance operations in the surrounding area, and top cover for convoys transiting through. They did not have the availability to permanently fly top cover on convoys, so they tended to move in and out of it, sometimes dropping in to a top cover role on the way to and from surveillance missions.

It appeared that two Apaches were always designated as an airborne response force to react to incidents of troops in contact in the valley. It was the avoidance of these Apache that was the main challenge to the IED teams, who had to prevent themselves from being picked up on the Apache surveillance systems following an attack.

It was also apparent that the Regime battle group had designated Harrisonburg as the main seat of government in the valley. They considered the 'Battle of Harrisonburg' as a hard won victory, not the bloody nose that it had been, and were now moving on to reconstruction operations. They were following the 'clear, hold, build' doctrine.

As well as the FOB, the Regime forces had established a fortified 'government center' in what remained of the battered town center. They had civil affairs and psychological operations teams working the area, trying to get people to return. They had brought in some civilian development staff, Army Corps of Engineers, political officers, as well as civilian security teams to move them around to and from the government center and between the various reconstruction projects they had going on.

As a result of the activity of a covert close recon team that Jack sent down into the town, the information came back that the Regime was running development and reconstruction operations out of the government center, as well as a registration and RFID chip office. They were offering food and reconstructed housing to those who were willing to return to the town.

Regime patrol activity in the town had overmatched the local militia and driven them underground. Arrest operations were ongoing, raids often resulting from information supplied by turned townsfolk who decided to take the RFID chip and the food. Many of the militia simply disappeared after nighttime raids. It appeared that the Regime had picked up the incumbent Mayor, who had turned, taken the chip, and become a puppet for the Regime.

The Regime was making a big effort in Harrisonburg, paying willing contractors in electronic money and food handouts to work on reconstructing the town. They had started on the town center and persuaded several shops to reopen. They also sponsored a bar/restaurant/night spot only a block from the HESCO fortified government center.

The restaurant became a regular spot for the Regime civilian and military staff as well as some of the battle group officers to socialize, along with numerous collaborators. It was a night spot for the local Regime elite, both civilian and military, to hang out with various cronies and collaborators.

It was around 2100hrs on a spring evening in Harrisonburg town center. The Regime squad patrolled tactically through the streets on a security patrol. There were two teams, a slight distance or 'tactical bound' between the two. They were armed with the usual M4 rifles with a SAW gunner in each team.

They rounded the corner into the street where the new Regime restaurant was located. It was down a ways on the left and as the squad moved down the street they could see a small convoy of vehicles pulled up at the curb. There were two military Humvees and two civilian SUVs. A couple of soldiers stood around the Humvees and a little way down were a small group of civilian security personnel.

The squad was led by Olson. He looked exactly the part, because he had once been the part. They had all shaved and cut their hair. As Olson moved down the sidewalk his squad was split in a file formation on both sides of the street. He could see a lone guard on duty at the top of the three steps that led up to the door of the restaurant. Light and music was spilling out from the windows into the street.

Olson walked up the steps towards the door. The guard looked surprised, he was expecting the patrol to keep moving down the street. Suddenly, Olson kicked him backwards through the door, at the same time raising his rifle and following through into the restaurant, followed by Gibbs with the SAW. As they burst through the doorway in pursuit of the falling guard, they pushed left and right, clearing the fatal funnel of the doorway, shot the guard, and opened fire into the restaurant.

Phillips and McCarthy stood at the bottom of the steps and engaged the surprised soldiers and security guards, while the second team also supported, rapidly gunning down the loitering guards. The second team pushed forwards, double-tapping the prostrate guards, and took up security positions by the vehicles. Phillips and McCarthy then pushed through the door and joined Olson.

Inside, it was carnage. It had been a lively evening; drunken Regime elite were sitting about and propping up the bar, waitresses wending their way between the crowded tables. In a couple of places, escort girls sat on officers laps, scantily dressed.

Gibbs had gone cyclic with the box of two hundred rounds on his SAW, arcing the weapon back and forth across the crowd. Olson was supporting him with short bursts, paying particular attention to anyone with a weapon, as they were joined by the other two as they came through the door.

The team was not aiming for the waitresses and escort girls, but they didn't make a special effort to spare them. They were collaborators. The storm of bullets ripped across the room, tearing into flesh, sometimes passing through multiple bodies before coming to a stop.

The covert reconnaissance had suggested that there was a private room upstairs, and as soon as the restaurant area appeared pacified, bodies heaped, Olson and McCarthy took off up the stairs. They left the other two to work over the crowd, making sure none were moving.

The pair raced up the stairs, pausing at the door to the upstairs room. Olson kicked it open, McCarthy tossed in a flashbang, and as soon as it detonated they were through, going left and right and covering the room.

As Olson scanned across the scene, he took in a young girl curled up naked on the bed and then his weapon lighted on a civilian in the corner of the room. He was sat knees to chest, naked, his hands over his ears, a pistol held in one of them. He was terrified, and any thought of resistance had passed with the fury of the assault on the room. Olson shot him several times. He was the newly assigned senior political Commissioner.

Olson scanned back to the girl on the bed. She looked around twelve years old, half-starved and barely pubescent, her face bruised, tears running down her cheeks as she sobbed. Olson grabbed her arm and dragged her off the bed, throwing a blanket around her as they exited from the room.

As Olson returned downstairs, he scanned the room. He saw a bartender and waitress hiding down behind the bar. Another waitress was sobbing over by the restrooms. There were windrows of bodies in the room, a pile over by the bar and several in the center of the room around the tables. Entangled among the Regime civilians and military, a couple of the escort girls lay dead.

Olson addressed them all, "Don't collaborate! Pass the message! Get out now!"

He pushed the waitress by the restroom towards the door, his men doing the same with the others behind the bar. As the squad left, taking the girl, one of his men tossed two thermite grenades into the corners, setting the place on fire.

Outside, they jumped into two of the Humvees and drove away from the scene. The assault had taken three minutes. A block away, the QRF from the Government Center had not yet got into their vehicles.

Later, patrols found the two Humvees several miles from town, burning. There was no sign of Olson's squad.

Two days later, the girl was handed over to Megan at Victor Foxtrot for medical care. She had been victimized by the Commissioner. From the story, it appeared he liked young girls, the younger the better, and she was one of the latest that had been supplied to him. She had been repeatedly raped and beaten.

Her name was Juliet. Her parents had been militia Patriots, 'disappeared' by the Regime, and she had been taken. Once the physical wounds had been treated, she was moved down to Zulu for some love and mental healing from the women.

As part of the defensive plans for Zulu, Jack needed a bug-out plan, an alternate location for the families if the base were ever to be compromised. He sent a reconnaissance team out to the west, with orders to look for a secure location deep in the forests as the trees and ridges marched westwards into West Virginia. He thought somewhere between thirty to fifty miles away from the current location would work well.

It took them a couple of weeks, but they came back with a good location, very similar in terrain to the current one. It was forty miles to the west, deeply forested and well hidden. But it also had access both by hiking trail and close enough access by a combination of country roads and fire roads. This meant that they could move their vehicles and heavier equipment there.

Jack sent the plant equipment away from Zulu to be loaded up and sent to the new location, along with a work party. His orders were simple: they were to dig in a basic version of the current base, so that if they had to evacuate to it they could get the families underground and out of the way of thermal surveillance. They were also to dig defensive foxholes around it. But other than that, there was not to be much else, nothing to attract the attention of any passing hunters, just some well hidden bunker entrances and foxholes.

Bill came on a visit and they sat and discussed the new defensive and evacuation plans for Zulu. Bill mentioned that he had sent a loyal man down to Texas to set up a liaison and they now had a secure coded communication link. Bill had a lot more updates on what was going on in the outside world.

Texas has seceded from the Union along with a block of southern States. They had taken with them their National Guard for those States as well as a large chunk of the active duty military that had either been based down in the southern States, where there was a large military presence, or had since defected from the Regime.

It appeared that the southern secession block consisted of a linear block of States based around: Arizona, New Mexico, Texas, Louisiana, Mississippi, Alabama and Georgia. It was known as the Southern Federation.

There were currently no open hostilities between the Regime and the southern block; after the initial fighting around the separation, it had become a hostile stand-off with demarcation lines drawn, the two sides facing each other, an uneasy truce punctuated by occasional limited hostilities. The Regime was not only busy with the Patriot Resistance in general, but also with the Resistance attempts to create another secession block in the 'American Redoubt' based around Idaho, Montana and Wyoming.

However, to Jack all that was almost to be expected, and was nothing compared to the big news. China had attacked the United States. The U.S. Pacific Fleet had been defeated and Hawaii annexed. There were rumors that the Chinese were planning an invasion of the Pacific coast, and perhaps even an allied Russian invasion of Alaska.

Part of the reason for the uneasy truce between the Regime and the Federation was the concern over this potential course of action. The Regime was moving assets west, and the Federation was massing forces in Arizona in order to defend against an invasion. However, there may have been a mutual enemy, but this certainly did not mean that the two sides were interested in working together.

The Regime still held the balance of military power by a considerable advantage in combat power. The Regime had created several new strategic commands: a Pacific coast command (USPACOM) that operated west of the Rockies and was the primary defense against Chinese invasion; Atlantic Command (USATCOM) which included the eastern seaboard; and a central command (USCENTCOM) which included the Great Plains and northern central States.

Where a southern command would have been, was the southern block of secession States, so elements of USCENTCOM and USATCOM were tasked with operations in the south of their areas to contain the Southern Federation. They also had to contend with the suppression of Patriot Resistance operations across their areas of responsibility.

There was a demarcation line that roughly followed the straight lines on the northern state borders, across the top of Arizona and New Mexico, cutting down across the northern Texas border, then splitting Arkansas and then following the northern borders of Mississippi, Alabama and

Georgia before splitting South Carolina to the Atlantic coast.

The demarcation line consisted of a demilitarized no-man's land, along the north and south side of which the Regime and the Federation conducted defensive patrolling operations, with the main defensive positions covering Interstate access routes across the demilitarized zone and major centers of population. It was a strategic game, but neither side could defend everywhere and with the Chinese and Russian menace added to the mix an uneasy stand-off continued.

The situation, with this threat to the United States now from enemies both foreign and domestic, was certainly a dislocation to Jack's thought process. It was odd to consider American soldiers being shipped west, from both the Regime and the Federation, in order to fight a foreign invader, while the Resistance fought the Regime, and it was only a matter of time before the Regime and Federation forces had to go at it.

However, the Regime was a domestic enemy of the American people and the Constitutional tradition of liberty. The Resistance would not attempt to get into bed with the Regime, even if the Regime would tolerate it. Better to allow the Chinese and Russian threat to bleed the Regime and draw heavy combat assets west of the Rockies. Once the Regime was dealt with, the Resistance and the Federation would then have to deal with any continuing foreign threat.

Chapter Twelve

F ollowing Bill's visit, Jack threw himself into planning for an attack on the Apache FOB at Bridgewater Airpark. It was evident that degrading the Regime attack helicopter capability in the valley would greatly benefit the freedom of movement of Resistance operations. Jack gathered his command team and started them planning their various pieces of the operation.

The FOB was situated in a rural area, farmland, south west of Harrisonburg. The I-81 ran north-south some three kilometers east of the FOB, as the crow flies.

The Regime forces had HESCO walled off a four hundred meter square area of the airpark. The access road, State Route 727, ran past the front of the FOB in a north west to south easterly direction. The FOB itself and the airstrip were between this road and a river to the north east, which ran roughly parallel to the road. There was a distance of about eight hundred meters between the road and the river behind the FOB.

From the north and east there were only two access points to get on to route 727 that ran past the front of the FOB. One was to the south east, where the river bent into a southerly direction. Here, three and a half kilometers from the FOB, the road dog-legged hard left to run north easterly along the edge of the river for four hundred meters before turning rapidly east and crossing a bridge before joining Route 11.

The other access point was also a bridge, three kilometers to the north west, where the 727 joined the 42 at a T-Junction. Three hundred meters north east of that junction the road crossed a bridge into Bridgewater.

The enemy had walled off the main area of the airpark where the buildings were. There was an entry control point (ECP) directly off the 727 on the south west side. The access road from the ECP ran north easterly into the compound and bisected the buildings inside the FOB, leading to some taxi and aircraft parking areas at the back.

There was also a grassed area inside the FOB on this north east side. The actual airstrip was behind the buildings and ran north west to south east, but it had been cut off by the HESCO wall on the north west side of the FOB.

There was also a secondary road that paralleled the one inside the base, running along the outside of the south east HESCO wall from the 727. Halfway along this south east perimeter there was a secondary ECP, directly off the road. The area surrounding the FOB was open fields with very free access for vehicles and fields of fire.

The south east half of the inside of the FOB consisted of some open parking areas, the open pan area to the north east out the back for aircraft parking, and a couple of large buildings. The closest building to the secondary ECP was a large L-shaped two story building that was being used as accommodation for the guard force. The long part of the 'L' ran parallel to the south east perimeter wall and the bottom part of the 'L' was on the south west end, pointing towards the secondary ECP.

The north west half of the base was dominated by a large aircraft hangar, roughly seventy five meters square. On the main ECP side of this hanger, facing the gate and close to the internal bisecting road, was a two story building that was being used as the squadron headquarters and pilot accommodation.

Jack and his team were studying the OP reports in detail, as well as the photos that had been taken. There were guard bunkers on each corner of the FOB. The ECPs were on two sides, the south west and south east, and as such there were guard bunkers there also. There were also bunkers built halfway along the walls on the other two sides of the FOB.

The enemy guard bunkers were a cross between a raised bunker and a watch tower, built on the HESCO wall out of additional HESCO bastions, sandbags and wooden beams. The area where the guards sat manning their machine-guns was quite open, a sandbagged timber roof

247

held up by four corner pillars, thus allowing observation but also reducing the protection from incoming fire.

The two platoons of Regime infantry were guarding the FOB and they were equipped with MRAPs, which they were not using in their static role. The vehicles were parked up in a motor pool close to their accommodation building. Two of them were being used as the 'gates' to the ECPs. They were parked across the road in the gap between the HESCOs, and driven out of the way if access was needed. The support machine-guns from the turrets on the MRAPs were mounted in the guard bunkers.

The Apaches were kept parked up on the pan to the north east side of the FOB, sometimes taken into the large hanger for repair and maintenance work.

The Resistance OP over-watching this Regime FOB was located eight hundred meters to the south west. Here, there was ridge covered in scraggly trees running in a north west to south easterly direction. The ridge overlooked the FOB and due to its elevated position could see beyond the HESCO wall. There was a draw between the ridge and the FOB, and behind the ridge to the west was an area concealed from view of the FOB. The ridge was accessible from vehicle navigable roads and trails from the west.

The OP position, or in the vicinity of it along the ridge, was an ideal location for a fire support base. Given that it was ideal to assault at a ninety degree angle to your fire support base; this would mean approaching and assaulting the base either from the north west or south east flanks, along the 727.

Jack also had his team, and Jim in particular, look at the two bridges and the photos that he had a recon patrol take of their structure. He needed to consider dropping the bridges with demolitions to slow down any QRF moving to assist the FOB under attack.

Once his team had decided that the plan was viable, Jack gave it the go ahead and they moved into battle procedure. Warning orders were issued to get things in motion. There was task organization, administration, logistics, weapons, ammunition and vehicles to ready for the operation.

Jack decided against deploying down into the valley with a small recon team to conduct an additional commander's reconnaissance. He did not want to risk compromise of the OP and he had sufficient information. He trusted the competence of his team. The OP would remain in place and the fire support base would link up with it prior to the operation. That would also allow passage of the latest information on Regime forces activities.

Jack gave his verbal orders around a scale model of the Regime FOB and the surrounding area. The positions of his various elements were marked on the model and he was able to talk through the scheme of maneuver and the specific mission and tasks allocated to each of his subordinate elements.

The plan was for a night attack, going noisy at 0300hrs. This was the time of the enemy's lowest ebb, when most of them would be sleeping except for those on guard duty. The OP had also observed a pattern of life from the Apache squadron that they never conducted missions at this time. There was a window between around 0200hrs and the start of the next day's operations at around 0500hrs when they seemed to do all they could to not be flying.

Jack wanted to catch the attack helicopters on the ground, because if they were airborne, things would go badly for his fighters. This was a go/no go criterion for the attack and as such surprise must be absolute.

The idea was to achieve surprise and concentrate force to fix the enemy on the FOB and destroy the helicopters in place. The priority was the destruction of the Regime Apache helicopters with the secondary objective of killing as many pilots, flight personnel and guards as possible.

The night of the raid, the various elements had infiltrated, in small packets by multiple routes and staggered times, lights off, into an assembly area to the west of the objective.

A courier pair went forward and linked up with the OP, gathering the latest reports. The operation was on radio silence; this would continue until compromised or when the operation went noisy as planned. Then, radio silence would not matter beyond OPSEC on the net.

The fire support base consisted of the mortar and machine-gun squads. They were mounted in the pickups, which were not being used as firing platforms but simply to carry the heavy weapons and large amounts of ammunition needed for the operation. They moved up Route 698 from the west and then cut across the fields to a rally point in the dead ground west of the ridge. They were guided across the fields by a dismounted security party.

The mortar squads stopped in the low ground behind the ridge and set up their mortars, stacking the mortar bombs ready, with the vehicles close by for a further resupply. The mortar fire controller stayed with the machine-gun squads as they walked up the back side of the ridge, where they linked up with the rear group from the OP. Their ammunition carrying vehicles stopped short of the ridgeline.

The machine gun teams carried their 240s and .50cals up to the ridge, stopping short. They set up the tripods in the low positions and mounted the machine-guns on top. The gun teams carried the tripods with the guns mounted and stealthily moved into position atop the ridge. They carried first line scales of ammunition; the resupply would come from the vehicles which would be able to drive up closer once the raid went noisy.

The machine-gun teams set up on the ridge, their guns mounted on the tripods set low to the ground. The .50 Barrett sharpshooters also set up, as well as the mortar fire controller. The other MFC would be with the assaulting party, ready to call for fire or switch fire as necessary.

One of the key things about a night attack was the use of control measures to prevent fratricide. The Company had acquired limited amounts of night vision equipment, but not enough to rely on it for everyone. The raid would have to go noisy with the use of white light. They were unable to use measures such as IR glint tape as the Regime forces did in conjunction with their NVGs, so they would use phase lines to initiate switch fire. They would also use cyalume sticks hung out of windows to mark the progress of the clearance as the fighters fought through the objective.

Concurrent to this, a small party had moved up to the northern bridge and rigged it for demolition with explosives. The demolition had been planned and the team briefed by Jim, who had marked on the photographs exactly where the explosives needed to be placed. He had trained the demolition teams to be able to rig and drop the bridge. Once the bridge was rigged, the team sat in an over-watch position with the detonator attached to a command wire, waiting for the call.

To the south east, Jack had allocated 2nd Platoon the task of demolishing the bridge and providing flank protections. This was the most likely route that a QRF force would come if they moved from the Harrisonburg FOB with the intent of reinforcing the garrison at the Airpark.

The platoon rigged the bridge for demolition and then set an ambush overlooking the four hundred meters of dogleg road that led from the bridge towards the Airpark. They were able to get in and conceal themselves amongst some farm buildings that sat atop a slope looking down towards the dogleg portion of the road, from the north.

The other two platoons waited in the two dump trucks, along with Jack's tactical headquarters, in cover on the road to the south west. They had remained in the assembly area while the fire support elements had pushed forward to occupy their positions on the ridge.

They had rigged the dump trucks for machine-guns. On the front wall of the armored truck bed were mounted two 240 machine-guns, and on the front ends of both sides were mounted two more, to make six mounted guns per truck. These guns were manned by a dedicated force, while the three squads of each platoon sat down in the back of the dump trucks. They had also fitted dozer blades to the front of the trucks, giving them a ramming capability.

Jack was in the lead assault truck with his small tactical HQ including the MFC, and also Caleb's 1st Platoon. Jim was in the second truck with a team of his demolitions guys and Alex Lambert's 3rd Platoon.

As 0300hrs approached, Jack moved the two vehicles containing his assault groups up to just short of the junction with Route 727, south of the FOB. It had been confirmed earlier while they in the assembly area, after the couriers had met up at the OP, that all eight Apaches were on the ground, no activity. The base was quiet. The assault force was one kilometer from the enemy FOB.

Jack got on the radio, "Juliet One Five, this is Zero Actual, send."

The OP came back, "Roger, Alpha Golf," the code that the birds were still on the ground, no activity.

"Tango, Tango, Tango," Jack said into his radio, the agreed code that the operation was a go.

There was a pause, seeming like an eternity, as the silence persisted. Then, there was the detonation as a mortar round fired. An eternity later and there was a pop up in the sky as a parachute flare bloomed in the darkness, bathing the enemy FOB in murky light.

Again, a couple of seconds delay as the gunners acquired their targets, before the fire base erupted in a wall of fire directed at the Regime base. The gunners had been allocated specific targets to ensure that the base was effectively suppressed, and the Barrett shooters were aiming in particular at the guard bunkers to kill or suppress the enemy gunners.

The MFC up with the fire base called for fire from the mortars behind him in the low ground. Because they knew both their and the enemy's location the initial salvoes of mortar rounds were fairly accurate, adjusted by the MFC to primarily suppress the rear area of the FOB where the Apaches were, not primarily to potentially damage the aircraft, but to deter any flight crews from attempting to start them up and take off.

The enemy's response was faltering. Fire was initially returned from the bunkers facing the fire base, but the gunners were soon suppressed or killed and it dwindled. The bunkers on the other sides were struggling to bring their weapons to bear in the right direction. The QRF was deployed into stand-to positions and the troops sleeping in the accommodation were rudely awakened, hustled out of bed by screaming NCOs to take up fire positions.

Jack had planned for approximately five minutes of preparatory fire before moving the assault force, to suppress the guard bunkers and allow the mortars to bed in and adjust fire on their targets. Five minutes later, the MFC on the ridge got on the radio and confirmed that the mortars were on target. Jack got on the radio and gave the code word for the assault force to move, for the benefit of both them and the fire support base.

As a response to Jack's radio order, the demolitions team to the north fired the charges, blowing out the structural steel underneath the bridge and sending it crashing down into the river. To the south, the flank protection platoon sat in their ambush position, watching their bridge. One door was closed, the other remained open.

The two assault trucks rolled down Route 727, heading north west towards the FOB. Jack was stood in the front of the truck bed between the central two gunners manning the 240s bristling out. He could see the red tracer arcing down from the ridge on the left, across the road and into the FOB on the right.

One round in every five was a tracer round and it was deceptively harmless as it gracefully arced down into the objective, the sound a 'tick, tick, tick;' from the sonic crack of the rapid long bursts of the 7.62 guns and a slower deeper sound from the .50cals. It was like a laser light show, with tracer rounds sometimes ricocheting off the targets in the FOB and zipping off up into the night sky

The guns were in the sustained fire role mounted on the tripods and were firing long bursts into the Regime FOB. Jack knew that the 240 gunners would be sat by the guns, their index finger and thumb the only contact as they pulled the trigger, sending the tracer down onto the enemy.

The mortar squads were putting up constant illumination rounds from one barrel while the others worked under the direction of the MFC stonking bombs into the Regime FOB. Jack could see the flash of the detonations in among the enemy buildings and hear the concussive 'crump', distinctive to mortars.

Short of the FOB the assault trucks took a right turn out into the field and headed diagonally towards the secondary ECP in the south east wall. They were moving into 'danger close' range of the mortars but it was a calculated risk to keep the enemy suppressed while they breached the walls, and the platoons were protected by the steel sides of the assault trucks. As they took the right turn Jack called the phase line over the net to let the fire support know.

The trucks came line abreast and stopped out in the field two hundred meters from the wall, fifty meters apart. The machine-gunners opened fire on the FOB, suppressing the secondary ECP bunker and the one on the eastern corner. The two assault trucks then started to fire and maneuver in fifty meter bounds, one moving while the other covered, as the assault force closed with the enemy wall from the right flank.

As the two assault trucks advanced on the enemy, the mounted machine-guns poured bursts of red tracer fire towards the Regime base, targeting in the main the guard bunkers and any muzzle flashes they could see in the semi-darkness of the mortar illumination flares. In return came the enemy fire, flicking over the top of the two assault trucks, red tracer coming back the other way, cracking overhead.

Occasionally, the enemy fire would hit home, smacking into the armored sides and cab of the assault trucks, often ricocheting away into the darkness. Jacks gunners stood firm, firing at targets in the Regime FOB.

Just before the last bound of his truck to the secondary ECP, the MFC with Jack called for fire to switch to the north to suppress the far side of the base. With the other assault truck suppressing, Jacks truck accelerated towards the secondary ECP, the gunners firing on the move. Just before they reached the MRAP blocking the gate, the truck slowed, Jack called "Brace, brace, brace!" and the assault truck hit the MRAP, gunning through and pushing the MRAP out of the way as they drove through the gate.

Jacks truck pushed through and moved to halfway between the gate and the 'L' shaped barracks building, twenty five meters from the closest windows on the end of the building. The truck gunners were firing at any identified targets as their support fire from the ridgeline switched left away from them, concentrating now on the headquarters building and the remaining guard bunkers.

They were in amongst a storm of fire, and as Jack stood in the front of the truck bed he could see the muzzle flashes of enemy fire coming from the windows of the building in front of him, the crack of the passing rounds just more noise amongst the cacophony around him.

The second truck came through the gate and swung to the right to where the Apaches were parked. The truck drove over and through the Apache ranks, stopping on the far side with the gunners providing covering fire. The platoon leaped out of the back and took up fire positions in cover around the Apache park while Jim led his demolition team to the helicopters.

Just then, the gunner just to the right of Jack was hit in the shoulder. He gave a gasp of pain and dropped back into the truck bed. Jack grabbed the 240 and started to send bursts of three to five rounds through the closest windows where he could see enemy muzzle flashes. Jack felt a hand on his shoulder and moved to the side to let one of his fighters take over the gun, allowing him to resume his command role.

Jack gave the order and his truck advanced to the 'L' shaped building, parking right up against the end of the foot of the 'L'. Caleb's platoon was waiting in the truck and as soon as it stopped they were up and posting grenades through one of the end windows, their chosen breach point.

As soon as the grenades went off, the entry team was in. They used white light flashlights mounted to their weapons once they were inside the building, and Olson pushed his squad through to clear through the first few rooms.

Caleb's squads started to systematically clear the upper floor of the building. The squad leaders controlled their men, breaking down into four man teams to clear the rooms. As they went they hung cyalume sticks out of the windows of cleared rooms to show their progress to those providing fire support.

As soon as the last of the assault platoon was inside the building, Jack moved the dump truck away from the building, off to the left, to where the gunners could suppress into the depth of the FOB and also cover the lower floor of the 'L' shaped building and any escaping enemy..

In the building, there was a central corridor with rooms off to the sides that had been offices but now had been largely co-opted into accommodation. Some of the rooms had entry points only off the corridor, others had internal connecting doors. This gave the squad leaders the choice of moving through the connecting doors if they were available, or room to room down the corridor if they were not.

It largely came down to communication and the use of link men, with leaders sequencing and organizing the teams to flow through the rooms. They had to hit each room with aggression and try to seize the initiative through the use of aggression and grenades while they still had a supply.

The rooms were not that large and they usually used a single team to hit each one, a two man assault team breaching the room with the team leader following rapidly on their heels. The fourth man would act as link and cover man in the corridor. If there was a connecting door the next team in sequence would usually flow through the room and that door, or if not they would move down the corridor to the next door and breach through it.

Coordination had to happen between the teams clearing each side of the corridor to ensure the team on one side did not pass an un-cleared room on the other.

It was tough fight inside the building, room to room, blasting their way through initially with high explosive fragmentation grenades and then moving to flash-bang stun grenades, until they even ran out of those. Sometimes if a room looked like it would be a tough breach the team leaders would step in to lead the entry by example, but in general it was more effective with them in a command and coordination role.

At one point Olson's team rotated back to point squad and they pushed down the corridor to breach the next door on the left. They had already turned the corner and were clearing the long side of the 'L'. McCarthy and Phillips were the breach pair up front with Gibbs behind him as the link/cover man. McCarthy and Phillips stacked on the door with Olson close behind them. Gibbs pushed out right so he could cover down the corridor.

McCarthy checked the door while Phillips prepped his high explosive grenade. The door was locked. McCarthy moved out in front of the door, looked at Olson, who nodded. McCarthy then looked at Phillips, nodded, and front kicked the door. It went flying inwards and Phillips tossed the grenade low through the door just as McCarthy moved back into cover. The door hit the wall and rebounded. As it came flying back, a burst of fire from inside punched a series of holes in it. Just then, the grenade exploded with a concussive crack.

Olson screamed, "Go, Go, Go!"

McCarthy went through the door, followed closely on the heels by Phillips. He shouldered the door aside to the right and went left, swinging his barrel through the center of the room and then towards the corners. His white light illuminated the room as it arced across, furniture scattered around, the smoke from the detonated grenade still obscuring the air. Phillips went right, mirroring the procedure. Olson came in and stepped to the left side of the door, the 'fatal funnel'.

No targets, no enemy.

The room was cluttered with furniture. McCarthy and Phillips moved towards the opposite corners. As he moved along the wall, McCarthy hit his shin on a cot bed, tripped, and went flying forwards over it, ending up in a tangled heap. As that happened, there was a burst of fire from the far left corner, from behind some sort of filing cabinet. The burst passed over the top of McCarthy, stitched along the wall, and hit Olson in his ballistic plate, also hitting the bolt assembly on his M4, disabling his rifle.

Olson grunted as he was punched back into the wall, winded. He dropped to his knees, let go of his M4 and rapidly transitioned to his pistol on his battle belt, firing into the darkness of the corner.

Phillips was in the far right corner and he started rapidly firing rounds into the furniture that was scattered around on the outer side of the room. McCarthy rolled up, kicked the cot bed from where his legs were entangled in it, and pointed his light into the corner. He caught sight of a Regime soldier crouched behind the filing cabinet, fully geared up in body armor and helmet.

McCarthy started firing into the corner, panicked, to no effect. He saw the soldier swing his M4 back towards him, the white light on McCarthy's weapon giving away his position.

Get a grip. Hips and Heads, Hips and Heads.

McCarthy lowered his barrel and shot the man several times through the hips. The soldier screamed and fell back into the corner. McCarthy got up, crossed the room, and finished him with a shot to the head.

They checked behind the rest of the furniture before calling out "ROOM CLEAR, NO EXITS!" The call was passed back to the next team in rotation by Gibbs in the corridor. Olson grabbed the dead guy's M4 to replace his, and they got ready to go again.

"What the hell was that McCarthy?" Olson said to him, punching him on the shoulder.

"What's that?" said McCarthy.

"I never told you to get your kip on. What's the deal with you, every time you see a freakin' cot bed you have to try and get in it. And what was all that rolling around on the floor showing off about? Douchebag!"

"Yea, screw you McCarthy," chimed in Phillips, grinning.

"Assholes," said McCarthy, "next time I'll just not bother saving your sorry asses."

Olson shook his head.

They all grinned, the adrenaline coursing through their bloodstreams.

Brothers in arms.

As soon as they had cleared the upper floor of the 'L' shaped building Caleb pushed his squads to the north west windows and started them suppressing into the depth of the base, focused on the headquarters building. Jack moved the truck up level with them so the gunners could also engage.

Jack then called in 3rd Platoon to clear through the lower floor of the 'L' shaped building. They moved in from the right side, covered by their assault truck, which was parked on the opposite side of the building to Jack.

Tracer fire was streaking in both directions across the FOB, from Jacks fire support and his assault trucks, and from the machine-gun and rifle positions of the Regime defenders. The Regime forces had abandoned the lower floor of the 'L' shaped barracks building and fallen back to the headquarters building. This made 3rd Platoon's clearance job easier, but they still had to enter and clear each room to confirm it empty.

As much fire support as the Resistance had, they could not suppress everyone, and it was a tough fight.

The mortar rounds, once they had initially switched fire, had smashed up the large hanger building pretty well and then switched fire again onto the far perimeter. Concurrent to the assault onto the 'L' shaped barracks building Jim had led his demolitions team and was laying charges on all the Apaches.

They were using a design of Jims that modified the EFP to breach the armor on the Apaches, and they were placing the devices to do as much irreparable damage to the aircrafts essential systems as possible. As well as the modified EFPs, they were also using thermite charges to melt and burn as much of the metal parts as possible.

Now, with Jack's assault trucks and Caleb's 1st Platoon in support, 3rd Platoon now rapidly pulled out of the building and reloaded onto their assault truck, driving forward under heavy covering fire, crossing the gap between the 'L' shaped building and the headquarters building and parking up below the windows.

3rd Platoon breached into the end of the building just as Caleb's platoon had done and began the systematic room clearance, trying to kill as many of the Apache squadron as they could find, as well as the infantry who had withdrawn to the building.

There was still sporadic fire coming from the far perimeter and also from isolated groups of enemy who had withdrawn towards the north west side of the FOB.

The MFC now called a cease fire due to the proximity of Resistance fighters. The mortars stood by to provide fire on call, perhaps to suppress any reinforcing or fleeing enemy. The one barrel continued to put up illumination.

Jim came on the net and gave the code word for charges set, which also meant that they had only ten minutes left before they blew. Jack called the platoons back to the trucks, which meant the fight in the headquarters building had to be abandoned, and they started pulling back towards the gate.

The battle had lasted about an hour by now and the armored Regime QRF column from Harrisburg had rolled down the I-81 and cut across the back roads towards the bridge. It was a mixture of armored Humvees and MRAPs, the heavy armor would have taken too long for such a rapid response task. The QRF was mounted in twelve vehicles.

The first four vehicles crossed the bridge and turned left onto the four hundred meter stretch where the ambush lay. As the fifth vehicle, an MRAP, was on the bridge there was an explosion and the bridge fell away, taking the MRAP down to splash massively into the river below.

2nd Platoon's ambush opened with a volley of daisy chained EFPs, hitting and knocking out two of the vehicles.

Two MRAPs remained, their turret gunners firing up the slope towards the winking muzzle flashes of the Resistance ambush. The AT-4 rockets came streaking down the hill, impacting into the remaining MRAPs. All four vehicles were destroyed, two of them burning on the road with ammunition starting to cook off inside.

A gunner tried to get out of one of the MRAPs, the flames licking up around him from inside the vehicle, catching his clothing on fire. He pulled himself out of the turret and then fell, rolling down and slamming into the road. He was soon put out of his agony by the impact of multiple 5.56mm rounds.

The remainder of the Regime column, halted across the river, was able to engage and they brought heavy machine-gun fire down onto the ambushers. There was a group of farm buildings around which the ambush party had set up and they started to break contact and withdraw through the buildings.

Under Alex Lambert's direction they broke contact and headed away to the south west and into the woods where they had stashed their vehicles.

Meanwhile, Jack had pulled the assault trucks back to the secondary ECP, loading the platoons up on board. He halted there to cover the Apaches and interfere with any attempts to remove the explosive charges. The truck gunners were still engaging enemy within the FOB.

The charges began to detonate, the concussive boom of the explosions massive even after the firefight.

The fuel in the Apaches caught fire and the flames lit that side of the FOB with an orange flickering glow, punctuated by the continuing sound of the detonations

Jack moved the trucks out and they burst out of the gate and headed back towards the assembly area, covered by the resumption of fire from the guns up on the ridge. The MFC also brought the mortars back into action, the crump of the mortar bombs landing combined with the detonations of the demolition charges.

As soon as they were clear past the junction, Jack called for the guns to cease fire and the gunners started to break them down and move back to the vehicles. The mortars remained in place, bringing a steady barrage down onto the FOB. Then, once the gunners were clear the mortars finally ceased fire and the whole fire base mounted up into the vehicles and started to extract back to the assembly area.

Caleb's platoon had several walking wounded casualties in the back of the dump truck. Another of them was seriously wounded and he died on the drive back to the assembly area. He had been hit several times under his body armor in the abdominal area and it looked like he had bled out internally; it was possible that his aorta had been nicked by the bullets causing massive internal hemorrhage. There was nothing they could do in such a case.

As soon as they got back to the assembly area they were marshaled in and placed out in all round defense. The casualties were moved to Megan at the mobile aid station and she quickly went to work on them with her team, including Dr. Davis.

As the elements came in, they were accounted for and as soon as the exfiltration packets were complete they were sent on their way back to the designated rally point. The serious casualties were loaded into the ambulance vans where the medical staff could work on them while they moved. Soon, they were all gone into the pre-dawn darkness.

Once the Regime QRF sent back their situation report they were ordered to move their remaining vehicles around to the south where Route 11 crossed the river further down. They had to take a long route to the south and back up towards the FOB. Another QRF was dispatched to the ambush area to aid the stricken convoy and check for any survivors.

By the time the initial QRF reached the FOB, it was daylight and a few of the surviving defenders were walking around exhausted and dazed. The FOB was burning, the remains of the Apaches black stricken hulks sitting on the scorched tarmac. Some supplies of aviation fuel in bladders had apparently caught fire and added to the chaos. It was going to take the Regime forces a couple of days to clean up the mess, searching through the remains of the FOB for survivors and bodies.

Chapter Thirteen

The attack had been an amazing success. The Company was euphoric. They had taken video footage from the fire support base using a night vision camera. It had caught the massive weight of tracer fire pouring down onto the FOB, the crashing assault of the two dump trucks and the destruction of the Apaches. Before the cameraman had moved out with the machine-gun teams, he had caught footage of the continuing detonations and the fires raging throughout the FOB.

Given the resource problems posed by the possible Chinese attack on the west coast, the fighters were hoping that there were not sufficient Apaches available to replace the ones they had destroyed. It was likely that if Apaches continued to be deployed on operations in the valley, they would have to be based outside of it. Clearly they had demonstrated that they could not be protected even on a heavily fortified FOB in the valley.

In the weeks that followed, this allowed the ramping up of the small team IED patrols, with attacks and ambushes along the routes through the valley. They did not see any more Apaches, although occasionally other helicopters, of the utility type such as the Blackhawk and the Chinook, would fly top cover. They were not as deadly as the Apache, but not to be underestimated; if the fighters were spotted these aircraft with their door gunners were still a potent threat.

Jack got a message from Bill confirming that the Chinese had apparently invaded the west coast, the Russians crossing into Alaska to seize oil resources. The reports were sketchy but it appeared that the Chinese had landed in California, coming ashore in a combined amphibious and airborne operation launched from their Pacific fleet and the toehold they had in the Pacific on Hawaii.

There were mixed feelings to the whole Chinese invasion piece. Clearly, it was American soil and the Chinese had no place invading. Some of the guys commented that it was only California, broke and socialist, so the Chinese could keep the place, but they didn't really mean it.

Bills message alluded to huge battles in California between Regime forces and the Chinese. Caleb joked sarcastically about whose side the Chinese population in California would be on, going on to paint Chinese restaurant owners as Chinese sleeper agents and domestic terrorists, to the great amusement of all.

The Chinese invasion was bleeding combat resources from the Regime. Bill speculated based on the information from his sources about an alliance between the Chinese and the Russians. Russia appeared to be primarily after the oil resources in Alaska, while China wanted land resources to solve their massive over-population and scarce resource problems.

One of the odd things that Bill put in the report was that there was a 'feeling' amongst his contacts that the Regime leadership, and in particular The Leader himself, were not really putting in a great effort to defeat the Chinese invasion. It was odd, and there were talks about divisions within the military leadership over this.

Indeed, it seemed that in the USPACOM region, the commanding general had not so much been appointed by the Regime, as he had risen internally through USPACOM to his position due to his competence, which was a most unusual development in the political game of general officer selection.

The current USPACOM commander was General Wall. It appeared the usual preening careerists had proved unequal to the task when faced by hordes of advancing mechanized Chinese forces, plastering the American positions with fire. It was a different animal from espousing COIN doctrine, rules of engagement, health & safety and the wearing of luminous safety belts from a safe FOB in Kabul. The sycophants had peeled away, mostly back to the Pentagon, and General Wall was taking the fight to the Chinese in California.

Reports said that potentially General Wall would be striking out with USPACOM on his own campaign strategy to defeat the invasion, despite such disloyalty to the Regime being likely to result in an 'accident' fatally impacting his health. Some generals, it appeared, were true Patriots deep down below the political careerism.

It was summertime now and the Virginia heat and humidity lay like a blanket over the valley, the ridges and amongst the forests. Insects, mosquitoes and no-see-ums abounded in the woods. The constant humidity was unpleasant but it had to be borne. The Resistance and their families had gone through the harsh winter and now the challenge was a different one, such was the temperature range in the region.

One of the problems they were facing was shortage of food. They were still getting supplies through the network but it was becoming generally harder as the country suffered through the aftermath of the collapse, the power grid outage, and the ongoing strangulation by the Regime.

Jack never ceased to be amazed by the lack of common sense, the almost mental illness, in the thinking of the progressives. It was all about agenda and nothing about practicality. What really needed to be happening was that production, in particular of food, needed to be a priority. But instead the Regime focused on the subjugation of the people and trampling of liberty and self-determination.

The Regime tried to mandate food production, in a similar way to the Soviet five year plans, but they were squashed by their own bureaucracy and cronyism. Much property in the 'safer' areas in the federal controlled zones had been seized and reallocated to loyal Regime bureaucrats. Other farms on the edges of those same zones had been redistributed and settled by groups of the entitled. Of course, it went the way of the Zimbabwe farm seizures, the new sitting tenants having no idea how to run the land.

Val was a twenty eight year old army veteran. Her MOS, or military operating specialty, had been civil affairs. She had deployed to both Afghanistan and Iraq and because it was the job of civil affairs units to get out on the ground and interact with the local populace she had seen plenty of action.

She had a four year degree and had been pushed towards a commission as an officer, but by then she was over the whole army thing. She was tired of the endless bureaucratic incompetence, the power games, and the reverse discrimination.

As for being an officer, she saw most of them as a joke. She felt that the commissioning process left a lot to be desired in the U.S. Army simply because there was no real selection for aptitude, character, and leadership ability. Basically, if you had a four year degree, you were in.

Of course, she would never have said this to anyone for fear of reprisal, but she could also never figure out why there were so many Chinese officers, particularly in the military intelligence field. And by Chinese, she meant real Chinese 'straight off the boat'. These were the characters whose first language was Chinese, whose Facebook accounts and phones were in Chinese, and whose families were in China. What sort of security procedures gave these jokers top secret clearances?

Hello, elephant in the room anyone?

So she had stayed enlisted, never getting further than E4 Specialist, which she had been given at basic training anyway due to her degree. She had a bright future ahead, and had submitted her packet for promotion to E5 Sergeant after her last tour to Afghanistan. It had gone wrong after that.

She had gotten out after the attempted rape. It was true that the military system in general was simply broke, and that all the talk of equal opportunities was just ticking the box. Sexual discrimination was rampant.

The night the drunken battle buddy had tried to rape her had been awful. It was a violent drunken assault that would have succeeded if she had not successfully fought back. She had reported it, but of course the black eye he was wearing went against her.

Remember, self-defense will always get you in trouble, better to be the victim hey?

The assailant was a black NCO, who she thought she could trust, but he was rising through the ranks on the unspoken 'reverse discrimination' policy and the case was quashed. After that, the harassment had begun; the petty bullying from the NCO buddies of her assailant. She had even faced disciplinary action for failing to clear her mail from the mail room. It was petty and vindictive, using the bureaucracy to award her negative counseling statements and punish her for being a victim.

The thing was she was not the victim type. Val was not her real name; it was shortened from her nickname, which was The Valkyrie, awarded to her during the training at Victor Foxtrot over the winter. She was now either Val or 'The Val' to some. She was a big muscular blonde, beautiful and all woman. She had played rugby before the collapse and had been a rising star on the USA Rugby scene. Her nickname then had been 'The Bombshell'.

Val could run, carry a ruck, fight and go on forever. She had fought stalwartly in the Battle of Harrisonburg and been part of the assault on the Apache FOB. Some of the females in the Company who 'batted for the other side' had mistaken her for one of them, but she was not. One of the guys in her training squad had also made the mistake of getting too fresh, and ended up on his ass with a bleeding nose. He was moved.

Val had become a team leader, despite her lack of infantry experience. She got it, she understood tactics, she had balls, and her team loved her for it. She drove them hard and did not tolerate bullshit, but at the same time they knew she loved them back and would do anything for them. She was utterly selfless.

Sergeant First Class John Cobb was from the 82nd Airborne Division, and he originally hailed from South Carolina. His platoon had been attached to the mechanized battle group in the valley to make up for casualties sustained in the

275

Battle of Harrisonburg. They were occupying a platoon sized COP in the northern end of the valley, overlooking the I-81. The platoon was responsible for patrolling an area of operations, including a stretch of the I-81 and surrounding countryside.

SFC Cobb was disillusioned. He did not support the Regime and he was not happy to be fighting for it. Most of his men felt the same, and there was much mutinous talk. The current situation in the United States was a tragedy, and they sympathized with the Resistance. However, they felt trapped, they were part of the machine, and there was nowhere to go. Desertion was punished by death by firing squad.

The general feeling in the platoon was that they did not want to be fighting for the Regime. But they felt their alternatives were limited. They also had a political officer to contend with, allocated to their COP. If he felt you were disloyal to the Regime, you would find yourself extracted for 'reeducation'.

How to get out of it and where to go?

Two days ago, there had been an IED attack on the I-81 and SFC Cobb had taken out a half platoon patrol in armored Humvees into the surrounding area to try and pick up any sign of the insurgents.

Since the successful attack on the convoy, Val had been moving on foot with her team through the valley. They were moving away from the site of the ambush on foot before they would head back to where they had hidden their vehicles and then back to base.

Val knew that food supplies were getting low. For the current patrol, they had one MRE package per team member per day. The MREs had come 'off the back of a truck' and found their way through the Resistance quartermaster network to Victor Foxtrot. They preferred to use the MREs for patrols because they were packaged, did not go bad, and had the chemical heaters.

Val had led the patrol in single file along the drainage ditch to a known food drop. The food drop was a couple hundred meters out the back of a private home, near to a dilapidated shed. Checking inside the concealed five gallon bucket, they had found a stale loaf of homemade bread. It was better than nothing. They had moved into the shed, posted security, and eaten.

It was mid-afternoon.

They had a set of NVGs that they used when it got dark, one sentry handing them off to the next.

Late afternoon, SFC Cobb took his Humvee patrol along an old track to a copse of trees. He parked up the vehicles in a defensive formation in the trees and posted security. They were overlooking a private house and out back was a large yard with a dilapidated shed at back of it.

A farm dog down at the house started barking up at them and the door opened. Out came the widower who lived there. She was a proud American and that is why she supported the Resistance, leaving what she could when she could in the food cache. She had little, but she had been into food storage and homesteading, she baked her own bread, and would leave a loaf in the cache whenever she could. It was often taken.

As SFC Cobb looked down at the house, the old woman looked up and saw the vehicles parked there. She went over to her car and started to honk the horn. It was a common thing that had been adopted in the valley; residents would honk their horns whenever they saw a Regime patrol, in order to warn any Resistance in the area.

SFC Cobb admired her for her courage, because many Regime troops had taken to simply lighting up any vehicles that did it, often with .50cal fire, on the excuse that they were supporting terrorism. It made him sick. It was just simply wrong. It was murder of American citizens.

Val's team was alerted to the presence of the Regime patrol by the car horn. There was little they could do. In the cold light of the proximate threat from the patrol, it was evident that the shed they were occupying was badly positioned.

It was on the edge of an open field and the only covered route in or out was the ditch they had approached in. That ditch led in the direction of the small hill and copse that the Regime patrol sat on. They were trapped for the time being, so they hunkered down, going to fifty percent security, two on duty at any one time.

SFC Cobb had decided to stay in position for a few hours. He had one of his security positions scanning with a portable thermal imager. He had a feeling about this. Late that evening, he was called over to the sentry position.

The soldier on the imager thought he could see something in the shed. SFC Cobb had a look. It was indistinct, but there seemed to be a heat source coming from the dilapidated building, heat leaking out from the inside through the broken down door. He decided to investigate.

He got his squad ready to move on foot, donning their NVGs, while detailing the rest of his group to provide over-watch and potential fire support from their Humvee mounted guns. He gave them express orders to only open fire on his order.

Using the concealment of the copse, SFC Cobb took his squad down the backside of the hill and then around to the ditch. In single file with this squad behind him, he crept up towards the shed.

When the squad was twenty meters away from the shed, the fighters inside opened fire; the rounds went cracking over the top of SFC Cobb and his patrol. It had gone noisy now, so there was no more need for stealth.

"Stay low, get on line!" shouted SFC Cobb to his squad. "Hold your fire," he said on the radio to the fire base back in the copse.

By now, all of Val's four man team was firing, the rounds whipping over the top of the squad in the ditch.

"Hold your fire, hold your fire!" shouted SFC Cobb to his squad. Then, sticking his head up he called to the shed, "Cease fire, cease fire!"

The lack of incoming fire confused Val and her team and she told them to cease fire. There was nowhere to go except back over the open field or forwards into the ditch to assault the enemy. None of those looked like good options. Silence descended over the fields again after the furious outbreak of fire.

"What do you want!" called Val.

"Surrender!" called back SFC Cobb.

"We're not taking prisoners today!" called Val.

Cobb chuckled, "No genius: you surrender!'

There was a pause.

The silence drew out.

"Hold your fire, I'm coming out!" called Cobb. "Don't try anything; you are covered by my gunners on the hill."

SFC Cobb handed his weapon off and climbed out of the ditch. He stopped just short of the shed. Val appeared in the doorway, looking perplexed.

"Hey," said Cobb.

"Hey," said Val, "what's this?"

"You from the Resistance mob in the hills, the mountain men?"

Cobb took her silence as confirmation.

"Look," Cobb continued, "we want to come over. My whole platoon."

Val considered this for a while. "How are you going to prove to me this is no trick?"

The balance of power had shifted to Val. She was now holding the cards, despite being outgunned and in a bad position. Val thought some more.

"Ok, here's the deal," she said, "If you want to come over, you have to prove to us this is no trick. You have to do something for me. Meanwhile, we need to send two of mine back to let my boss know of the arrangement."

"Ok, let's hammer this out," said Cobb.

They sat and discussed it, coming up with a plan. Val knew that they were short of supplies and she also needed these Regime troops to show her they meant business. It was too easy for it to be a trick. Once they had chatted for a while at the shed, Val being very careful with OPSEC, both groups moved back up to the Humvees to discuss this further. Val's team kept their weapons.

SFC Cobb had to make sure that his men were fully onside, and both he and they had concerns for their safety at the hands of the Resistance. Val wanted to make sure that this was genuine, so she had demands too. It was a surreal time, both sides forcing themselves to trust each other a little, while trying to ensure their own safety and searching for signs of treachery in the other.

Val and Cobb were culturally the same, and came from similar army backgrounds, so they could empathize with each other and that made the trusting easier. But Val also had to make it clear to both Cobb and his men that she was from the Resistance and what that would mean to them. She spoke to the group, and outlined what they would have to do. There was no going back from this.

Val wanted to know why these soldiers wanted to come over. SFC Cobb and the others were able to articulate this well, it was something they had believed and talked about amongst themselves for a long time. However, they had not had the means or opportunity to do something about it until now.

The platoon was generally onside, but Cobb told her that the platoon leader, Lieutenant Rider, was pro Regime. There were a couple of others that could not be relied on. The plan involved going back to the COP, taking it over, and then ambushing a supply convoy that Cobb knew was due.

Meanwhile, two of Val's team would go back and let Jack know about an agreed RV point up in the hills. Val, her remaining team member, the defecting platoon and the looted supplies would move to that grid. Val also informed him that they would have to disable the blue force tracker and tracking transponders in all their vehicles before they headed into the hills.

With Val and her team keeping hold of their weapons, they climbed into the backs of the Humvees while SFC Cobb got his guys back together for a brief. They were all with him, but they knew a group back at the COP was not. SFC Cobb briefed them on the plan agreed with Val.

The patrol rolled back into the COP at dawn. It was a small group of farm buildings surrounded by a HESCO wall, the usual guard bunkers on the perimeter. They parked up the vehicles and as per the pre-arranged plan they rapidly rounded up those they knew were loyal to the Regime. They held them outside the TOC in the yard.

SFC Cobb alerted Val and her team and they joined the group. There were six prisoners, including the platoon leader and the Regime political officer assigned to the COP. Their wrists were zip tied and they were forced down onto their knees.

SFC Cobb spoke to them, "We are going over to the Resistance. You are the only ones in the platoon who are not with us. This is your chance. Join us, or you will be executed. But be advised, you will be called upon to fight with the Resistance, so if you are just saying it to save your hide, think again."

All of them came over, with the exception of the lieutenant and the political officer.

"Ok Cobb," said Val, "this is your moment, show me whose side you are on."

"Last chance LT, don't be an idiot," said Cobb. The lieutenant tried to get up and charge, but Cobb kicked him down to the ground. Cobb pulled his handgun, walked over, and executed Lieutenant Rider with a shot to the head. Val drew her handgun, walked behind the political officer, and executed him with a round to the back of the skull.

It was a defining, sickening moment. The platoon stood around in shock. Cobb turned around, handgun raised. "Anyone got a problem with that?" he shouted, his voice shaking.

No answer.

"Ok, the convoy is coming through tomorrow afternoon. Squad leaders to the TOC for a planning meeting. Val, with me. All radios turned in to the TOC now! Specialist Evans: take care of accountability on that. If anyone has second thoughts and tries to get word out, they will be killed. Everyone else, get back to your duties."

Val dispatched her two team members with the coordinates of the RV. It turned out that the platoon all had their original reverse US flags in their upper arm ACU pockets, under the Regime flags. They pulled them out, threw the Regime flags into the dirt, and stuck the US Flags onto the Velcro. They buried Lieutenant Rider and the political officer round the back in a shallow grave.

Taking the convoy was easy. It was a relatively small supply convoy, a few MRAPs guarding five LMTVs, the version with the armored cabs. The trucks were full of rations. SFC Cobb quickly planned a fake IED on the I-81 just south of the COP. They had the area cordoned off and diverted the convoy to the COP. There was a large enough parking area inside the HESCO perimeter for this purpose.

As the convoy drivers and escorts were relaxing and getting out of their vehicles, the COP turned their weapons on them, SFC Cobb demanding their surrender. There was an awkward moment of confusion before the unprepared convoy escort troops made the collective decision not to do anything. There were twenty two of them.

Utilizing the psychological shock of capture, the convoy troops were disarmed and corralled on one side of the compound. Cobb and Val spoke to them, explaining what was going on. They were then given the option: join the Resistance or remain prisoners.

They all came over.

The next day, the enlarged convoy including SFC Cobb's platoon made its way to the west, into the hills. They wound up the roads into the forested ridges. Val was with them and she had ensured that SFC Cobb had disabled all the transponders in the vehicles.

They arrived at the RV location that Val had given. It was a clearing off the road. Stuck into the field just off the road was a wooden post with a piece of white cloth hanging from it. Val walked over and saw there was a note attached to the pole in a plastic cover. She opened it. Inside, was a new set of grid coordinates. She smiled. She had given the coordinates fairly arbitrarily, and Jack was building in some additional security in case she was compromised.

They drove for thirty minutes to the next set of coordinates. It was a clearing off the road, overlooked on three sides by wooded higher ground. Again, there was a post with a note. Val read it and passed on the message.

The defecting troops were very nervous. They were in a perfect ambush killing area deep in Resistance territory, a place where the Regime had not dared so far to send ground troops for fear of the obvious ease of ambush on the heavily wooded roads.

The instructions were to strip off body armor and weapons and move away from the vehicles. The covers on the backs of the trucks had to be opened. The soldiers had to wait in formation in the center of the clearing. There was a lot of muttering about this, but they had little choice.

They stripped down to their basic uniforms and formed up. Val was with them.

They waited.

Jack was up slope in the tree line with Jim. He had the ambush site covered by his fire support platoon. He also had air sentries keeping an eye and ear out for any supporting aviation. They kept the formed up soldiers under observation for an hour.

"What do you think Jim?"

"Well boss, it looks legit. What about you?"

"Yea, looks good, let's go down and see them."

They both emerged from the tree line and walked down the slope towards the formed up soldiers. Val came towards them. They met out of earshot of the troops.

"Hey Val," said Jack, "if this is what it appears, you have done very well."

"It was just luck. If it was a different unit, we would be dead or captured by now."

"What do you think?"

"I think it's for real, but a few of them, mainly the ones from the convoy we captured, had a stark choice to make so I am not sure how much their heart is in it. But I don't think there are any actual infiltrators amongst them, it was all too spur of the moment."

"Ok, let's go talk to them," Jack said.

They met with SFC Cobb and walked amongst the troops, questioning them about the Regime, what they thought, and their motivations. After another meeting, they agreed that it seemed legitimate and they would take the troops into the organization. It was a trust moment, a certain level of faith and intuition was at work.

As soon as the decision was made, Jack called down a platoon and they had the troops grab their personal gear. They allowed them to keep their personal weapons. Some of the Resistance platoon jumped in the vehicles, checked the transponders were destroyed, and drove them away as per Jim's instructions. They would be moved to one of the hide sites, hidden, and the rations moved into the Resistance stores.

There was one other thing. RFID chips. When Jack told Val and Cobb what had to be done, there was a look of shock on both their faces. Cobb had genuinely forgotten.

"Yea, they chipped us all. Just like a regular formation for shots or whatever. We had no choice. It was either that or UCMJ action," said Cobb.

"Ok," said Jack, "they have to come out now. I would have preferred it if they had come out before you moved here, but now is better than never."

Jack introduced Dr. Davis and Megan, and along with their medical team they ran an impromptu surgical clinic. Dr. Davis and an assistant administered lidocaine to numb the skin, then he whipped out the chip with a quick incision to the forearm, before passing the soldiers on to have the wound sutured. It was quick and efficient, and afterwards the chips were piled up and burned.

There were forty eight soldiers, the platoon and convoy combined. Under the escort of another platoon, they marched for several hours on trails through the woods to the training compound. They did not go anywhere near Zulu or Victor Foxtrot, but to the farm complex that the Company had used as their urban training site. This was to be the quarantine area, to ensure all was as it seemed.

Jack and Jim together interviewed them all, with Val and Cobb there to assist with their background knowledge on them. Eight of them did not appear to be trustworthy, having just gone along to save their skins. Either that or they were not prepared to fight in the Resistance. They were segregated and confined.

A week later, they prepared to move the forty they trusted to Victor Foxtrot and integrate them into the organization according to their skill sets. This would have the effect of splitting them up.

Jack and Jim discussed what to do with the eight. It was a hard call. As far as the defecting units command knew, the unit had just disappeared with no sign. If they released the eight, not only would their command know what had happened but they would be able to glean significant intelligence from debriefing them. Maybe even getting geographically close to where the Resistance bases were.

It was a hard call to decide what to do with them. Killing them was mooted, and it was agreed that if it became necessary it would be an option. But these soldiers were not active Regime members, nor were they an active threat for betrayal. Their hearts were just not in fighting for the Resistance. In the end, it was decided to keep them prisoner at Victor Foxtrot, using them as a labor force for menial tasks, and see how the situation developed.

Chapter Fourteen

Jack had come to the conclusion that it was time to move the families out of Zulu. He felt that it was only a matter of time before one of the bases was discovered, and given the success of Resistance operations in the valley he felt that the Regime would only concentrate more force as time went on.

Things were different than he and Bill had originally conceived. They had planned on Zulu being a remote safe base up in the wooded ridges. Resistance operations were supposed to have spread out from initial beginnings in the Shenandoah Valley, further to the east, towards Manassas and as far as the I-95.

The opposite had happened. The valley had become a crucible of combat, with the Regime reacting to Resistance successes by reinforcing defeat in order to try and bring more combat power to bear on the Company.

This had the effect of containing much of the combat inside the valley, but it also meant that Zulu was vulnerable to any concerted push into the hills. Victor Foxtrot had originally been conceived as just a training base, but it had morphed into their forward operating base.

Jack considered that it was only the concealment measures and the discipline enforced in these bases that had prevented them from being picked up by Regime aerial surveillance up until now.

Following recent operations Jack managed to get a few days leave down at Zulu with his family. It was so wonderful to see them and to have a bit of time to spend with them. The summer months were pretty tough for them down in the gulch in which Zulu sat. However, they were doing well and the environment was a wonderland for the kids, even given the lack of television.

Food had got pretty tight at one point, as it had for all of them, but that had been alleviated by the resupply from the supply convoy. Caitlin was now working alongside Paul Granger running the administrative side of Zulu. Jack suspected that she was really running it. Jack was able to sit down with them and discuss the logistics of moving the base, putting the preparations in place.

Once back at Victor Foxtrot, Jack got things in motion. They had to move the forty miles to the new location over a mix of trails and roads. All the while operational security had to be paramount. The first thing Jack did was segregate a force of originals from the newly arrived soldiers. He selected the fire support platoon mainly because they had the vehicles. This would leave him his three maneuver platoons in place as well as the Company headquarters and ancillary elements. He still had one of the platoons down to the north of Zulu in the patrol base Zulu Delta.

When it came time to move the large group of families set out on foot in a strung out column. They moved on the trail to the south of Zulu with the full complement of gators and ATVs, loaded with supplies, equipment and some of the younger or infirm family members.

The able bodied carried their rucks and self-defense weapons. They were escorted by the defense contingent from Zulu; the platoon from the patrol base also conducted satellite security patrols ahead and to the flanks as they moved.

They had to move over five miles of trail before making it to an RV. This had been selected where a ravine provided cover close to a fire road that the fire support platoon could access with their vehicles. Here, they were split into groups and driven in the dump trucks and pickups to the new base. They were dropped at another concealed ravine site which had been secured in advance.

Once the civilian group had reassembled at the far RV, they walked the three miles in to the new site. A work party made several trips back to Zulu to strip out as much of the moveable and reusable equipment, including the camouflage netting. They then transferred it by road, including the gators and ATVs, to the new site.

Rudimentary construction had already happened when Jack originally sent the plant forward, and now they went into a further work phase to get the place inhabitable and concealed. The defense force again provided security at the new location, supplemented in security and work details by the fire support platoon.

Jack felt that because he was not currently conducting any concentration of force type deliberate operations, he could spare the fire support platoon. For the time being, the only assets he had back at the original locations were the platoon at the Zulu Delta patrol base, two platoons up at Victor Foxtrot, and the supplements from the defecting soldiers. He kept the new location secret from the new draft, at least for now, to keep a firewall up between any potential treachery and the families.

Equipment and supply transfer operations went on for a week, moving vehicles from the various laager locations and the excess food and fuel supplies. Jack intended that once it was complete, and the fire support platoon was freed up to return to Victor Foxtrot, he would be left with a light force freed up from logistical stores and family members. Thus, Zulu would no longer be a factor and Victor Foxtrot could easily be abandoned if compromised. The bulk of stores would be at the new location, which they had named Yankee.

For the duration of the move operation, Jack had pulled all patrols from the valley, so he had all his forces either at Yankee, at Victor Foxtrot, or at the Zulu Delta patrol base. He had also sent a coded message on the network to Bill, letting him know that operation 'Cold Hearth' was underway.

2nd Platoon was currently occupying the patrol base Zulu Delta down by the now abandoned Zulu. They had remained in place to provide protection and a patrol screen to the recently completed take down operations that had been going on, with Zulu now finally stripped of all they could take. Jack was going to pull them out over the next couple of days and consolidate at Victor Foxtrot.

Jack and Jim were up at Victor Foxtrot with the tactical headquarters and 1st and 3rd Platoons. They were doing some maintenance training that was also designed to integrate the new draft of soldiers into their ranks.

The guys from Cobb's 82nd Airborne platoon fitted in well, they were trained and experienced light infantry soldiers. In contrast, the convoy troops left a lot to be desired, and it was a steep learning curve for them. Some of them were moved out to supply roles and similar, to which their level of fitness and motivation suited them better. Only a few proved suitable for the teams, and they were integrated as battle casualty replacements where possible.

Cobb would have preferred to have kept his men together, but Jack agreed with Jim that this was not a good idea. Granted, the two groups had moved past the trust point by now, the turned Regime soldiers were too far into it to be forgiven by the Regime. However, it was partly to split them up for security reasons, but also to make sure they became integrated into the mindset and experience of the Company, rather than continue in a regular army mindset. Jack's fighters were after all Resistance fighters who could operate in small teams or alternatively concentrate up to Company level, as they had trained and demonstrated so well.

What Jack agreed to do as a compromise with Cobb was to let him keep each of the individual squads of the 82nd soldiers together. The three squads would be bolted-on to the three infantry platoons. This would mean that they would not follow the exact same model that the fighters had been trained in, and would not be able to operate as IED teams, but they would add value as infantry squads as an asset to each platoon. They could also be used as an organic fire support asset for each platoon, utilizing their support weapons training.

Val was in 3rd Platoon, and Jack put Cobb and his squad in with her. The two of them had developed a bond since their joint adventure and it seemed like a good idea to keep them together. The second squad went to Caleb's first platoon and the third one was allocated to 2nd Platoon but would wait up at Victor Foxtrot until they rotated out of Zulu Delta.

Duty at Zulu Delta was not exciting. It was good operational patrolling experience, and battle discipline had to be maintained. It was not a camping trip, despite whatever was happening up the valley in Zulu itself; it was a tactical operation.

The patrol base itself was defended by a routine of sentry duties, while squads or teams would push out one at a time to conduct patrolling and surveillance activity in the valley.

It could be interesting work. The woods were by no means empty, although it was not that frequent that they got hunters or survival groups this far into the hills. They got some though, but if they were out here they tended to be self-reliant hunter types.

Zulu, and now Zulu Delta, had always tried to be covert and avoid any attention from travelers or hunters passing through. It posed a dilemma. If a patrol came across anyone, they aimed to remain covert, observe, and report back to base.

Occasionally a hunting or survivor party had stumbled into Zulu before Zulu Delta was in place. It posed a problem, even now with the patrol base. What to do with them? So far there had not been any Regime foot patrols – the assumption was that aerial surveillance would be the method of choice - but there had been unaffiliated survivors.

It had never led to a firefight because the training of the patrols and sentry positions had so far led to the Resistance getting the drop on any approaching groups. On the rare occasions that they had encountered anyone and been compromised they had ended up detaining and questioning them. In those instances they had absorbed the survivors willingly into Zulu. It had seemed preferable to word getting out and the intercepted survivors had been happy to find food and shelter.

A day or so before 2nd Platoon were due to pull out back to Victor Foxtrot, a four man team was out on patrol two kilometers to the north of Zulu Delta. They were patrolling slowly northwards on the slope above the trail that led down to the south to Zulu. They were hand-railing the trail, some hundred meters upslope above it, occasionally stopping to observe the trail through the trees.

Mid-morning they moved into the cover of a slight depression in the slope, obscured by some undergrowth, and went into listening watch mode. They had moved just upslope of the small game trail they had actually been following.

They were in position for around fifteen minutes when a bird broke cover from the trees in noisy flight some hundred meters to the north. The team tensed and waited, observing.

A short while later some figures came into view on the game trail. They were moving slowly south, following the game trail in single file, apparently doing exactly what the team was doing but in reverse.

As they came closer, it was obvious that these were soldiers, but not line infantry. There were four of them and they appeared to be wearing some sort of highly effective non-standard camouflage clothing. They wore plate carrier chest rigs covered in magazine pouches, and they wore it easily in a professional manner that appeared to sit lightly on them. They had daypacks loaded with gear. Their helmets were without fabric covers and cut high, boom mikes extending forwards across their faces. They had Special Operations Forces written all over them.

As the team observed, the Regime team stopped and went to one knee. They made no sounds, accomplishing this with a quick hand signal. The point man was observing forwards, scanning the trees with an optic on his weapon. The rear man turned to kneel facing the rear. The center two faced outwards, opposite to each other.

The second man appeared to be the leader. He pulled what looked like a GPS out of a pouch and looked at it, then looked around him. Then he pulled some sort of monocular optic out of another pouch. He proceeded to look around, peering up the trail with one eye glued to the device. He then scanned slowly to the flanks, passing the optic towards and then over the position where the Resistance team lay.

As the enemy leader's gaze passed over the team, he barely appeared to pause. There was possibly a slight glitch, the Resistance team leader Billy thought, before he scanned on, obviously dismissing what he thought he may have seen. The enemy leader put the device away. He then quietly tapped his magazine with a finger, getting the attention of the point man who had otherwise not taken his gaze off his forward sector.

The enemy leader passed a quick hand signal to go back the way they had come. The patrol peeled back down the trail and headed slowly and deliberately away north back down the game trail. The rear man never looked back.

Billy was excited. This was some serious stuff. As soon as the Regime SOF team was out of sight Billy told his team they were going to follow them down the trail and see where they had come from, before reporting back to Zulu Delta. They would not send a real time radio report except after enemy contact, to maintain net security and avoid Regime direction finding, so the report would be verbal on return to base.

The team moved out onto the tail and proceeded to patrol north. Billy was on point and he kept catching glimpses of the enemy rear man through the trees, but again he never looked back.

After four hundred meters, Billy emerged round a bend in the trail and realized that he had lost sight of the enemy rear man. As he led his team down the trail, there was an area of thicker cover upslope to the right.

The Resistance patrol never saw it coming. The Regime SOF patrol had broken track ahead and peeled back into the cover above the trail into a hasty ambush. Billy had been trained in the technique by Jack, so he should have known better, but hindsight is a bitch.

The SOF patrol opened up with an ambush weight of fire into Billy's team at a range of ten meters. All of the team was hit instantly, but due to their body armor it was not fatal for two of them. They managed to return fire, and even went into a break contact drill and tried to peel back down the trail, but the enemy was too close, they were both wounded, and they were shot to the ground.

The Regime SOF team wanted to capture one of them, but the fighters fought so hard they had no opportunity but to finish them off with rapid fire. The Regime SOF team broke cover to clear their bodies and search them, before calling in the contact to higher.

The grizzled SOF team leader surveyed the bodies. Addressing his team, he simply said, "Good kill. Let's move out." *Aren't those handheld thermal imagers a bitch. Suckers.*

Back at Zulu Delta, they heard the sounds of the firefight echoing around the valley. Stand-to was called and the remaining two and a half squads stood ready in their two man foxholes with overhead protection and thermal screening. There was no 'troops in contact' call over the net from the patrolling team, but the gunfire came from the vicinity of where they had been due to be, so it did not bode well.

Concurrently to the SOF patrol's move up the valley a Reaper unmanned aerial vehicle, a UAV drone, was in the air above the valley. The drone was conducting surveillance and target acquisition in support of the SOF patrol mission to locate Resistance bases. There were in fact multiple patrols in the surrounding area that day but as soon as the contact happened, assets were directed to support it.

There was also an AC-130 Spectre gunship loitering on station to provide support to the SOF patrol mission as required. The gunship had been circling out to the east for a couple of hours to prevent its engine noise alerting anyone down below.

Unfortunately, just as stand-to was called and the platoon at Zulu Delta took up positions in their concealed foxholes, a buddy pair was attending to a call of nature at the latrine. One of them was taking a dump. The drone operator picked them up on his FLIR camera, but it was indistinct through the trees. He watched as they hurried to complete the business and move back to their foxhole, where they promptly disappeared.

As this was going on, the airborne reaction force for the operation was spun up at the order of Director Woods. The regional ARF hunter-killer company had been moved forward in their Chinooks to the Harrisonburg FOB for the duration of the operation. Director Woods had also asked for more troops, and had been allocated two more Ranger companies from the same battalion, both also now forward based and waiting at the Harrisonburg FOB.

Now that the drone operator was reporting a likely Resistance location following the hasty ambush, he was tasked to look for a landing zone (LZ) suitable for the Chinooks.

The AC-130 gunship moved into a 'pylon' racetrack pattern above the valley, always keeping the left side of the aircraft pointing towards the ground. The **40mm Bofors cannon and the 105mm M102 howitzer pointed out of the left side of the aircraft to provide a potentially massive weight of fire directed at a single point on the ground.**

As Captain Brooking's hunter-killer ARF Company flew south down the valley to the selected LZ one kilometer north of the suspected Resistance position at Zulu Delta, the AC-130 gunship opened fire at the location reported by the drone operator.

The cannon and howitzer mounted in the side of the aircraft rained explosives down into the area around Zulu Delta. Fortunately given that the positions had overhead protection in the form of a couple of feet of dirt, they could not be picked up on the thermal imagers mounted in either the drone or the gunship.

It was a shocking display of firepower, but it was ineffective. After a couple of minutes of this display and having failed to draw any Resistance fighters into the open, the gunship ceased fire and continued to run a racetrack pattern above the valley. They still considered the targeted location as the most likely site for a Resistance base; they were just frustrated in not being able to confirm it.

Meanwhile, the ARF descended in their Chinooks into the LZ in the clearing, ramps lowering and the platoons running off the back. There was an operational pause while the company oriented themselves and then they set off in formation through the woods. It was an advance to contact in a southerly direction, towards the site targeted by the AC-130.

The hunter-killer company moved in echelon, which meant that there was a lead platoon, followed by company tactical HQ with Captain Brookings, and then the other two platoons in column behind. The lead platoon had adapted its formation to one better suited to fighting in forests. The platoon leader had pushed two squads up front in an extended skirmish line, with the other squad providing the flank protection, a team to either side trailing back off the ends of the skirmish lines as they patrolled.

The hunter-killer company was a light infantry formation based off the Ranger Companies from before the collapse. Today, they had left their fire support elements behind, taking on a purely light infantry role with fire support provided by aerial assets. Given Jack's background as an Army Ranger, the way he had trained his fighters was very similar to the way this force was trained, without the insurgency aspect tacked on.

Jims Special Forces background was a larger part of where that insurgency side had come from, and Jacks fighters certainly had an 'X' factor of unconventional tactics to fall back on.

Up at Victor Foxtrot they had heard the distant small arms contact followed by the bombardment from the AC-130 gunship. There had been no communications from Zulu Delta either before or after, but that was to be expected.

On the one hand, it was obvious what was going on and they did not want to compromise locations or intentions by using radio communications. On the other hand, it would have been nice to have more of a situation report to react to.

Jack mobilized the two platoons and the Company elements that he had up at Victor Foxtrot. He prepared the two platoons to move rapidly to reinforce the platoon at Zulu Delta. The vehicles that he had remaining at the training base were ordered by road to the south, to the ERV that had been designated. It was to be the same one used on the trek out by the families in Zulu.

He had his communications and medical elements with the Company, including Megan. The ambulance vans were sent to the ERV. All their heavy packs were also sent with the vehicles.

This left the two platoons, Company tactical HQ and a small logistic/medical element on foot and dressed in light order, just their tactical vests and daypacks. They had as much ammunition as they could carry, plus water, some basic medical supplies and some high energy foods.

This was a compromise situation, so the training base was rapidly sanitized of anything useful to the Regime Intel people. As part of the contingency planning for this type of situation, Jack had created ERVs; emergency rendezvous. There were not too many, to reduce complications, but the idea was that if the force had to break up, they could head for the ERVs to reform.

In this case, there was the ERV to which the vehicles had been sent and another one where the vehicles had dropped those going to the new base at Yankee. Jack had kept the location of Yankee itself known only to a few. If the close ERV was compromised, then teams could move to the far ERV. The only problem was that it was thirty five miles further away as the crow flies over hilly ground.

Jack organized the order of march with 1st Platoon leading, followed by Company tactical HQ, then 3rd Platoon and the logistics tail. Jim was bringing up the rear and Jack made a snap decision to put the three 82nd airborne squads with him as a reserve force, with Cobb as the platoon leader. He felt he had not had enough time to fully bolt them onto the platoons as fourth squads at such a critical time.

They had over five miles to go to get to Zulu Delta. First, it was a short climb to the ridge, and then it was five miles of undulating ground contouring north up the valley, trending downwards to Zulu and then Zulu Delta.

Jack told Caleb to hustle, and the Resistance Company set of at a fast patrol pace towards the ridge.

Zulu Delta was situated a little over one hundred meters above the trail and on a relatively flat piece of ground on the valley side, suitable for the defensive triangular patrol base position with the ground sloping up to the ridge to the east.

The foxholes were very well concealed, and behind them the fighters had constructed low hooches of branches and ponchos. These were designed to be living shelters so that they did not have to live permanently in the actual foxholes. The idea was that they provided thermal and camouflage concealment, but that in a stand-to situation the fighters would move into the foxholes. The hooches were above ground and although well camouflaged were more visible than the foxholes.

It was summertime and the leaves were out in full on the trees, creating a full canopy. Viewed from the air it was certainly true that the impression of tree coverage was always sparser than that from the ground. Aerial views always emphasized gaps in the canopy. However, it was also true that the foliage, although not providing perfect concealment, did interfere with the observation capabilities of the Regime surveillance assets.

Both the Reaper and the AC-130 were using FLIR thermal imaging devices. In the areas where the crew and operators had gained most of their experience before the collapse, such as the Middle East, tree coverage was often not an issue. Open deserts worked very well for aerial assets. The forested slopes of the George Washington Forest and surrounding areas were a different matter.

People could certainly be picked up under the tree canopy, but tracking them was harder. It was a friction that degraded the effectiveness of the Regime aerial assets and thus reduced the quality of fire support available.

2nd Platoon was stood-to in their triangular harbor position. They had endured the initial bombardment from the AC-130 and knew that they were concealed from the FLIR by the several feet of earth that comprised the overhead cover on their foxholes. The fire from the AC-130 had been directed at their general area and it added to their impression that the position had not been fully revealed to the enemy.

1st Squad was on the side of the triangle that faced north up the valley. 2nd Squad faced west and overlooked the trail just over one hundred meters away and slightly below them. 3rd Squad was reduced to one team after the killing of Billy's team, and faced to the rear, oriented in a south easterly direction. Platoon headquarters was in two foxholes in the center.

The AC-130 came back over and made a couple of gun runs from its racetrack circuit, firing into likely areas and trying to get a response and positive target identification. Despite the fact that they were clearly compromised and should bug out, the platoon leader did not want to move while the AC-130 was overhead; it would be suicide if they were picked up moving through the tress. Possibly there would be some good cover back at the abandoned bunkers at Zulu, but getting there would be a problem.

2nd Squad was observing to the west and they identified the point platoon of the hunter-killer company moving across their front. They were moving in their skirmish line formation through the trees between the trail and Zulu Delta. It appeared that they were hand railing the trail. Their frontage was around one hundred meters, their right flank anchored on the trail, and the left flank protection elements were going to pass very close in front of 2nd Squad's foxholes.

The skirmish line was in enfilade to the 2nd Squad's foxholes, with the flank protection teams trailing back from the outside edges of the line, platoon headquarters central to the formation. A tactical bound behind that first platoon followed the Company tactical HQ, perhaps a little too close with an impatient company commander, and the rest of the formation was lost in the trees to the north.

The squad leader reported the situation to the platoon leader on the dug in landline field telephone. Owen Westbrook passed the order back: engage.

2nd Squad occupied four foxholes, each one dug in, concealed and protected with overhead cover. Each foxhole was ten to fifteen meters apart and the end foxholes contained the squad SAW gunners.

As the Regime point platoon line moved up central to 2nd Squad's foxholes, the squad leader opened fire, joined instantly by the rest of the squad. They generated enfilade fire that scythed along the line of the enemy skirmish formation.

The closest enemy, including the flank protection team, stood little chance. The Resistance fire poured into them at close range. Several of them were hit in the initial onslaught. The closest enemy that survived the initial fire took cover as best they could, pinned down.

The saving grace for the enemy was the close country and the large number of trees that provided both cover and concealment.

In response to the sudden noise and violence of the contact, the rounds whipping through the forest and impacting into trees, the Regime platoon went to ground.

Those not pinned down or lying dead or injured close to the Resistance foxholes located the source of the fire and began to return it, passing along the general location of the Resistance fighters. They had the general location, but the concealed bunkers were hard to spot and it was going to be hard for the Regime troops to fully locate and suppress the dug in fighters. Many rounds were wasted firing through the low hooches, thinking the Resistance fighters were in them.

After the initial fusillade the Resistance fighters began to conserve ammunition, watching and shooting, waiting for an enemy to reveal themselves. The enemy platoon had started to reposition itself, trying to get on line to orient its fire upslope, and they accomplished this by a mix of short dashes by individual soldiers or more safely by crawling up behind the trees. The shouts of squad and team leaders resonated in the trees along with the crackle of disjointed return fire.

The Regime platoon leader was assessing the situation, He realized that he was not in a position to assault the Resistance positions and relayed this in his contact report to the company tactical HQ. Captain Brookings told him to stay firm and establish a fire support position. He was preparing to assault with his second platoon left flanking, or from the north.

The Regime point platoon had started to consolidate into a rough line around fifty meters from 2nd Squad's positions, but it seemed an insurmountable distance through the trees. Rounds continued to crack back and forth between the two forces, with the Regime point platoon hunkering down in as best cover as they could find due to the accuracy of the incoming rounds from the Resistance fighters. They started to take more casualties, at a steady rate.

As the remainder of Jack's Company crested the ridge they heard the outbreak of gunfire, the furious staccato hammering of the firefight. Jack passed the word up the line: "Double time!" They had five miles to go on a steadily downwards trending incline, broken by slight uphill's as the trail passed through draws and over small spurs.

The Company was in light fighting order, which really wasn't light at all. They had their tactical vests, based either on body armor or plate carriers festooned with magazine pouches. They were not carrying their rucks, but their daypacks were loaded with ammunition, water, medical supplies and some rations. They carried around seventy pounds each, varying on each individual's load and weapon system.

They were strung out along the trail in single file, a company snake. As the order to double time was received, none of the fighters had any doubt as to the urgency. They started to shuffle run down the trail. On the flats and the downhill's they shuffled and jogged, on the uphill they leaned into it and drove themselves up the slope.

Those that started to drop back were passed. There were not many of them, some simply due to previous wounds sustained. Megan was at the rear with a small medical team for anyone that needed medical help, along with Jim who was kicking butts as required. The key was to get the majority of the Company's combat power down the trail to rapidly reinforce 2nd Platoon. The others could catch up as they arrived.

As the Reaper drone circuited the area looking for targets, it picked up the activity at Victor Foxtrot. The Company was at that time cresting the ridge to head down to Zulu Delta, but a handful of the logistics guys were trying to rapidly load the last vehicles and bug out. The feed was relayed to the controlling RTOC video screens at the fusion center. Watching the video screens, Director Woods felt a surge of excitement and gave the order to engage.

As the last three vehicles took off down the driveway they were hit by AGM-114 Hellfire missiles fired from the Reaper, destroying the vehicles in flaming explosions. Shortly after, the two 500lb GBU-38 Joint Direct Attack Munitions (JDAMs) carried by the Reaper were dropped, impacting into the farmhouse and barn and disintegrating them in massive explosions.

The blast freed the eight incarcerated defectors who had been locked in an outbuilding. The door was blown off and they came staggering out into the open. The Reaper picked them up and fired another two hellfire missiles, killing them instantly, the bloom of the explosion filling the operators TV screen.

Video games.

The damage was surveyed on the video at the RTOC, the Reaper circling overhead. Two and two were put together and at the advice of the senior Ranger liaison in the RTOC Director Woods ordered a second hunter killer company from the assigned Ranger Battalion to be dispatched in Chinooks to clear and secure the terrorist base.

Meanwhile, a third company was loaded onto Chinooks and sent to the LZ in the valley where the original hunter-killer company had landed, in order to reinforce the troops in contact.

At Zulu Delta the firefight still raged between the 2nd Squad and the enemy point platoon, consolidated in a linear position fifty meters downslope, sheltering behind trees.

The nature of the fight in the woods, close and personal, meant that indirect fire, or aerial barrage, was not an option. To hit Zulu Delta with such fires, the hunter-killer company would have to break contact and withdraw to a suitable distance, not easy under such circumstances.

The Regime hunter-killer company commander, Captain Brookings, had organized a flanking assault utilizing his second platoon. They pushed upslope and pushed down towards Zulu Delta from the north, effectively a left flanking assault from the enemy point of view, coming in at right angles to their point platoon downslope to the west.

The Regime assaulting platoon also adopted a skirmish line with flank protection. It was the best formation for fighting in the woods. They knew that contact was imminent so they came forward by bounding over-watch, working in pairs along the length of the line, in short rushes from tree to tree.

As they reached fifty meters from the front of 1st Squad's line of foxholes, which remained unseen by the Regime troops, the fighters opened fire. The enemy immediately went to ground in their ragged skirmish line formation and a firefight developed between the two sides. Again the foxholes were hard to spot and the advantage remained with the defenders.

The Regime hunter-killer company was breaking like waves on the rock of the Resistance triangular defensive position. The flanking attack was bogged down, and casualties were screaming in the trees. Calls for medic were shouted along the line.

Captain Brookings pushed up towards the fighting in the center, his third platoon waiting in reserve. He had to be careful about deploying the third platoon to flank further round to the east of the Resistance position, because at some point they would end up opposite his point platoon to the west, with the Resistance position in between, and thus they would be in each other's sectors of fire.

He decided to keep his third platoon in reserve for now, pushing them upslope to the north east a ways, but keeping them back from the action. Meanwhile, a stalemate developed at Zulu Delta. The enemy was taking steady casualties, but the fighters had to conserve ammunition. The fighters could not withdraw, but the enemy was unable to press the assault.

Chapter Fifteen

I t took the Company fifty minutes to make the five miles down the trail. 1st Platoon emerged on the edge of the old Zulu ravine, breathing hard with sweat pouring off them. Caleb pushed them across the draw into a position lining the far side.

Jack joined him with his tactical HQ. 3rd Platoon pulled rear security while Alex Lambert joined the group. Three hundred meters ahead they could hear the firefight, the noise ebbing and flowing with the action.

Jack assessed the situation, listening and reading the battle as best as he could. Unfortunately, they had pulled out the landline communication between Zulu and Zulu Delta so they could not communicate with 2nd Platoon securely. Jack did not want to compromise his intent by asking for a situation report over the insecure net.

Jack gave his platoon leaders quick battle orders, giving them an opportunity to question and clarify. Once they were happy, he sent them back to their platoons. He then got on the net and briefly sent to Owen: "Got your back." He got a double click response. This allowed Owen to pass out the news to his men to be on the lookout for friendlies from the south, thus reducing the chances of fratricide.

As the platoon leaders organized their platoons, Jim established a casualty collection point in the Zulu gully, using the three squads from the 82nd to provide security for Megan's team.

Caleb's 1st Platoon formed into a skirmish line with flank protection, anchoring the line on the trail to the left. They eerily mirrored the formation the enemy point platoon had adopted as they had moved south down the valley. Caleb mirrored them as he prepared to move north, aiming his axis to the left of the patrol base. It was to be expected, they had all learned their light infantry tactics in the same schools.

Alex's 3rd Platoon formed up on the right. Their intended line of advance was upslope of Zulu Delta, to take them to the east, uphill and on an axis to the right of the patrol base. Alex adopted a different formation, a platoon column. He had his point squad moving in a skirmish line, followed by his tactical HQ and then the other two squads in a travelling over-watch echelon column behind.

Caleb's platoon started to move forward; as they got to within two hundred meters of Zulu Delta they broke into bounding over-watch in pairs. This meant that along the frontage of the skirmish line, each buddy pair moved together, while keeping the integrity of the line as a whole.

Alex's platoon also started to move forward on the right. As they closed with the sound of the firing his point squad also began moving by bounding over-watch, in short rushes from tree to tree, the rest of his command following behind.

At Zulu Delta, the enemy was starting to get a stranglehold on the defensive position. It was not easy for them, and they were being held at bay by the accurate fire from the concealed foxholes. However, as the firefight continued the hunter-killer platoons started to get a better target identification on where the bunkers were.

Captain Brookings was too far forward for best command and control, but he was an honorable and brave man and his men were in harm's way and he wanted to lead by example. Just then, his tactical HQ group were being suppressed by fire from a Resistance bunker and the radio operator lying next to him passed over the handset.

"Sir, it's call sign Overlord. He's demanding to speak to you no.!"

"Overlord? What the hell?" said Captain Brookings as he took the handset. "This is Falcon Alpha, send over."

Director Woods screamed into the radio microphone back in the RTOC, "What the fuck Brookings, what's taking you so long?!"

"Sir, we have dug in enemy, heavy resistance, we are pinned down."

"Brookings, I don't give a fuck. You are a coward. Get onto that position and kill those redneck hick fucks. Think about the welfare of your family Brookings. Get moving!"

"Roger that sir. Out."

Captain Brookings passed the handset back, the radio operator looking at him wide-eyed, seeing the shock on his face.

"Right, let's get some momentum going," said Captain Brookings, his face red with anger, "we need to press this attack." He grabbed the handset for the platoon net and started to give orders.

The hunter-killer company started to hit Zulu Delta with 40mm grenades from their under-slung M203 grenade launchers, carried by two men in every squad. They were only effective against the foxholes if they got them in through the bunker firing ports, which they were unable to do when faced with the effective fire from the Resistance fighters.

Then, they brought up some SMAW-D bunker busting rockets. These were the equivalent of the AT-4 anti-tank rocked, one shot throwaway weapons designed in this case to destroy enemy bunkers and hard targets.

A team moved forward towards 1st Squad's line of foxholes, given covering fire by the enemy platoon that had faltered in the assault and was static in the trees. The

SMAW-D team crawled up to the line and was given directions on the location of one of the identified bunkers.

The first soldier knelt up with the SMAW-D launcher on his shoulder and was immediately thrown back, shot in the chest above his plate. His team leader dragged him into the cover of a tree, picked up the launcher and took aim around the tree trunk. The rocket fired with a concussive thump and went streaking towards the bunker, whipping over the top and detonating beyond Zulu Delta in the trees.

The response from Zulu Delta was immediate, as they went to rapid fire and began to suppress the area where the rocket had been fired from, dust still floating in the air from the launch. The Ranger team leader was a brave man, and he pulled another rocket towards him and readied it behind the tree. He swung out, acquired the target, and fired.

The rocket impacted the farthest east foxhole on 1st Squad's line, killing the two occupants instantly. There was a ragged outburst of cheering from the Regime firing line as the remaining foxholes reacted with furious rapid fire. The tide was beginning to turn. Slowly, but it was turning all the same.

1st Platoon was moving north in their skirmish line through the trees. They were approaching Zulu Delta, it was up on their right. Suddenly, the near end of the enemy point platoon's line came into view. The enemy was firing off to the right at Zulu Delta but they had a couple of guys facing south pulling flank security.

There was an outbreak of firing as both sides collided, Caleb's skirmish line running for cover. Caleb himself was just behind the line and he urged his men onwards. They were facing the end of the strung out firing line of the enemy point platoon, and they continued to fire and move in their pair's forwards towards the enemy.

For the Regime troops, this new development was highly disturbing. They had been flanked by an unknown force and were in serious danger of being rolled up from their right. Their right flank started to fold and they began to pull back to the north, Caleb's advance supported by fire from the Zulu Delta foxholes upslope as he swept forwards.

Caleb pushed his platoon forwards until his right flank anchored on the southern foxhole of 2nd Platoon. His left flank was anchored on the trail and he ensured that he placed a team there facing west over the trail in order to provide flank security. This gave him an elongated 'L' shape orientated east-west, facing north.

The enemy point platoon was pulling back to the north by pair's fire and movement, continually under fire from the foxholes in Zulu Delta as they moved. They were almost combat ineffective due to the accumulation of casualties. Those that were wounded but not immobilized were crawling and dragging themselves out, while others were dragged out by their buddies.

Meanwhile, on the right flank Alex's platoon pushed northwards along the slope. They passed in front of Zulu Delta about one hundred meters to the east of the patrol base. Shortly after, the lead squad bumped into the flank of the hunter -killer platoon's firing line. Again, there was a furious exchange of fire.

As this happened, Jack had been following 3rd platoon with his tactical HQ. He peeled out from the back of the platoon column and moved into the back of Zulu Delta. With the other three in his tactical HQ team he bounded forwards and they got into the spare foxholes on the rear south east side, where the team there occupied only two of the holes.

As Alex's point squad went to ground and began engaging the enemy, supported by fire from Zulu Delta to the west, Alex pushed up to where he could observe the action. He called his two rear squad leaders forward and issued quick battle orders.

His second squad pushed around to the right, right flanking, in a squad wedge formation, followed by Alex. Behind him followed his third squad in echelon.

The second squad pushed through the trees and then turned west in their wedge. They hit the east end of the enemy firing line. Again this enemy platoon was faced with being rolled up. They began to withdraw, facing the fire from the squad to the east and the combination of Alex's first squad and the remaining three north facing foxholes from 2nd Platoon.

As the enemy began to bound back through the trees, Alex pushed his third squad up beyond his second squad to keep the pressure on the Regime forces.

Jack was observing what he could see of the battle through his optic, scanning along the trees. He was looking towards the center of the enemy line when he saw through the trees one of the Regime commanders up on one knee, frantically shouting and giving orders in the face of the flanking assaults by Jack's force, his radio operator beside him.

Jack focused in through his ACOG, looking to take the shot and take the man down. As he did so, the target looked in his direction. It was impossible for him to see Jack, but the man's eyes appeared to look right at him. Suddenly, recognition flashed.

Aaron. Shit.

Jack stared down the scope, finger on the trigger.

He couldn't take the shot.

There was suddenly a flurry of activity from the enemy as they began to withdraw, and just like that Aaron was gone into the trees. The opportunity was lost. Jack was stunned. The enemy had always been nameless, faceless shapes on the battlefield. Aaron had been his friend, and now they were enemies locked in combat.

As the enemy platoons withdrew, Jack got the situation reports on his radio. He ordered Caleb to stay in place with his platoon, while Alex's platoon were to consolidate in place in a triangular defensive position some one hundred yards from Zulu Delta, upslope to the north east.

This gave the effect of two triangular defensive positions, Zulu Delta with its foxholes, with 3rd Platoon one hundred meters north east in their own position. Caleb's platoon was in a line from the bottom south west corner of Zulu Delta, strung out to the trail to the west.

As soon as they confirmed their positions, Jack gave the order to dig in and put up the thermal ponchos. Furiously. They took their entrenching tools out and started to dig in buddy pairs, one man covering while the other knelt and furiously carved out a shell scrape from the forest floor. Anything that lowered their profile below ground level would protect them from incoming rounds and high explosives.

Casualties had been light on the Resistance side, but Jim was up and cutting about the positions with a working party, collecting casualties and the bodies from the blown foxhole.

The story among the Regime soldiers was a little different. There was a tideline of a couple of dozen bodies surrounding Zulu Delta, where the Regime troops had crouched in the woods behind trees trying to gain fire superiority, before being rolled up from the flanks and having to withdraw.

Captain Brookings was not a happy man. His two platoons were forced back in disarray, on the verge of combat ineffective due to the losses sustained. He ordered a withdrawal three hundred meters north and formed a defensive position. He then called for air support.

The AC-130 was still on station and it requested that the hunter-killer Company pop smoke to identify their location in the trees. They did so, and also relayed the coordinates of Zulu Delta to the gunship.

The AC-130 was finding it hard to pick up the exact position of the Resistance fighters below the canopy. It identified Captain Brookings's new defensive position. The bodies lying around Zulu Delta were still warm, some wounded and some even trying to crawl away. This confused the picture, which was further confused by the fact that the AC-130 could not see the foxholes and the other two Resistance platoons were now under thermal ponchos beneath the leaf canopy.

The AC-130 relayed a request to the RTOC for confirmation of fire coordinates. Director Woods was watching the live feeds on the monitors. The thing was, he hated the military; they had always been the bad guys to him, spreading oppression and death around the world, killing Muslims. He had been enjoying the spectacle of the redneck terrorists and the Rangers fighting it out and killing each other in the forest.

Director Woods knew that the Resistance base was down there, and he did not care that some of the warm bodies on the monitor from the Ranger Company may still be alive.

He gave the order, "Weapons free, engage it."

Lieutenant Jefferson was over by the map board, watching all of this.

"Sir, those are most likely friendly forces, some of them are our wounded!"

Woods turned on him, "Get the fuck out of my RTOC now, you traitorous piece of shit!"

Lieutenant Jefferson was about to start towards him, military discipline forgotten, when he was intercepted by two of the Director's security team who were stationed in the RTOC and hustled out of the room. Woods smiled as he was pushed out of the door.

Director Woods announced to the RTOC, "Those heat signatures are confirmed Resistance, that is the enemy position, engage it now."

He turned to the senior Ranger Liaison, "Jefferson, he's fired, I don't want to see him back here, see that he is sent for reeducation." He turned back to the monitors.

The AC-130 pounded the area around Zulu Delta with its 40mm Bofors cannon and 105mm howitzer. What the aircraft could pick up through the gaps in the tree canopy was mainly the bodies of the dead and wounded Regime soldiers, some of them still alive and trying to crawl away, having been left in the hasty withdrawal.

After a ten minute bombardment of the area the AC-130 called to return to base for re-arming and refueling, both of which were now depleted by the long mission.

Back in his defensive position, Captain Brookings linked up with the second company commander, who had brought his command in from the LZ to the north. They huddled together to work out a plan of attack. As they did so, the obligatory call came in from Director Woods on the satellite phone.

If it had not been plain before, it was plain now. The Resistance would be crushed today, or Captain Brookings's family was going to the camps.

As the bombardment from the AC-130 had raged around them, Jack's 1st and 3rd Platoons had huddled in their shallow scrapes, as much as they could have dug before the bombardment started, while the high explosives and shrapnel shrieked through the trees.

On the ground around Zulu Delta, it was carnage. The Regime soldier's bodies, both the dead and those that had only been wounded, had been blown apart, shredded and scattered through the trees, body parts and intestines thrown around and hanging from branches. It was a horror show.

As soon as the engine noise of the aircraft receded, the fighters were up on their knees frantically digging their scrapes deeper.

A few of the fighters had been wounded to various degrees and Jim was having them brought into Zulu Delta before moving them back to the collection and treatment point back at Zulu. He was also organizing redistribution of ammunition to resupply those squads who were low.

Fortunately, Jim had the foresight to plan ahead and Zulu Delta itself had a dug in ammo cache and the foxholes themselves had been stocked with extra ammo that simply remained there as platoons rotated through, so the Company was able to replenish their reserves.

Thirty minutes later, they came under mortar bombardment from the LZ to the north, where the Regime had flown in fire support elements as well as the additional hunter-killer company.

It was now mid-afternoon.

Jack had been in the process of making arrangements to withdraw to the south when the new bombarment began, forcing them to hunker down in the scrapes and foxholes.

Getting mortared in the woods had its pros and cons. On the one hand, the trees soaked up some of the flying shrapnel. On the other, sometimes the mortar bombs would burst in the trees, instead of in proximity to the ground, which effectively created an airburst and would send shrapnel and wood splinters down onto those in the open below.

Mortars are an area weapon and they were hard to target in the woods without direct observation. It appeared that the enemy was stonking the general area and the exploding shells were largely ineffective against the sheltering fighters. The bombardment did have the effect of fixing the Resistance force in place.

Fifteen minutes later, the bombardment ceased. It was 'danger close' for the assaulting hunter-killer companies. The fresh company came in from the north in a platoon column formation, the lead platoon colliding with

3rd Platoons triangular defensive position up to the north east.

Captain Brookings had reorganized his command into two platoons and came in from the low ground to the west. He had put the previous reserve platoon in the lead, with the mauled combined platoon in echelon behind.

Both companies hit together, working at right angles to one another, one from the north and one from the west. As the western force bumped into Caleb's flank protection from across the trail, he called his right hand squad down. They were the one that abutted on the right side with Zulu Delta, and they peeled out and moved down to reinforce the left flank. He then moved another team to cover the south, effectively his new left flank, from enemy flanking movements hooking round to his left/rear.

In both the north and west, the contact between the two forces went as before, with the Regime troops going to ground and ending up in a firebase around fifty meters away. The difference this time was the pressure and the volume of fire directed at the Resistance fighters. The two direction simultaneous assault was also psychologically difficult to deal with, and the expectation was that now that the two sides had reestablished contact, the Regime forces would now try and flank.

Before the enemy was able to bring too much weight to bear on his forces, Jack ordered 3rd Platoon to withdraw to the south, back the way they had come. He wanted them to move back in-line with Zulu Delta.

As the Regime advance broke itself on his triangular position, Alex ordered his squads to begin to withdraw. He pushed his rear squad back out of the way and moved his two front squads in tandem, fighting back in buddy pairs within their teams. He managed to gain some breathing space from the enemy as he moved back through the trees, getting back online with Zulu Delta, his third squad covering to the east to prevent a flanking assault from upslope.

The sudden withdrawal just after contact had been made had prevented the enemy building too much pressure and had the effect of skipping out from under the hammer blow before it could fall.

As his point platoon made contact with Caleb's flank protection, Captain Brookings pushed forwards, shouting for his men to advance. They were pinned down, and the fire increased as Caleb brought his squad down to reinforce his flank.

Captain Brookings was getting desperate, he was under so much pressure from Director Woods and he feared for his family. He could not force the issue; his men simply could not move further forwards under the withering accurate fire from the Resistance fighters.

Captain Brookings took his tactical HQ group and moved round to his right, trying to flank the Resistance line. He pushed forwards, showing reckless bravery, trying to skirmish forwards on his right flank, desperate to flank and break the Resistance line.

McCarthy was in a fire position towards the left of Caleb's flank protection line. He saw the rush of Regime soldiers bounding forwards through the trees, trying to keep up with their commander. The officer was a brave man; he came on firing his weapon as he skirmished through the trees.

McCarthy lined him up in his sights and pulled the trigger, aiming for his belly below his body armor plate. He took the shot, it slammed into Captain Brookings. The round took him in the abdomen, rupturing his aorta and severing his lower spine, sending him crashing to the ground to lay in no-man's land between the two forces, bleeding out internally into his abdominal cavity.

As he lay there with the life draining out of him, Captain Brookings' last thoughts were of his wife and two children, and Director Woods's promise to send them to the FEMA Camps.

Once 3rd Platoon were accounted for and shaken out Jack then ordered 2nd and 3rd Platoons to move back together with a two squad frontage per platoon. The third squad from each platoon would move south ahead of the withdrawal and act as the reserve for their platoons.

Jack told Caleb to begin peeling his platoon southward. Caleb began to do so, peeling one squad at a time back behind the others along the east side of the trail. His force was now oriented westwards, firing over the trail and peeling south, which provided the whole company flank protection from the Regime company assaulting from the west.

Jack began to coordinate the whole show moving back to Zulu. The four squad frontage from the combination of 2nd and 3rd Platoon moved back to the south, oriented north, with 1st Platoon hanging off the left end and covering the flank to the west.

They managed to break contact with the enemy. The jaws of the two pronged attack slammed shut too late, they had avoided its clutches.

Arriving at Zulu, Jim had the casualty collection point packed up and Cobb had his squads covering north along the rim of the ravine. Jack moved his platoons into Zulu into a defensive position before rapidly giving orders for a withdrawal to the south down the valley towards the ERV.

Jack grabbed Cobb and asked if he was ok to use his squads to help carry the casualties, of which there were five who were on improvised stretchers unable to walk. Cobb was ok with it and started to organize his men into teams to carry the stretchers. 1st Platoon took over their security duties.

Jack gathered his commanders and rapidly outlined the plan. It was a move south in a company snake to the ERV. There was no more time to get any more complicated than that. The order of march was 2nd Platoon, tactical HQ, 3rd Platoon, the medical section with Jim and his logistics section, the 82nd platoon with the casualties and the rear guard provided by 1st Platoon.

Jack was moving everyone with a sense of urgency and just as 2nd Platoon started to head out of the ravine on the trail south the Regime forces appeared again in the woods to the north and were engaged by 1st Platoon.

1st Platoon suppressed the lead elements of the Regime force while the rest of the company started moving south along the trail as rapidly as possible. The casualties slowed them down.

Once the Company was clear, 1st Platoon broke contact again and moved south along the trail.

It was now evening time, still light because of the summer. They had been moving for about an hour. There had been no further contact, the two Regime companies somewhere further to the north.

What they did not know was that following the assault on to Victor Foxtrot, with the third Regime company finding it deserted, that company had been ordered to push west over the ridge and down into the valley. They had been tasked with ambushing the Resistance egress route as it went southwards from where the battle was being fought to the north.

As the valley went south it narrowed, gained in height and became more rocky and upland in nature. The Regime Company had pushed down into the valley and found the trail. On the slope just east of the trail was a linear rocky outcrop, back in the trees about fifty meters from the trail.

The outcrop formed a small cliff like feature, only about eight feet high that overlooked the trail down below. At this point the trail ran beside a rocky creek, just to the west of the trail.

The Regime company had placed a hasty L-shaped ambush on the outcrop. Two platoons formed the kill group, lined up along the top of the outcrop, just back far enough to be in the cover of the trees and vegetation. The third platoon formed the blocking bottom arm of the 'L', across the trail to the south and facing the Resistance fighters as they walked south.

Unfortunately for Jack's Company, they were withdrawing in haste and using the trail. They also had not taken the precaution of putting out flankers along their line of march. They were bugging out as rapidly as they could.

As 2nd Platoon reached the far limit of the killing area, just before they hit the blocking force, all of 2nd platoon, tactical HQ and half of 3rd Platoon were in the kill zone.

Suddenly the quiet evening was torn apart by a massive weight of fire pouring into the kill zone. The elements in the ambush itself were overwhelmed by the Regime forces fire and immediately sought cover by the side of the trail and in the creek itself.

The point squad of 2nd Platoon found themselves facing a cross-fire from ahead and to the left and had to orientate themselves to try and fight back. Some in the kill zone were hit, but it was hard to tell the numbers of casualties because everyone was instantly in cover after the initial bursts, now pinned down by the weight of fire.

The saving grace was that it had been a hasty ambush with small arms fire only, no claymores. The use of automatic fire to initiate the ambush also meant that much of the fire had been inaccurate, terrifying yes, but much of it passing over the heads of the Resistance fighters down in the defile.

Trying to recover from the initial shock of the ambush those in the kill zone tried to rally to return fire as best they could, but many remained pinned by the weight of fire now striking all around them.

Jack had dived into cover behind some rocks at the stream edge and he now grabbed the radio and called out the direction of the ambush. Enemy fire was cracking overhead, smacking and zinging off the rocks, with ricochets occasionally whining and buzzing away.

The two platoons inside the kill zone were pinned down and it was essential to extract them from the ambush.

Val was leading her squad and found herself just on the edge of the kill zone as the ambush was sprung. Her squad hit the ground, the rest of her platoon ahead were in the kill zone and pinned down. She saw the SAW gunner ahead of her hit and killed and she crawled up and grabbed the machine-gun from him.

Val heard Jack come over the net giving the ambush direction. She looked up and identified the enemy fire coming from on top of the linear outcrop to the left of the trail. She could also see that where she was the outcrop faded out into the slope of the valley side, where the end of the enemy firing line was located. She looked back and saw Jim behind her squad, taking cover with the medical section, and back behind that was the 82nd platoon, dragging the casualties they were carrying into cover.

Val shouted, "Ambush left, left flanking! Let's go!" and spurred herself into action. She stood, carrying the SAW and shouted to her squad, "Follow me!"

Val rushed forwards, her squad fanning out on either side of her. She stopped to brace herself and fire the SAW, using it like an oversized M16. She was trying to hit the ambush from the flank.

Jim instantly grasped the situation. He shouted to Megan to stay down and rushed after Val's squad. He looked back down the trail to see the three squads from the 82nd platoon running up the trail towards him. Jim waved them on and kept running.

Val's angle of assault was just too acute to the ambush. The rush of her squad was seen by the gunners on the end of the Regime line and they switched fire towards the skirmish line as it came towards them. Val's squad didn't stop, they didn't fire and move, they simply ran at the enemy firing, in their desperation to get to grips with them and rescue those in the kill zone.

One of her men was hit, then another, both going down. Val had the SAW firing from her hip in short bursts as she ran forwards, her squad fanning out on either side. Then, she was hit in the plate and knocked down.

The charge faltered and the man next to her ran to her aid. She rolled to her knees, got up and charged forwards into the enemy fire, hammering at them with the SAW, and then her head snapped back as a round smacked into her helmet, her blonde ponytail whipping around as she crashed to the ground. Jim came running through the middle of the squad.

"Let's go!" he screamed as he charged the end of the Regime line. The remainder of Val's squad let out a shout of fury and followed Jim as he charged at the enemy, screaming as they came on.

Something changed psychologically at that moment. The Regime gunners on the end of the line felt it. They panicked in the face of the onrushing screaming Resistance fighters, filthy in their mismatched gear, unkempt 'mountain men' beards and hair. The enemy on the end of the line broke as Val's squad clawed their way up the end of the outcrop and onto the position.

It went hand to hand.

Jim expended his magazine, drew his handgun and laid about him with it until he emptied the magazine on that also. He ended up rolling on the ground with a big 240 gunner, smashing his head in with a rock snatched up from the ground.

Then, in a rush, Cobb and his three squads poured in, hitting the Regime ambush line from the north and starting to roll them up. They pushed past Jim and the remainder of Val's squad and started to fight down the line. The enemy was breaking and pulling back.

Jim, on his knees, looked back to where Val had fallen. Megan was there, out in the open.

Don't you ever listen?

Megan was treating Val, who appeared to have been concussed but was still alive. Jim shook his head.

Bloody heroine, saved us, broke the enemy.

Back in the ambush kill zone Jack felt the pressure lift. The fire slackened. He stood, calling "Fight through, Fight through! Move it, let's go!" and advanced towards the ambush, firing. Around him a visceral yell went up and the fighters began to fight forwards in bounds, then simply charging the enemy ambush line.

All along the line the will of the Regime forces broke and they started to fall back in the face of the assault, the rebel yell rising along the line of Resistance fighters. The Resistance Company had seized the moral component of the fight.

The charging fighters reached the linear outcrop and scrambled up it, chasing the enemy back. The Regime NCOs were trying furiously to get control back over their troops and have them fight back towards the ridge and a rally point. Some of them succeeded and groups started to coalesce and fight back to safety.

Jack got hold of Caleb on the radio and told him to make sure he had security covered back down the trail to the north, in case the enemy companies arrived from that direction. With that thought in mind, Jack called a halt and had the platoons withdraw back to the ambush site.

The charge took some stopping, the shouts going up and down the line to pull back to the trail, some of the hotter heads taking a little longer to get the message.

The medical section had already been moving around the kill zone treating the casualties they could find. Jim was cutting about organizing again and they loaded the additional casualties onto ponchos and set off again for the ERV.

Val was walking, propped up on the shoulders of two of her squad members. She had a possible broken rib from the plate strike and a bloody crease down her temple where a round had passed through her helmet, clipped her head, and passed on. She was concussed and groggy but insisted on walking.

An hour later they reached the ERV without incident. Jack was very aware of being compromised and hit in the ERV so he acted with a sense of urgency.

Between the ambulance vans and the other vehicles there was enough transport to move the various wounded, including the walking wounded and the medical and logistics teams. Jim organized them quickly into small packets, loaded the vehicles and sent them away to the secondary ERV via different routes.

Jack then gathered the remainder, made sure they had the grid coordinates for the secondary ERV thirty five miles away, and told them to split down into four man teams and exfiltrate. They would meet at the secondary ERV to reconsolidate the company and rest up.

He stressed the need for stealth, using unobvious routes, and the use of the thermal ponchos. He split the Company into the basic components of four man teams and they then bomb-burst out into the woods.

The Company was gone, fading like ghosts into the trees.

Back in the Fusion Center RTOC, Director Woods was frustrated. The terrorists had just disappeared. The Reaper drone had picked up two pickup trucks racing away down a forest trail, and they had seen on the cameras the wounded laying in the back of the trucks, medics leaning over them.

Director Woods had given the order to engage and the two trucks had been destroyed by hellfire missiles, the explosions blooming across his TV monitor. The drone had then picked up a small group of terrorists moving through the trees, but the men below must have heard the drone overhead because they just simply disappeared from sight, including from the FLIR TI feed.

Woods had a date that night back at his compound with a hooker and a few lines of cocaine. All in all, it had not been a bad day. Although they had failed to annihilate the terrorist fighters, he had been able to orchestrate much death to two groups that he had a deep seated hatred for: the hick terrorists and the Army Rangers.

Ultimately, they were all cut from the same cloth, white supremacist redneck Special Operations Forces veteran types, whichever side they were on. Once the Rangers had outlived their usefulness, they would be 'disappeared' into the reeducation camps as the revolution progressed and the Homeland Corps was ramped up to take over domestic military duties.

Director Woods's security team was made up of 'Black Panther' members who had remained loyal to him since his Chicago voter intimidation days. Two of them were with him in the RTOC, dressed in the blue fatigue uniform of the Homeland Corps 'blue shirts' with tactical vests and M4 rifles slung from their fronts.

As Director Woods left the RTOC for the day, he headed down the corridor flanked by his two security guards, on his way to the elevator to the parking garage, where the rest of his detail awaited with the armored vehicles.

Suddenly, around the corner ahead of him stepped Lieutenant Jefferson, M4 rifle raised at the ready position. In a rapid succession of shots, the two security guards were gunned down, Jefferson advancing down the corridor to finish them with a shot to each of their heads. Director Woods stood between the two bodies, frozen and stunned.

Woods snapped out of it, "What the hell is this?! Stand down!"

Jefferson advanced towards him, rifle held in the ready position. Woods put his hands up defensively, but Jefferson jabbed the rifle muzzle into his mouth, smashing Woods's front teeth. He followed up with a muzzle swipe to Woods's temple, knocking him back against the wall, blood smeared across this forehead and running from his smashed mouth.

Woods's defiant confidence evaporated, leaving just the cowering bully that he was. Leant against the wall, he held up a hand imploringly.

"Jefferson, wait, wait. You are one of us, you're a brother. You're a black man; you have to be on my side. We can take care of you. I was wrong about you," said Woods, his tone wheedling.

"No Sir, I'm not like you, I'm an American. I'm a U.S. Army Ranger. My color is the color of my uniform. You, Sir, are a traitor, a coward and a disgrace. Your racism sickens me."

Lieutenant Jefferson shot Director Woods twice in the chest, knocking him back against the wall. He shot him again through the forehead and Woods slumped to the ground, leaving a red stain across the wall as he slid down it.

Suddenly, two military police came round the corner, handguns drawn. Jefferson swung his weapon around, firing rapidly as the two MP's ducked back round the corner into cover.

Then, he ran, desperate to get out of the building.

Chapter Sixteen

J ack drove his team hard. He had to get to the RV to be
there to account for and organize his people. He took a
direct route to the ERV, cross graining the generally
north-south running terrain features and ridges as he
moved west. They only paused for brief water rests and a
couple of times for a little longer to eat what rations they
had.

Jack could feel the exhaustion in him as he walked.
His legs no longer had spring; he felt the leaden weight of
them as he was walking uphill, the exhaustion embedded
deeply in them.

As they continued to walk, they had to constantly
snack on high energy foods. They were not hanging
around, they were moving fast, and their blood sugar was
always on the edge. A couple of times Jack felt his vision
narrow and dim, and he had to eat something to get his
blood sugar up. Hypoglycemia was the danger, and as soon

as the sugar hit his bloodstream he felt himself come alive again.

Jack was amazed by Ned. He was older than Jack, but his endurance was impressive. However, the long march took its toll. As they were cresting a particularly nasty climb up what had seemed an endless slope to a ridge, the team sat down at the top to take a rest. They were some ten miles from their destination.

Ned was exhausted, mumbling and slightly incoherent. Jack tried to feed him an energy bar, passing pieces into his mouth. Ned sat there, trying to chew, and then he just let it all dribble out down his chin and over his shirt. Jack just couldn't get him to take food on board.

However, Ned never gave up. Jack was exhausted, and would have found it hard enough to keep going without taking energy on board, but Ned never stopped.

Twenty four hours later his team walked into the ERV and was met by the security party.

Jack set up an OP over-watching the ERV itself, in case any of his teams had been captured and gave away the location. The OP included some guides who would meet incoming teams. They would be guided to a further checkpoint for accountability and then an assembly area one mile away.

Once at the assembly area they would be provided food and water and allowed to rest up.

Over the course of the next week, all of Jack's teams trickled in, with the exception of those in the two pickups which had gone missing. Some had experienced adventures, pursued by Regime elements or drones, and had taken long diversions or been forced to lie up under the thermal ponchos, others were simply exhausted.

Jack decided to take a different approach with the Yankee patrol base. They were too far inside West Virginia, away from any realistic target areas, to carry out operations from here. He decided that they needed to rest up and plan their next move.

Jack set up a treatment center under Megan for the various wounded personnel, located tacked on to Yankee to make use of the people there to help with the healing and management of the wounded fighters.

He established his fire support platoon co-located with the fighting vehicles in a laager area. They were to be used as a quick reaction force for a mobile defense in case of a Regime incursion into the area.

He now dispersed the three 82nd squads to the three platoons and had each platoon set up a defensive patrol base dispersed around Yankee. This gave him a defensive screen round Yankee where the families and recovering wounded were being housed.

Once the defenses were set up, they went into a busy period of equipment and weapon cleaning and maintenance, as well as physical rest. They conducted a light patrolling program into the surrounding area.

Jack realized that to get back in the fight, he was going to have to move his forces back into a position where they could begin operations against the Regime again.

Two weeks later, Bill arrived. Jack was amazed. Jack had moved his TOC into a bunker he had had built just outside of Yankee, in order to be central to the defensive positions around the base. They grabbed some hot water from the central kitchen, made coffee, and walked up to his bunker where they sat inside on camp chairs by the light of a kerosene lamp.

They had a lot to talk about. Bill wanted to go over the after action reports from the recent combat, and Jack wanted news from the outside world. The big strategic question was about what was next for them.

The war against the Chinese was still ongoing west of the Rockies, with General Wall leading USPACOM. There were no significant breakthroughs to report either way from that theatre as yet. The demarcation line still held to the south with the Southern Federation, but there were rumblings of war.

"Listen Jack," Bill said, "I want to get your buy in on a plan."

"Ok, run it by me."

"Remember the guy I sent to Texas?"

"Yea."

"Ok, well they know all about your Company in Texas. Jack's Juggernauts, aka the Mountain Men," Bill chuckled. "You are famous, and very well regarded. I have been in negotiations and my guy reports that Texas is offering sanctuary to the families, on the basis that we move the Company to Texas. You will have to submit to operational control from the Federation chain of command

and they will use you to further the Southern Federation's military agenda."

"You say 'you' – where do you fit in to this?"

"I would stay here, at the farm, and continue to run the network. Intelligence gathering."

"I see," said Jack, "but how do you feel about this? This is your Company, you created it, and we would no longer be fighting in Virginia?"

"I appreciate that Jack, but actually you need to give yourself more credit. I started this thing, but now I'm the network guy. You have fought and bled with this Company, it is yours. I want to see the families safe, and I think we could hit back at the Regime more effectively with the support of the Federation military. Anyway, they are likely to send you back in to conduct operations once the families are safe in Texas."

Jack mulled it over.

"Ok Bill," he finally said, "Let's get some of the main players together and see what they think, and if they agree then we can run it past the group."

It was not just a military decision. They got the commanders together along with the leaders from the civilian side, including Caitlin and some of the other key women such as Gayle who ran the place.

It was unanimous. They wanted to get to Texas. It would keep the families and kids safe, and then the Company could join the fight again secure in the knowledge that their loved ones were out of harm's way. From a military point of view, they would no longer have to allocate combat power to protecting the families.

The next question was how?

Bill wanted to keep some OPSEC around this one so he pulled Jack aside and told him: C-130 Hercules aircraft. STOL operations, which stood for 'short takeoff and landing'.

Texas was prepared to send in Texas Air Guard aircraft to extract the Company along with the families in return for the agreement that they would fight for the Southern Federation.

Bill outlined the plan: he would hang around until they could find a suitable landing field. Once that was established, he would return to his farm, allowing suitable travel and planning time, and pass the message to Texas. On a specified day, the aircraft would come in and lift them out.

They needed a suitable dirt field three thousand feet long. They did a map recon and located some potential locations, following up with recon patrols. They found a suitable location on some upland pasture land dotted with occasional trees and low shrub. It was located in a small valley. It was perfect for two thousand feet and had three thousand feet of clearance available at a pinch.

It would need a little work but it was only a mile from Yankee. Jack had some work parties set to work clearing the few trees and the bushes, creating a dirt landing strip.

Meanwhile, allowing for time to get the landing strip ready, Bill took the coordinates, set a date with Jack, and headed back to his farm. They set an initial date for a daylight pickup, with further dates if they first one was missed for any reason.

They had agreed, in accordance with information that Bill had brought with him from his coded radio exchanges with his agent in Texas, to go for a dawn pickup time. This would allow the Texas Air Guard aircraft to fly in by night, but give them the advantage of daylight to conduct the STOL landing on an unknown and less than ideal landing strip.

Ten days later the Company was waiting in a defensive position in the trees at the end of the makeshift landing strip. It was just a flattish grassy field which they had cleared of trees and bushes. The fighters had a perimeter around the families, who were organized into four 'chalks', one for each aircraft.

They only had their basic gear with them, weapons, tactical vests and rucksacks. The larger support weapons, ammunition, food and equipment had been placed into the dug outs at Yankee and camouflaged, making it into a huge cache, while the vehicles were hidden under netting deep in the woods, including the military vehicles liberated by the defectors.

If they ever came back out this way, for whatever reason, they would be able to break out the gear from Yankee.

Under Jim's supervision, day-glow panels had been placed out to mark the landing strip.

They waited in the pre-dawn light.

Shortly after the sky lightened, the first C-130 Hercules came roaring over the treetops above them, the first of four. It came over and buzzed them low after flying 'nap of the earth' up from Texas, hugging the terrain contours at two hundred feet to stay below Regime radar.

There was a separation between aircraft and the first circled the landing strip, getting eyes on the terrain, followed by the others. They came around in a loop and lined up for the approach.

The first aircraft came in and lined up on the airstrip. As it came in its nose dropped towards the strip and then it went to 'full flaps' as it swooped in to land, taxiing down towards the end of the strip. As each aircraft landed, it taxied down to the end of the runway and made space for the ones landing behind.

Once the fourth had landed, they put their engines in reverse and rapidly backed down the airstrip in a single file to where the fighters waited with their families.

As the aircraft sat there with the engines 'turning and burning' the rear ramps lowered and a small security detachment ran off the back of each to secure the immediate area. The loadmasters walked down the ramp and gestured to the waiting chalks.

The four lines of families and fighters walked out towards the waiting aircraft carrying their gear, some of the wounded carried on stretchers. As they reached the ramps at the back of the aircraft they felt the heat coming off the roaring engines, seemingly threatening to burn their faces as they waited for those ahead to get up the ramp.

Some of the kids and those who had never experienced it were shielding their faces and turning away from the heat as the engine noise roared around them. Some of the younger kids were crying, scared by the noise, held by their moms.

The flight crew was directing them to fill into the red webbing seats that lined the outer skin of the aircraft and also a central island down the center. The rucksacks and wounded on stretchers were secured in the open space by the back ramp, between the two side jump doors.

As soon as everyone was loaded, the ramps went up and the aircraft raced forwards one at a time, taking off over two thousand feet in the same direction that they had landed.

The C-130s lurched into the air and took off; banking sharply to the south and going straight back into nap of the earth flying at two hundred feet.

The constant low level flying over the hilly terrain, along the valleys and lurching over the ridges was rough. The passengers could feel the aircraft pulling G's as they roared south. The aircrew went amongst them handing out sick bags to those who succumbed to airsickness and little boxes of juice drinks with straws to the kids.

Several hours later, they landed at Dallas Fort Worth. It was a definite culture shock. They emerged off the rear ramp straight from the Virginia woods, where they had been surviving at a basic level. They were met by air-conditioned coaches on the pan and driven to a large aircraft hangar, where there was power. Inside, they were met by a reception committee of Texas Guard dressed in the old style green BDU uniforms.

There was food and drink laid out, and a medical team waiting to help with the wounded. Jack was amazed at the forethought: they had it all set up in the large hangar, the medical tents off to the side, so that they did not have to separate anyone from the group, which may not have gone down so well with the close knit Virginians.

The senior officer present was a Colonel Bridges. Jack shook his hand and felt good about it. He seemed like a genuine stand-up guy. Colonel Bridges explained that they had set it up so that they would keep them in the hangar for OPSEC purposes, and to allow them to recover, clean up and decompress.

After that, they would make plans to integrate the Company with the Southern Federation forces, arranging for a place for the families to stay longer term.

Colonel Bridges did not bat an eyelid at the heavily armed and geared up Resistance fighters. He simply mentioned to Jack that they had built a weapons unloading bay at the entrance to the hangar and for safety reasons it would be best to clear the weapons for their stay. Jack agreed and passed the message.

They ended up spending a week decompressing in the hangar. With Megan's agreement and that of the families of those that had family with the group, some of the wounded were moved to a nearby hospital. Trust was developing easily and the group was starting to relax. The hangar had been divided up into male and female areas and there were rows of bunk beds laid out with bedding provided.

It appeared that Colonel Bridges was to be their main liaison go-to guy and he and Jack developed a good relationship.

There was a laundry service organized and in the meantime a bunch of military surplus and charity clothing was dumped off at the hangar, allowing the group to get on some clean clothes. The fighters found themselves outfitted in fresh green BDU uniforms, which led to a lot of joking about looking like smart real soldiers.

The Guard had brought in some mobile shower units, one male and one female, and everyone was able to get clean. It was luxury after being in the woods in the heat and humidity. They had also set up a projector in a corner of hangar along with a laptop and big selection of movies. The children spent a lot of time that week sitting about watching kid movies.

After the week, they were moved to the Double Tree hotel just down the road from the airfield. They had exclusive use of the hotel, there were no guests, and the hotel was running on generators. The staff was working and although the service was not the usual hotel standard, they ran a good buffet in the dining room. It was more of a makeshift barracks than a hotel, but to the Company and their families it was luxury.

The best thing about the hotel was the hot showers. Jack had a quiet word with Andrew and had him and Vicky take the kids away for a few hours, allowing him and Caitlin the free use of the hotel room. It had been a long time since they had been able to spend some quality alone time, and those few imitate hours were priceless.

Colonel Bridges was meeting with Jack every day and two days after the move to the hotel it became clear what they were going to be asked to do. It was time to pay the piper.

"Jack," said Colonel Bridges, "we have reviewed your report of the actions your Company participated in. We have seen the video footage of the battles. I have met your soldiers and spoken with many of them. They are excellent people, and you have all done a sterling job."

"Thank you," said Jack.

"It is also clear that amongst your command you also have a number of historically airborne qualified personnel."

"True," said Jack, thrown a curveball.

"Well, we want you guys for a high risk high reward airborne mission that we have in the pipeline."

"Ok."

"But I can't tell you more until you are in isolation. We need to get you across to Fort Benning for parachute refresher training; we will isolate you there, and you will get the full mission brief."

"Ok, but I need to make something clear."

"What?"

"I will take all of my fighters, airborne qualified or not, if they want to go."

Colonel Bridges grinned, "I thought you would say that. That's fine, but just so you know; we only have enough 'chutes for one practice jump."

"Roger that."

Jack got his Company together in the conference room. He explained the situation and asked for volunteers. Everyone volunteered, including the three squads from the 82nd.

The next day, they said goodbye to their families and some of the wounded who were not medically cleared to go on the mission. They grabbed their gear, loaded onto the buses, and drove to the airfield for the flight across to Fort Benning, Georgia.

For many of them, all the airborne qualified personnel and in particular the Rangers, it was a trip down memory lane. The base was now being run by Southern Federation troops and they had set up the jump school using the equipment that was still in place.

They ran through a week of parachute school, compressing the course from the usual three week school into that one week. They pushed through ground 'week' and tower 'week' in the first five days and moved onto jump 'week' on the seventh day. It was a refresher for all of them, new for many of them.

It was certainly a strange sight to see them go through jump school, dressed in their ragtag of clothing despite the issue of the new green BDUs, and wearing beards and unkempt hair. Some of them had trimmed and groomed themselves a bit, but not many. Jack grinned to think how this would have gone down in the super strict jump school of times past.

How priorities change.

During the week, Jack was given top secret briefings that allowed him to begin to understand what they were up against. He had to keep the information close hold from the Company until they were in isolation following final jump qualification.

The Southern Federation believed that it was time to attack the Regime. They were planning a game of 'kill the king'. It was a two part combined airborne and ground assault. The ground assault would break the Regime line in South Carolina and push north up the I-95 towards Washington DC. It was to be massive armored and mechanized push.

The preparatory operation would be a surprise airborne assault onto Washington DC, the Capitol itself, to attempt to cut the head off the snake. It was a high risk operation.

The idea was to use Jack's Company as part of the airborne assault. If it failed for any reason, or the ground component did not make it to link up, then the thinking was that Jack's fighters could lead the Southern Federation forces in a withdrawal out of DC back into the Virginia woods, to continue Resistance operations.

The planned drop zone (DZ) for Jack's overhead assault mission was the Washington Mall itself, then rapidly assaulting onto the White House.

Jack had some input of his own on this plan. While serving with the Rangers, he had participated in an exchange with the British Parachute Regiment. Jack had been long dismayed with the direction that the US had gone with its parachuting capability. He had some opinions that he would have liked to have seen implemented.

The classic T-10 parachute with its four second deployment count was being phased out for the T-11, with its six second count. All this meant that the direction the US military was taking was to jump from higher altitude, thus creating greater risk to the aircraft and the paratroopers.

When he had jumped with the Brits, they were using the 'LLP', or low level parachute, that deployed rapidly but had a slower rate of descent. It was regularly jumped in training at six hundred feet, and could be jumped in combat at two hundred and fifty feet, without a reserve parachute since there would not be time to deploy one.

In contrast, US military training jumps took place from altitudes around one thousand feet. Jack had also seen that the Brits had perfected the low level 'overhead assault' and had a simple system to rig for it. Knowing that he did not have access to the LLPs, but that he was jumping into a potential hornets nest on the Mall, Jack asked for a jump height of four hundred feet using the older T-10 parachutes.

Jacks plan was approved and he implemented this into the training. For the final, single jump on the seventh day they would jump at four hundred feet. He also showed his Company how to rig for overhead assault.

Once they were wearing the parachute on their back, they used a piece of paracord tied to their rifle, like a sling. It was measured by holding the rifle out, almost like a bow, and pulling the paracord back to the elbow, almost like a bowstring.

Once the paracord was rigged, they laid the weapon muzzle down behind their shoulder, resting against the parachute container, magazine rearwards. They then looped the center of the paracord under their arm and through the left upper D-ring attachment point for their reserve and clipped their reserve in place on their front.

The reserve held the weapon in place by the paracord, with a further piece of paracord rigged as a quick release to tie the weapon muzzle down along their side. The idea was that once under canopy they could pull the quick release and raise the muzzle of the weapon up, thus getting it out of the way of their leg for landing, and once they unclipped the reserve the weapon would be immediately available to fight with.

They would jump wearing their tactical vests, and on landing they would simply pull the quick releases on their shoulders to let the risers go, freeing them from the parachute canopy. This meant that there was no need to get out of the parachute harness itself, which they would leave on at least until a lull in the assault allowed them to remove it. It was all about being fast into action on the drop zone.

For their equipment, which would consist solely of a daypack containing ammunition, water, communications equipment, spare batteries, night vision and an MRE, they would dispense with the usual equipment straps and lowering line. Usually the equipment container would be lowered on a fifteen foot line once under canopy. In this case, there was no time.

What Jack did was modify the way the daypack was rigged. It normally sat below the reserve on the jumpers thighs, let down on the fifteen foot line once under canopy by pulling on a release. They removed the release and simply had the daypacks attached to the lower D-rings on the harness, sitting on the jumpers thighs. Once on the ground, the jettison device alone would be used, releasing the daypack from the D-rings and allowing the jumper to extend the daypack straps and throw it on his back.

Keeping the daypack on the thighs would be uncomfortable for landing, but there would be no time under canopy from a four hundred feet jump height to mess about with lowering the container. The daypacks were not over heavy, not in the realm of one hundred and ten pounds which was the permissible weight for a full sized container. The jumper's would just have to suck it up and drive on; the priority was with the desire to jump low and be fast on the ground.

As soon as the risers, reserve and the daypack jettison device were pulled on landing, the paratrooper's weapons and daypack would be immediately available to go into the fight with.

With this system, it was possible to jump weapons up to the size of the 240, laid alongside the jumper's body. Spare ammo belts for the guns would be loaded into the daypacks. This meant that the Company would land in light overhead assault order with limited scales of ammunition, with resupply in their daypacks. They would have no mortars or anti-tank weapons.

Jack spoke to his Company before the practice jump, explaining that he could not go into the detailed plan due to OPSEC, but that there was a reason for the specific overhead assault modifications to what the veteran jumpers were used to. He was aware that he was addressing both veteran jumpers and novices.

"I realize that some of you are getting a very fast introduction to parachuting. Just remember that parachuting itself is simply a means of delivery to the battlefield. I have no doubt of your courage, and once you make the first jump you will be ready for the operational one.

"Parachuting itself is not complicated. Simply get out the door, keep your feet and knees together, and accept the landing. The important thing is to walk away. In this case, get rapidly into action once you hit the ground.

"It is what you do on the ground that is the important thing, and which distinguishes paratroopers from simple parachutists. You have all proved yourselves in combat, and I have absolute faith that you will shine in the chaos of a hot drop zone."

The practice jump was made successfully and the Company was moved into isolation for battle procedure.

The broad plan was for Jack's Company to jump in on the Mall and rapidly assault the White House in an attempt to kill or capture the Regime leadership. Kill the king, cutting off the head of the snake.

The Company would jump from three C-130s. They would be tactically loaded with the elements of the four platoons loaded in the same order inside each of the aircraft, the theory being that by doing so, once they hit the ground they would be roughly in the same place on the drop zone. The Company would rally by platoons to the north side of the Mall and assault onto the White House.

The drop zone itself was the Mall, running in from the east, the impact point was just to the north east of the Washington Memorial, allowing a drop zone length of fifteen hundred meters to just past the Lincoln Memorial. Apparently the shallow reflecting pool was empty now, and the jump height of four hundred feet would allow minimal drift, thus helping to keep the jumpers on the narrow drop zone.

There would only be one pass, the jumpers exiting in simultaneous sticks from the two rear side jump doors of each of the three C-130s. The Company would comprise one hundred and twenty parachute trained originals: 1st, 2nd,

3rd Platoons, the fire support platoon armed with 240s and a command element comprising tactical HQ, Jim's logistics team and Megan's team of medics.

With forty paratroopers per aircraft, twenty jumping from port side and twenty from starboard, it would allow enough room on the DZ to get them all out in one pass.

The plan was to hit the DZ loaded so that tactical HQ landed first to the east, then as the jumpers exited from the westward flying planes the order would be the fire support platoon, 1st Platoon, medics and logistics and then 2nd and 3rd Platoons.

Simultaneous sticks meant that the paratroopers would exit from both the port and starboard jump doors at the same time. Each jumper would exit with one second separation, the theory being that there was a half second stagger between the port and starboard doors.

To the north of the east side of the drop zone, in the area where tactical HQ and the fire support platoon should be landing, was a five to six hundred meter distance across the open ground of the ellipse and the south lawn, to the White House itself.

In conjunction with the overhead assault, a TALO operation (tactical air landing operation) would land a number of C-130s at Reagan National, close to the Mall just across the river. These C-130s would contain a light infantry battle group along with resupply loaded on gators, which would drive off the rear of the aircraft ramps on landing. This landing would also contain heavier support assets, such as 81mm mortars, that could set up at Reagan and provide fire support to Jack's fighters across the river.

The TALO assault was also a surprise shock action with the objective of securing Reagan National, the Pentagon and the dual bridges across the Potomac to the Mall and White House areas, thus allowing a link-up with Jack's Company.

Once the two elements of the airborne assault went in, simultaneously the ground assault would start up the I-95 from South Carolina, attempting to thrust north the five hundred miles to link up with the paratroopers in DC.

It was a bold, all or nothing move. If the plan failed, the paratroopers would have no option but to attempt to fade away into the countryside and back into an insurgency role.

Jack spoke to his assembled Company in the hangar before they donned their parachutes and gear. He had them gathered around in a group.

"There is no doubt that this is a risky, bold move. It is not only a parachute jump into the heart of darkness, it is a leap of faith. I have absolute faith in you, the men and women of this Company. You are lions, every one of you a hero. I have never been more impressed by courage and dedication as that which I have seen from you, even in our darkest days in the forests of Virginia.

"Remember why we do this. We do it for America, for the memories of those brave souls who founded this country, who fought for freedom and made this country great. We do it for the memories of those who went before us, fighting for liberty both here and abroad.

"But more importantly, we do it for each other, and we do it for our families and children, and our children's children, for their future. If we don't stand against the tyranny of the Regime, who will?!

"We will not go meekly into the sunset, our freedoms stripped from us. You, stood here now, are striking the blow for liberty, for our Constitution, for freedom, for America. I am honored to go into battle with you. Remember, when all this is over, it is either liberty or death!"

Jack paused, and a cheer went up from the assembled Company. Jack looked around him and saw the tears running down their faces.

"Let us take a moment to say the Ode of Remembrance, in honor of those that we have lost in this fight. Let us take a moment of silence afterwards."

They bowed their heads, and Jack recited:

"They went with songs to the battle, they were young.
Straight of limb, true of eyes, steady and aglow.
They were staunch to the end against odds uncounted,
They fell with their faces to the foe.
They shall not grow old, as we that are left grow old:
Age shall not weary them, nor the years condemn.
At the going down of the sun and in the morning,
We will remember them."

After a minutes silence, Jack looked up.
"Ok, let's roll."

Chapter Seventeen

The three C-130s flew nap of the earth in the darkness of the night, up the spine of the Appalachian Mountains, concealing themselves as best they could in the valleys, flying at two hundred feet, below radar detection.

Following them, separated by ten minutes, were the TALO assault aircraft designated for Reagan National.

In South Carolina, the armored and mechanized Division marshaled itself at the line of departure. It was a long column, laid out on the I-95, arranged into assault and support elements. As well as the main battle tanks, the armored personnel carriers and the self-propelled guns, there were engineer units with bridging equipment, supply and logistics elements, carrying everything that the fighting column would need on the five hundred mile dash to DC.

Inside the Company's three C-130s, it was horrific. They had been flying for several hours now. It was hot and cramped and the smell of vomit filled the back of the aircraft. The green glow of night lights was the only illumination. The paratroopers cramped inside could feel the pull of the g-forces as they followed closely the contours of the land, the lurching feeling deep in the pit of their stomachs, sometimes pushed down in their seats as the aircraft climbed rapidly.

Timed to coincide with the approach of the transport aircraft to DC, a squadron of Southern Federation fast jets had streaked up the coast towards the Capital. The Regime scrambled its own fighter jets and a long range modern-style aerial dogfight ensued on the approaches to DC. Missiles were fired, evasive maneuvers and flares used as the fast jets struggled for ascendancy,

Meanwhile, a second Southern Federation squadron of fast jets utilized the cover their brothers in arms were providing and rocketed through to DC itself, firing missiles and softening up the approach down the air corridor for the C-130s. The primary mission of this squadron was to destroy any ground to air missile sites and clear the approach for the paratroopers.

Inside Jack's aircraft the call of "Ten minutes!" was passed up the line of sitting paratroopers. Jack was sat down by the port (left) side jump door in the lead aircraft. He was number one, the first man out.

Next, the jumpmasters opened the doors, sliding them up on their tracks towards the roof of the aircraft and then swinging out the jump step, stamping it down into position. The rush of fresh air into the aircraft was a welcome relief. The jumpmasters were wearing parachutes – they would follow the sticks out the door – and they commenced to check the exit doors, hanging out of the aircraft to check outside.

Next came: "Stand up hook up!" and the paratroopers stood, stiff after so long crammed in wearing their equipment. They put away the red webbing seats by raising them and clipping them up, and hooked the end of their static lines onto the jump cable that ran above their heads.

The jumpmaster called out "Action stations!" and waved them towards the rear doors. Jack shuffled down at the head of his stick to stand in the open door, handing the slack of his static line off to the jumpmaster. The plane was moving and bucking beneath his feet and he put one hand out to steady himself in the doorframe, the other held the end of his reserve, elbow tucked in to his side. The little red jump light was on in the panel to the side of the doorway.

Jack stared south out of the aircraft door in the dawn light as the outskirts of the city passed beneath him, only two hundred feet below. He felt he could reach out and touch the rooftops. He watched as a fast jet went streaking past in the distance, headed for the drop zone.

They were getting close.

The massive wing of the aircraft was up to his right, its two propeller engines roaring and droning, exhaust tails streaming back into the dawn sky.

Superimposed on his view of the buildings below was a vision of Caitlin and the kids, laughing and at play. He loved them so much. The prayer was repeating itself in his head, on a loop, just the first couple of lines:

Yea though I walk through the valley of the shadow of death, I shall fear no evil, for thy rod and thy staff shall comfort me.

Jack thought of his family.

Please Lord, keep us safe. I don't want to die today, but if I have to, I do it for them.

The jumpmaster was holding him by his harness as the plane bucked and lurched. Jack saw some of the open parkland of the city center approaching and then the tracer fire began.

Red tracer began to arc lazily up from the ground towards the aircraft. As it got closer it appeared to speed up, an optical illusion, whipping past the open door. The sky was filled with tracer fire.

Jack looked up the plane at the stick ready to follow him out the door. He saw their pale resolute faces, some nauseous and sheened with sweat. Fear filled them, but they controlled it. They were lions.

He saw Jenny back down the stick, hanging on her static line, her eyes far away, a thousand yard stare. She had recovered from the shrapnel wounds to her legs.

He caught Caleb's eye, stood just in front of Jenny, and grinned at him. Caleb stuck his tongue out, grinning at him. Jack grinned back, shook his head and turned back to the door.

Greater love has no man.

Just then, a burst of enemy fire peppered down the side of the aircraft. One of the paratroopers was hit, falling to the floor. The man behind him unclipped the man's static line and dragged him to the side.

Suddenly, the aircraft lurched upward as it climbed to four hundred feet, the jump height. Jack felt the aircraft level out and then the pilot slammed on the flaps, slowing down to jump speed at around a hundred knots. The aircraft went slightly nose up and the tail dipped, making it a downhill run to the door.

The jumpmaster smacked Jacks arm down from the door and he put his hands on his reserve. Jack looked out and saw the Washington Monument, looking close enough that it seemed a real danger that the wingtip was about to clip it.

The red light in the door went off, to be replaced by the green light. The jumpmaster screamed 'GO!" and Jack was out of the door into the slipstream.

Five hundred miles to the south, the Southern Federation artillery began firing a massive barrage and the concentrated armored spear thrust itself into the Regime lines along the narrow frontage of the I-95.

The lead element of the Southern Federation attack was an armored battle group and under the cover of the artillery barrage they rolled forward to engage the Regime defensive positions.

The battle group smashed through and the barrage rolled ahead of them up the Interstate. Through the gap in the Regime lines poured a squadron of Apache attack helicopters, seeking out targets ahead of the advance.

The Regime forces on the demarcation line initially tried to rally but then they started to fold. The Federation column began rolling north up the I-95, engaging Regime targets to the flanks of the road as they moved.

As Jack exited the aircraft, there was no sense of falling, just a buffeting in the slipstream as his parachute deployed, yanked out of its bag by the static line. He felt the risers against the back of his neck as they deployed, pushing his helmet forward on his head. Then, he was under canopy.

Jack had a couple of twists in the suspension lines and he rapidly kicked out of them, as he span he saw the aircraft flying away from him, the parachutes of his men blooming in the sky behind it, tracer fire flashing past.

Next, he looked down and the ground was coming up fast. He put his feet and knees together and slammed in, 'oomph', failing to conduct anything close to a regulation parachute landing fall.

Jack rolled onto his back, released the risers from his shoulders, unclipped his reserve and popped the jettison device on his daypack. He got up on one knee and as he did so there was a series of explosions from the buildings to the north side of the DZ, followed by the sonic boom as one of the Federation fast jets raced over, taking out Regime positions.

He shrugged his daypack on, grabbed his weapon, and looked around him. The jump had been on target, the sticks drifting in to land to the west of him down the north side of the Mall. He saw a couple of his men hung up in trees. They rapidly released themselves from their harnesses and climbed down their deployed reserve chutes.

As Jack assessed the situation he saw that there was enemy fire coming from the north of the DZ, from the buildings and some Humvees. He noticed that the Regime troops that he could see were wearing blue uniforms.

So the reports were true, The Leader did not trust active duty army units within DC, and had entrusted his protection to a praetorian guard of blue shirts.

The paratroopers from the other two aircraft were landing around him, the three C-130s banking off to the south past the drop zone to begin their run back south to the Federation lines.

As the Company started to recover from the jump, along the line they were getting their weapons into action. The Company was still in the open on the grassy Mall and they needed to move. The fire support platoon was closest to Jack and they got their 240s into action, hammering away at the Regime forces to the north.

As the platoons rallied, they started to put down suppressive fire and move to the north, covered by the gunners of the fire support platoon. There were some stragglers, ones who had landed in trees or into the

Constitution Gardens Pond, straggling out soaking wet. Orders were to move once the elements reached seventy percent strength at the rally points, so the platoons were already moving on the objective.

This operation had to be bold to succeed, and there was no time to waste bogging down in an urban fight to the White House through the surrounding buildings. Jack got on the radio and ordered them to move rapidly north, as planned, and this spurred the platoon leaders into action.

1st Platoon began to run forward, fire and maneuvering by squads towards the ellipse. The resistance from the blue shirts was rapidly overcome. It appeared they lacked the moral or physical courage to stand in the face of determined opposition. 2nd Platoon followed 1st and soon the two platoons had eclipsed the fire support provided by the gunners so they had to cease fire.

Jack rapidly organized the Company into a classic formation at the southern end of the ellipse and they pushed north towards the White House.

Across the frontage of the ellipse 1st Platoon was on the right, 3rd Platoon was on the left, tactical HQ central and behind with 3rd Platoon following a tactical bound behind. The Fire support platoon was split with a squad to each flank and the third squad to the rear. It was a 'two up, one back' Company formation and they started to jog across the open ground towards the White House.

Enemy fire was light and sporadic, not effective. It seemed that at the heart of darkness, the eye of the storm, it was just a paper tiger.

The White House itself was an incongruous sight. Rather than the Stars and Stripes flying proudly above the building, it was the new Regime flag, looking entirely out of place.

When they were two hundred meters from the White House the Company encountered some effective fire and went into fire and movement, popping smoke and bounding forwards by squads.

Shortly after, there was a roar of engines and from behind the White House, to the north, rose up two Apache helicopters. The attack helicopters climbed into a hover, framing either side of the Regime flag atop the building. They fired their cannon towards the Company, who were forced to the ground, seeking cover.

Then, also from behind the building to the north, Marine One rose up along with two Chinooks. The helicopters turned and banked away, streaking away low towards the north west.

Jack screamed to engage them, but the Presidential helicopter was already gone, low over the city, followed by the two Chinooks. The Apaches were not making a serious effort to annihilate Jack's command; they rapidly turned away and followed the other escaping helicopters, flying escort.

Jack shouted to move and they were up again, running towards the White House. Resistance was fading away in front of them.

They fought across the south lawn, veering towards the west wing. They used breaching charges to smash into the Oval Office, through the bullet proof windows. Once they had gained entry the Company poured into the building and started clearing the corridors, moving through the West Wing and into the main part of the White House. There was no resistance, just a bunch of terrified staffers.

Jack stood in the Oval Office and looked around him. He saw the framed portrait of The Leader on the wall, above the fireplace, looking messianic. The broken glass from the blown windows was scattered across the rug. Jack walked over and pulled the portrait from the wall, throwing it to the ground. He also noticed that all the historical paintings had been removed. There were a number of other new paintings on the walls, all of famous socialist personalities. Karl Marx was in a prominent position, but not so as to eclipse The Leader.

Jack turned to Jim, "Looks like the bird has flown. Let's get that horrific flag down and get the Stars and Stripes up."

"Roger that Boss, it's about time."

Jack deployed his Company around the White House, the grounds and put OPs up on some of the key surrounding buildings. Ned set up the satellite radio and they sent the situation report back to the Federation Command.

Shortly afterwards the lead element of the light infantry battalion arrived. They had successfully landed at Reagan National and seized control of the airfield. Concurrently to their assault on the Pentagon they had seized the bridges between Reagan National and the White House.

The commander was a Lieutenant Colonel Dunn. He had left a Company at the airfield to secure it. In the planning they had been very concerned about the two bridges, the Rochambeau Memorial Bridge and the 14th Street Bridge that led directly from Reagan National across to the Capital.

Lt-Col Dunn had left two companies to protect the lifeline of the bridges, one at each end including a sapper section to check them out and ensure they were not wired to blow. He had advanced with a reconnaissance element and his tactical HQ to link up with Jack at the White House.

The Federation infantry had marched up the roads accompanied by several gators loaded with ammunition and supplies for Jack's Company. Lt-Col Dunn also informed Jack that the mortars were set up at Reagan and were available on call to support Federation forces in the area.

Now that the objectives were secure, they would await news on the ground operation and updates on when they could expect a link-up. In the meantime, Lt-Col Dunn was expecting to use the airhead at Reagan National for additional C-130 flights bringing heavier equipment and resupply flights.

It was all a little quiet. They had expected a harder fight. Could it be that The Leader and his trusted Regime cronies had simply fled? And where had they gone?

Jack gathered his commanders in the Oval Office. No-one sat at the desk; it seemed a form of sacrilege to do so. It was an incongruous sight, a bunch of sweating bearded Resistance fighters sitting on the sofas and stood around the room, the carpet covered in glass from the blown windows. Some of them still wore their parachute harnesses over their tactical vests.

Megan had set up an aid station in the West Wing, but casualties were light overall. It had not been the fight that they had expected.

Jack addressed his command team, "Ok gentlemen, we have seized our objective. Well done on an excellent operation. It looks like the Regime leadership escaped in those helicopters, I am not sure to where. I don't know whether the defense of Washington really has collapsed, or whether we can expect a counter attack. We need to dig in and be ready for it, to hold this position until relieved.

"Caleb, I want you to take your platoon on a clearance and recon patrol around the local area. Check for any surprises. As part of that, collect any suitable vehicles you can find. Blue Shirt Humvees, any suitable military stuff, whatever works. Also check out the garage for Secret Service armored vehicles, whatever is useful."

Caleb nodded, as Jack went on.

"We will now await news on the Federation assault up the I-95. We have linked up with Lt-Col Dunn and can expect resupply through the air bridge at Reagan National. Remember, if the ground assault does not link up, and we face an overwhelming counter-attack, we will be forced to withdraw from here. The rendezvous will be the cache at Yankee. If we can collect suitable armored vehicles, I aim in the case of our withdrawal to fight out of here in a strong armored column. Any questions?"

There were a few clarification questions before people dispersed to their various tasks.

The parachute and TALO airborne assault onto DC had been so bold and unexpected that it appeared that the city was in shock. Either the Regime had literally fled, leaving the city for exile, or they would be planning a counter attack using available military forces. The inability of the Regime to trust army units within the Capitol beltway had been a critical failure – their 'praetorian guard' had proved more useful for bullying and murdering unarmed civilians than fighting a force of determined American Patriots who wholeheartedly believed in their cause.

Either way, the Resistance and Federation forces were now in a honeymoon period.

Caleb returned from his patrol mission having collected a large number of abandoned regime armored vehicles, of various types. They had enough to mount and transport the Company and with the turret mounted support weapons on these vehicles, Jack rapidly moved to incorporate them into the White House defenses as a series of mobile bunkers and a quick reaction force.

As night fell, they were in a good defensive position, well-armed and supplied. Caleb had reported that the streets around the area were deserted; the place was a ghost town. Trash was piled up in the streets and it appeared that DC had become a nightmare of failed promises. The elites were provided for, while the people lived in poverty.

Jack relieved Caleb's 1st Platoon and moved 2nd Platoon into the recon role for the time being, assigning Owen to a series of vehicle mounted ground domination patrols in the surrounding area, in an attempt to gather Intel and detect any approaching threats.

Towards midnight, Ned reported to Jack that he had received a situation report on the secure satellite radio. It appeared that the ground advance had been halted in North Carolina, close to Fayetteville where the I-95 bridged across the Cape Fear River.

The Regime forces out of Fort Bragg, including elements of the 82nd Airborne Division, had staged a defense of the river crossing, blowing the road bridges. A huge battle had ensued, ongoing right now. It looked like it would last through the night.

According to the rather terse situation report, the Federation forces were attempting to seize the bridge crossing in an attempt to bring up engineer bridging equipment assets and continue the advance.

Jack grunted, deep in thought.

Those that fail to learn the lessons of history are doomed to repeat it; Operation Market Garden? A bridge too far?

Jack had passed back to the Federation command the news on the flight of the Regime leadership. There was no news back about where they may have fled to. Jack surmised that they would have likely gone to one of the underground nuclear command or continuity of government bunkers to wait out the attack and coordinate their forces to respond.

The Company spent a quiet night in and around the White House. Jack managed a couple of hours sleep on one of the couches. In the early hours before morning, waiting for the next situation report on the ground forces advance, Jack and his command team sat around in the oval office, drinking coffee.

Ned came in, looking excited, clutching some paperwork.

"Jack, take a look at this. It was partially burned, the staffers had the shredders going full out and had started to burn stuff in waste bins, but we stopped them before they got it all done. I've been looking through what was left overnight and this here is dynamite."

Jack took the partially burned folder. It was a classified folder and he could still see the words 'Red Dawn' typed on the front. He started to thumb through it but much of it was obscured and blackened.

"Ok Ned, give me the lowdown."

"Roger that. From what I can make out, it's a summary of an operation to entirely subdue and disarm the American population, including the military. The military is useful for now, but will serve its purpose.

"The Chinese invasion, you see, it's not really an invasion. The Regime enabled the Chinese to overcome the

PACFLEET defense of Hawaii using cyber warfare to shut down defense systems. The ultimate aim is for Chinese forces to integrate with Regime forces as a 'Peacekeeping' force across America."

Jack interrupted, "So it's grand treason by the Regime?"

"Yep. The kicker is, General Wall and USPACOM were not supposed to be so successful in blocking the Chinese in California. This is why the previous commanders did not try so hard, until he took over. Wall threw a spanner in the works. The next phase was supposed to be a 'truce' with Chinese forces and a joint military command working in the 'best interests' of America.

"The United Nations is going to support it. The motivation is the disarmament and subjugation of the American people because we are seen as the world's greatest threat to one world United Nations government, standing in the way of world socialism."

Jack interjected, "What, we hold our freedom too dearly?"

"Looks like it. There is a report here," Ned showed Jack the relevant section, "detailing the situation with General Wall and the options. One option is to 'terminate' Wall personally, but the report states that it may be hard to get to him. The other option is limited tactical nuclear strike to severely degrade USPACOM forces and allow the Chinese to overcome them."

Jack stared at Ned, and then he looked around at the shocked faces of his command team.

"Ok Ned, you did a good job finding that. Let's get what you can recover of the report summarized, and then get me Federation command on the satellite radio. We need to pass this up."

"Will do." Ned headed out.

"Oh yea, and let's see if we can get an update on the Federation advance?" Jack called as Ned turned back in the door. Ned nodded and walked out.

Jack walked over and looked out of the shattered windows of the Oval Office, over the south lawn as the dawn lightened the sky. He thought of Caitlin and the kids, and wondered how this situation was going to pan out.

Above him atop the White House flew Old Glory, fluttering in the dawn breeze. Just below, where Jim had strung it up, was the yellow Gadsden flag, the coiled snake with the words "Don't Tread On Me' inscribed below.

Now we wait.

Glossary of Abbreviations

A-10	- Close Air Support Aircraft 'Tank Buster'
AAR	- After Action Review
AC-130	- Gun Ship/see C-130
AFV	- Armored Fighting Vehicle
AH	- Attack Helicopter
AK	- 7.62 x 39mm semi-automatic rifle
Apache	- Attack Helicopter
APC	- Armored Personnel Carrier
AR-15	- .223 semi-automatic rifle
ARF	- Airborne Reaction Force
AT-4	- Anti-Tank Rocket
Barrett .50	- .50 caliber sniper rifle
C-130	- Transport Aircraft
CAT	- Combat Application Tourniquet
CH-47	- Large Transport Helicopter – CH-47
Chinook	- Large Transport Helicopter – Chinook
Claymore	- Anti-Personnel Mine, directional
Company	- 90-120 men, 3-4 Platoons + HQ
COP	- Combat Out Post
DZ	- Drop Zone
ECP	- Entry Control Point
EFP	- Explosively Formed Penetrator
EOD	- Explosive Ordnance Disposal
ERV	- Emergency Rendezvous
FLIR	- Forward Looking Infra-Red - TI
FOB	- Forward Operating Base
HEAT	- High Explosive Anti-Tank – Tank Round
Hercules	- Transport Aircraft
HESCO	- Fortification Bastion

HESH	- High Explosive Squash Head – Tank Round
HQ	- Headquarters
IED	- Improvised Explosive Device
IFAK	- Individual First Aid Kit
IR	- Infra-Red
KIA	- Killed in Action
LMTV	- Light Medium Tactical Vehicle – Army Truck
Lt-Col	- Lieutenant Colonel
LZ	- Landing Zone
M203	- 40mm under slung grenade launcher
M4	- 5.56mm semi-auto/auto rifle
MANPAD	- Shoulder fired anti-aircraft missile
MBT	- Main Battle Tank
MFC	- Mortar Fire Controller
MIA	- Missing in Action
MRAP	- Mine Resistant Ambush Protected - Vehicle
NATO	- North Atlantic Treaty Organization
NOD	- Night Observation Device
NVG	- Night Vision Goggles
OP	- Observation Post
Op Order	- Operations Order
OPSEC	- Operational Security
ORP	- Objective Rally Point
Platoon	- Approx. thirty men, 3 Squads plus HQ
QRF	- Quick Reaction Force
RPG	- Rocket Propelled Grenade
RTOC	- Regional Tactical Operations Center
RV	- Rendezvous
SAM	- Surface to Air Missile
SAW	- Squad Automatic Weapon
SF Role	- Sustained Fire Role
SITREP	- Situation Report

SMAW-D	- Bunker Busting Rocket
SOF	- Special Operations Forces
Squad	- Approx. 8 or 9 Men, 2 x Teams of 4
UAV	- Unmanned Aerial Vehicle (Drone)
VSI	- Very Seriously Injured
TI	- Thermal Imaging
TOC	- Tactical Operations Center
.50cal	- .50 caliber machine-gun
240	- 7.62 x 51mm machine-gun

Contact! A Tactical Manual for Post Collapse Survival

This manual is the result of a detailed consideration of a societal collapse and the civil shift and aftermath that would impact individuals and families who are intent on survival.

The purpose of this manual is to provide information to enhance security, tactics and survival skills of law-abiding citizens who are faced with civil disorder, lawlessness, violence and physical threat in a post-collapse environment.

The information in this manual is derived from years of experience gained from service with special operations forces (SOF) followed by years of employment as a security contractor in hostile environments including Iraq and Afghanistan. It is a distillation of military and security training, principles, and tactics, techniques and procedures (TTPs) adapted to the threat and environment anticipated in this type of scenario in order to provide knowledge needed to train to survive in a world turned upside down. It is no longer just survival of the fittest but survival of those prepared.

The manual will take you from self-defense as an individual, team and family, both pre and post collapse, and move on to tactics, techniques, procedures and training that can be used by tactical teams that you may need to form in order to survive. In a serious post-event scenario, one of total collapse with several months or years before recovery, families, groups and communities may be forced to create such tactical defense forces to protect personnel, loved ones and resources against marauders.

By Max Velocity - Available on Amazon

Rapid Fire! Tactics for High Threat, Protection and Combat Operations

The purpose of this manual is to provide information to enhance tactics and protection skills for those operating in high threat, protection and combat environments.

This includes the operations of the following, by no means exclusive list: special operations forces (SOF), specialized military teams, security escort teams, high threat protection agents, tactical law enforcement and SWAT teams, paramilitary law enforcement teams, and also civilians intent on improving their tactical skills and knowledge.

The information in this manual is derived from years of experience gained from training and operational service with SOF followed by years of employment as a security contractor in hostile environments including Iraq and Afghanistan.

It is a distillation of military and security training, principles, and tactics, techniques and procedures (TTPs) adapted to the threat and environment anticipated in this type of scenario in order to provide knowledge needed to train tactical teams to operate effectively in high threat and combat environments.

By Max Velocity - Available on Amazon